A Very
Merry
Temptation

A Very
Merry
Temptation

Kimberly Kaye Terry
Pamela Yaye
Farrah Rochon

HARLEQUIN®KIMANI ARABESQUE®

A VERY MERRY TEMPTATION

ISBN-13: 978-0-373-09141-6

Copyright © 2013 by Harlequin Books S.A.

The publisher acknowledges the copyright
holders of the individual works as follows:

'TWAS THE SEASON
Copyright © 2013 by Kimberly Kaye Terry

MISTLETOE IN MEMPHIS
Copyright © 2013 by Pamela Yaye

SECOND-CHANCE CHRISTMAS
Copyright © 2013 by Farrah Rochon

Recycling programs
for this product may
not exist in your area.

For questions and comments about the quality of this book,
please contact us at CustomerService@Harlequin.com.

Printed in U.S.A.

$6.99
9/29/13
DC

i13953266

TM www.Harlequin.com

CONTENTS

To my daughter Hannah, who always inspires me to be the best that I can be, I love you, Pooh Monster, aka Jr ;)

To my fly reading divas who support me, I love you all and, as always, keep it sexy ;) ~KKT

'TWAS THE SEASON
Kimberly Kaye Terry

Chapter 1

Nikki Danes took a small, cautious sip of the bright yellow sparkling wine. Her nostrils flared when the soft bubbles made contact. "Hmm," she murmured, and glanced down at the crystal flute, still nearly full after she'd taken the token taste. She tilted her head to the side, considering the contents as though deep in thought.

"Not too bad for wine," she continued, speaking softly to herself. She paused and narrowed her eyes, staring at the glass, considering.

If she didn't know better, she would swear she was drinking champagne and not sparkling wine, she thought, frowning. But as she'd never actually *tasted* champagne, and this was just a MagHard Interior Design–sponsored employee soiree, she assumed it was wine. Although the company she worked for treated its employees well, that didn't extend to spending thousands of dollars on champagne for the annual holiday event, aka an office party. At least that's what she assumed.

But as this was her first time attending one, she couldn't be certain.

"Whatever it is, I might as well enjoy," she said, and brought the glass to her lips. She tipped her head back and took a generous drink.

The golden liquid flowed easily down her throat and her eyelids floated partially down as she enjoyed the sweet yet sharp-tasting alcoholic drink...whatever it was.

"Hmm, delicious." She spoke aloud, softly. Again to herself. Not only was the taste delicious, it was...smooth. Intoxicating.

Nikki couldn't be called a connoisseur by any stretch of the imagination, but it most definitely couldn't be the corner-liquor-store variety of wine, she thought.

"So that's what the good stuff tastes like, huh? I'd better be careful. I'll be dancing on the tabletops if I drink too much of this stuff." Yet she took another sip.

She found herself swaying lightly to the music as the band started up. She'd never been a fan of live bands, but her friend and cubicle mate, Tony Morales, had informed her this one was on point. He'd in fact heard the group perform at many area clubs, both straight and gay.

She smiled, thinking of Tony. Most of the time his information was gotten via the Tony connect, which was what he called his gossip trail, but this time he put the special Tony connect *guarantee* on it.

"The bomb...dot, tic, mami! And those tight little black leather jeans the lead singer wears...mmm. *Caliente!* Yeah, mami, you are most def in for a treat!"

As Tony considered himself an aficionado of all things club, she figured he knew what he was talking about. She had been disappointed when Tony had informed her he wouldn't be attending, but really, she shouldn't be. As much as she liked Tony, she would be crazy embarrassed if her friend knew what she wanted tonight…and more so if the night went as she planned.

Best to keep some things on the down-low, she thought, her body swaying lightly to the beat. They began to transition from the opening song to an even more upbeat one and Nikki nodded absently as they began to sing a popular hip-hop tune, the catchy beat and tight lyrics immediately recognizable.

Tony was right. *Not too bad,* she thought as the group began to encourage the partygoers to get to their feet and dance to the music. Although it was still fairly early in the evening, the party room, which was a sectioned-off area of the one of the hotel's ballrooms, was already packed and an impressive number of her colleagues shuffled to the dance floor.

She brought the fluted glass to her lips again and drank as she surveyed the crowd.

Nikki rarely danced in public. Despite the mood-altering effects of the smooth-tasting wine, or champagne, or whatever it was she was drinking, it hadn't yet given her the courage to approach the dance floor.

She knew she needed to be careful with her drinking. She hadn't gotten around to eating the entire day, unless you counted the one Thin Mints cookie she'd gleefully found at the bottom of her backpack and devoured in less time than it took to snag it from the wrinkled plastic bag.

After pulling an all-nighter of editing a paper for her *last* graduate design course, she'd barely had time to take a quick shower before rushing to work, much less grab a bite to eat.

Nikki's stomach growled and she glanced around, looking for a waiter carrying a plate of hors d'oeuvres. She needed crackers, chips…something. The music was pounding and the beat was intoxicating, yet she stifled a yawn.

To say she was tired from a few nights of only getting three to four hours of sleep had to be the understatement of the year. She shook her head and blew out a breath, determined that she would enjoy the night and keep to the plan. She glanced around to see if the object of said plan was in attendance.

She felt a rush of disappointment at the same time that her stomach growled again. She needed to eat something quickly and shake off the fatigue from a demanding day.

Exhausted, she'd rushed to work hoping it would be a light day at MagHard Interior Design, the company she worked for on a part-time basis. After learning that Tony was going to be in after lunch, she'd concluded that she was going to have to work twice as hard. In half the time. She'd swallowed down an angry sigh of irritation. She'd do what she had to do, since there was a deadline assigned to their project.

That didn't mean she had to like it. She'd muttered and complained to no one in particular but done the work in the end, barely able to keep a pleasant disposition as she did so. Since she wanted to get hired as a designer with the company and transfer out of the accounting department, she needed to be seen as reliable.

Absently she continued her search for some type of sustenance from one of the floating waiters. "Where's a food platter when you need one?" she grumbled.

She felt a frown creep on her face and quickly erased it, vowing to stay calm. She was here to have fun. Just chill, relax and enjoy. No stress…and possibly get a little…sex.

Nikki blushed as the thought crossed her mind, but she firmed her spine and tossed her hair back over a shoulder.

She did a quick check around to see if anyone was watching her talk to herself and drink like a soldier on leave. The talking to herself was her normal routine, but the drinking wasn't, outside of the occasional glass at bedtime to help her relax enough to go to sleep.

She finished off the drink and felt warmth in her belly soothe the grumbling. Food would have to wait, she thought.

When a waiter glided by her, balancing a smoky mirrored platter topped with filled glasses on his shoulder, Nikki snagged a second flute quickly and, with a small smile, placed the empty one in its place.

Her glance ran over him as she took a sip and lifted a brow at his reaction.

The tall, blond, handsome young waiter smiled back at her, offering a dazzling display of his pearly whites... and nearly crashed into another waiter who was also staring at Nikki.

In direct contrast to his blond counterpart, this one was dark, the color of espresso with light brown eyes and a smile that nearly made her drop the glass of wine. The man looked so good.

Hmm, hmm, hmm...fine, fine, to-the-nth-degree fine, she thought, running her gaze over him from head to toe. From the top of his jet-black, hip-length locs, secured at the back of his head with a leather wrap, to his muscled body that the uniform in no way hid, he was superb.

"Hmm. Lord have mercy," she said, a smile growing on her face.

It grew until her face ached, her confidence boosted to the max by the attention and near collision of the two handsome waiters.

Not only had her confidence increased from the near accident, but she knew some of her coworkers had noticed as well, and that made her feel good. *Damn good,* Nikki thought, and ran her fingers through her curls.

She took another sip of the sparkling drink, then began

to feel the mellowing effect caused by the subtle but potent champagne. *This has to be champagne,* she thought.

She ran a hand over her hip, smoothing the booty-hugging, designer-knockoff dress down over her slim but curvy thighs, the hem stopping several inches from her knee.

Although the dress was a knockoff, she knew it not only looked like the real deal, but she was rocking the hell out of it.

Nikki smoothed the dress down again. The move was completely conscious. The hem of the dress hit her midthigh, and although she knew she looked good in it, she was still, truth be told, just the smallest bit uncomfortable, as it wasn't her normal modus operandi, so to speak, when she dressed.

When she felt her hands inching toward the hem again, she stopped herself before she started tugging it farther down.

Mental-check time: she had come to the party to have fun, be sexy and, if only for one night, operate under a different set of rules. The sort of rules where she threw caution to the wind and let her hair down, both literally and figuratively.

She found a tall table with an available bar stool, so she took a seat. Glancing around, she noticed George from accounting, who was eyeing her boobs like they were manna from heaven.

The creep. She suppressed a shiver.

Nikki knew he eyed any woman under the age of seventy like that. In fact, last week she'd caught his creepy ass eyeing Ms. Burke, the elderly housekeeper who cleaned the offices during the evening.

She shuddered and ignored him, barely hiding her laugh when his wife caught him staring, and without missing a beat in her conversation, reached a hand out and slapped him upside his head.

Although George's wife missed full-on connection, her hand—which was probably as large as any man's, since she stood six feet tall in stocking feet—glanced the side of his face as he ducked the blow.

Shamed, his pale face flamed with color as he swiftly rushed toward the bar to refill his drink. His wife continued to talk with one of the ladies from accounting as though the incident had never occurred.

Nikki shifted her focus and turned around to survey the room.

She remembered the rules. Her rules, unique ones she'd decided would dictate her actions and deeds tonight.

In other words, she planned to not only have fun, but she was going to do something…or at least attempt to do something she'd never done before.

Pick up a man.

But not just any man, she thought, tapping the table with her nails. She was going to be a different creature than she normally was. If only for one night.

She turned around to check out the growing crowd at the office party. Although this was her second year with MagHard Interior Design, this was the first time she'd attended their office party, and what an event it was.

She swayed slightly to the beat as she analyzed the guests, casually, so that just in case anyone was watching her, they weren't aware that she was…looking…for someone.

Fred and Ginger were just a few feet away, heads down, faces close together deep in conversation.

She covered her face and giggled…really, she needed to quit calling the pair Fred and Ginger, but everyone in the company did after the last holiday party. She had just started and hadn't felt comfortable attending, but she'd been privy to the gossip for weeks afterward.

That party had been small, much smaller than this year's extravagant affair, and had taken place in the office. Fred and Ginger, aka Bill and Esther, had both gotten so drunk they'd started dancing around the office, cranking up the music on the small iPod player, performing various numbers. From John Travolta's moves in *Saturday Night Fever* to a painful-to-watch rendition of *Dirty Dancing,* the two had danced as though there was no tomorrow.

Their last dance had, unfortunately, been their last performance of the night. Ginger had leaped onto the desk and slid into a full split, dress above her thick thighs, a smug expression on her round face…a feat that Nikki had to give praise to the woman for, as Ginger was by no means a *small* woman.

Demonstrating surprising agility, she'd gotten to her feet and then *attempted* to perform a tuck and spin that would have her landing into Fred's arms.

Despite the laws of physics seeming not to be on her side, the stunt might have worked, had Ginger not been so much bigger than Fred.

The paramedics had been called.

"But at least they had fun! And now look at them," Nikki said and giggled softly to herself. Before last year's party, the self-proclaimed nerds had been too bashful to talk to the other. But since returning from the ER, bandaged and bruised, the now inseparable lovebirds had been just about joined at the hip.

They would be celebrating their upcoming nuptials in the spring.

Nikki sighed, thinking of her own love life. It wasn't like she was jealous of Fred and Ginger—nothing like that—but she had come to terms with the fact that it might be a while…a long while before she found her Mr. Right. Which was why she'd decided that Mr. Right *Now* would do.

Between school and the job, she had zero to no time for anything serious. The problem was that she was, well… horny.

She felt her cheeks heat, but truth was truth.

She hadn't had good dick in… She frowned, trying to remember the last time she had.

"That is so sad," she mumbled to herself, and took another sip.

Nikki squared her shoulders. She had never been the type of woman to have sex for the sake of it, but she had needs. And those needs had cobwebs on them. It had been so long since they'd been fulfilled.

Oh, well, what the heck. 'Twas the season to be merry and all that, she thought, and brought the flute to her mouth.

Deciding she needed a healthy dose of courage, she downed the champagne in one swallow and started coughing. *Slow down…slow down,* she cautioned herself. The night was young and she was in need. And as she waited for the one she'd set her sights on to help clean her cobwebs out, she didn't need a trip to the doctor because of choking.

Damn. *So much for trying to be cute,* she thought as she tried to clear her throat of the liquid that seemed to have gone down the wrong pipe.

A nearby waitress quickly came to her rescue and thumped her so hard on the back she nearly pitched forward onto the table. She held up a hand and signaled the woman to stop her rigorous pounding. Then she handed the energetic waitress her empty flute after mumbling, "I'm fine, thanks."

Nikki hazarded a guess the woman was simply trying

to help, but something told her that the waitress was well aware that all that hard thumping had not been necessary. Nikki had caught the waitress checking out one of the waiters who'd been watching her during the collision. Not a worry. As fine as both waiters had been, neither one was on her menu for the night.

She grew impatient after checking the clock. She chewed her bottom lip. It was still early, but it seemed the entire staff of MagHard Interior Design had shown up tonight, and apparently had brought guests, as they'd been invited to do. The office party had grown into an all-out holiday ball, she thought. There were plenty of men in attendance, and Nikki knew she'd caught the eyes of several.

And she could probably pick one to help her out of her…situation.

But she didn't want just anyone.

There was only one whose dark emerald eyes she wanted to catch. Nikki bit her lower lip again, hoping he'd actually come to the swanky office party. From what she could ascertain from the office gossip, odds were he was coming. She'd overheard a few of the ladies in the secretarial pool discussing that very fact. She wasn't the only one who had her eyes him. Not even close.

She hadn't wanted to get her hopes up too high in case he was a no-show, but as usual her friend Tony had been the one who'd found out the info she needed. Tony had inadvertently given her the scoop when he'd informed Nikki that he'd heard it from Wanda, who worked in Accounts Receivable, who'd heard it from Linda, who worked in Human Resources, who'd overheard Sheila, the assistant to the assistant manager…that he was planning to attend.

Merriment made her laugh out loud at the string of *I heard it from*s that peppered that particular trail.

Max Stele.

Just thinking his name brought the image of the sexy-as-hell temporary employee of MagHard Interior Design to her mind's eye.

For two weeks Nikki had both avoided and sought to catch glimpses of the temporary office manager. And she wasn't alone.

Tall, dark and handsome was such a cheesy description, but that was exactly what he was: six feet five inches, two hundred and thirty five pounds of pure muscle, with dark, wavy hair that sculpted his perfect head and mysterious emerald-green eyes with midnight-dark eyelashes.

She knew his weight and height because Molly from Payroll had given her his stats. She had no idea how the woman knew and hadn't asked. Molly was odd like that—she knew some of the strangest details about people. But this time she hadn't chalked it up to the woman's proclivity to know unique statistics, but on the fact that *every* woman in the office was interested in knowing anything and everything about the handsome new manager.

Although Max was white, his skin had a deep golden tan, one that didn't come from any tanning bed but was strictly natural, just man and sun…. She shivered and grew warm just thinking of him. Which was one of the many, *many* reasons that Nikki had decided he would be the one to end her embarrassingly long drought.

She glanced up and saw one of the accounting managers making a beeline for her and nearly groaned. *No damn way,* she thought, not feeling the least bit concerned for her lack of kindness. If she got caught up chatting with Tom, she'd never get loose, and she needed to make sure she was free when Max finally showed.

Nikki hopped off the stool and looked for an exit, then blew out a sigh of relief when a woman she recognized from Human Resources put a hand on Tom's arm, forcing him to stop. She caught the frustrated look on his face and knew she'd been right; he'd been aiming right for her.

She felt bad, really uncharitable. It wasn't just because Tom was short and bald that she didn't want to talk to him, but Tom thought he had game and was a bit obnoxious, constantly bragging about his convertible coupe and expensive clothes.

Nope. Not even her type, she thought. Not on her worst day. She might be lonely, but she wasn't desperate.

Nikki began to walk through the crowd, keeping her smile firmly in place as she nodded her head, casually making eye contact with those she knew as well as the many she didn't. She took a sip from the glass she held. Tonight was all about the happy…and her mission. Again… there was only one man she was on the lookout for: Max.

He'd come to the office after the last manager's abrupt departure and would be around only long enough for upper management to find and train his replacement. Other than that, no one knew much about Max. His background was a mystery. Not that it mattered to Nikki. She had one thing in mind.

After she readjusted her girls discreetly inside her new, barely-there demi bra, she glanced to the side and saw the one she'd been looking for, Mr. Tall, Dark and Fine himself staring at her from across the room.

She felt as though her stomach had bottomed out. Dear God. Fine, fine, fine…ooh. The man was unbelievably fine.

She shook her head and bit back the groan…hoping he hadn't witnessed the coughing and the vigorous thumping that had ensued. Not to mention the dodging of Tom and all that talking to herself. She didn't want to scare him off.

She took a deep breath and smiled. Directly at him. Game on.

Nikki felt her confidence rise as she realized that although he had a gathering of both women and men surrounding him like bees to a honeycomb, she could feel his eyes on her even as he spoke to one of the other managers.

She stared in his direction. Thanks to the champagne, she felt bold. And thanks to the new dress and sticking to her exercise regimen, she felt sexy. Damn sexy.

And from what she'd gathered from her undercover intel, he wasn't really the kind of guy who went in for long-term relationships.

He was a get-it-and-hit-it kinda guy.

Good.

Because she wasn't looking for that type of relationship either. *Not anymore,* she thought.

If the grapevine was right, not only was he a get-it-and-hit-it type of guy, when he hit it…he hit it out of the park.

She squared her shoulders and put a little extra sway in her walk as she began to make her way casually to where Max was standing in the crowd.

Game…*on*…

Chapter 2

Maxwell Steele-Hardaway, aka Max Stele, had come to the office party for one reason and one reason only: to get Nikki Danes, in any way he could.

The gorgeous part-time accountant had captured his attention from the first time he'd seen her two weeks ago when he'd joined the staff of MagHard Interior Design.

Temporarily joined the staff, he corrected himself, quelling the surge of irritation.

When his mother had approached him to help out the family, she'd used guilt and motherly love, but especially guilt in her appeal to her only son to help her in what she called her "time of need." Time of need, his butt, he thought.

He loved his mother, but she was without doubt the queen bee of drama. Naomi Steele-Hardaway was also blessed with one of the sharpest business minds he'd ever known.

She ran the family's business, MagHard Interior Design, with all the precision and attention to detail of an army drill sergeant. She'd launched the company with his father more than thirty years ago, and since his father's passing when Max was still in high school, the business had earned the distinction of being on the Fortune 500 list, with affiliate offices all over the United States.

The fact that she'd used the trump card of her "time of need" was just her way of asking Max to come home. He shook his head. Scratch that. *Demanded* that Max come home.

The only question was…why.

Max pretended to listen to Michelle Grimes, one of the supervisors in Design, as she regaled him with stories about the manager he'd replaced while he contemplated his mother's reason for asking him to help…and searched for Nikki Danes in the crowd of partygoers.

The fact that his mother had fired the last office manager made her request more palatable. At least this time the alibi made more sense. But Max knew there was something more, another reason for her demand for him to come home.

"So if you'd like, we can discuss the changes over coffee Monday?"

Max frowned and looked directly at the woman in front of him. Michelle had been one of the first execs he'd met when he'd arrived at the Austin offices. Lucky for him, the office was one of the newer ones, and outside of top management, no one knew who he was. He'd told his mother he wanted to keep it that way. She'd agreed easily to his demand, which was odd, since his mother rarely, if ever, agreed to anyone making demands of her.

"Sure, no problem," he said to Michelle, without knowing what in the hell he'd just agreed to. When her face lit up like the Christmas tree, he felt apprehensive. Oh, hell…

what had he just agreed to? he wondered as he studied the woman. Damn.

Michelle's over-the-top flirting, starting the moment he'd arrived, hadn't gone unnoticed. But he'd hoped to hell she would get the hint that he wasn't interested.

She hadn't. Obviously. He knew that part of her attraction to him was the mystery surrounding exactly who he was. He had tested the waters by using his mother's maiden name, Steele, rather than the family name, Hardaway. But even then he'd added a twist and spelled it "Stele," just to make sure no one made the connection.

When he told his mother, she'd given him a butter-wouldn't-melt-in-her-mouth kind of smile and agreed.

He felt the frown deepen.

Damn it. He was here to enjoy, let go and have fun. And not think about his mother and what she was up to.

"Great! I'll uh…come by in the morning and we can go down to Starbucks. Or we can go to the new coffee shop that just opened up on the corner, near the office building. I've been wanting to check them out," she continued to babble, and it became incredibly difficult for Max to pay attention to the woman. He had one woman and one woman only on his mind.

Michelle continued to speak. "I hear they make a great café fresco and they have fresh pastries, homemade! Not like those made at—"

"I'll just bring the coffee to our meeting," he cut in, ending her enthusiastic soliloquy. Hell, if he didn't, she'd probably have him agreeing to crap he had no desire to agree to, as his focus was currently diverted.

"Do you want to meet at eight-thirty?" Michelle asked.

"I'm not always sure what time in the morning I will make it in. Depending on how late I've had to be up the night before," he murmured, letting the very obvious meaning sink in.

"Ooh," Michelle said, a bright blush staining her pale skin. Obviously she caught the hint he threw out.

Which was another thing he was aware of—the office gossip that he was a player, a guy who enjoyed women. But he made no attempt to rectify the rumors that circulated, both in the office and out. It helped to keep those at bay who knew who he was...or better yet, knew who his family was—and along with that, knew about the money. After convincing his mother that he wanted no one to know he was technically part-owner of the company, he'd finally agreed to help her out of the supposed bind she was in.

In actuality, his original reluctance at being at MagHard Interior Design had evaporated like steam the minute he'd walked into headquarters the morning he had started and seen Nikki.

He'd been on the elevator the first time he'd seen her.

The elevator had been crowded and he'd kept his eyes straight ahead, not in the mood to make eye contact with anyone. The packed elevator made several stops along the way, letting folks in and out and when the doors slid open, allowing the last passengers to leave, he'd breathed a sigh of relief.

Max had muttered, "Thank God," only to hear someone yelling....

"Oh, please hold that, *please!*" a breathy feminine voice had begged and although he would have loved nothing more than to have the last few seconds alone until he made it to his destination on the top floor, he had pressed a finger on the door-open button.

"Thank you so much!" the breathless voice had replied as a small woman hurtled herself into the elevator. Before

Max could really get a good glimpse of her, her perfume, light, unique and floral, had caught his attention.

"No problem," he had said, turning to glance down at her.

She had looked up at him as she readjusted the messenger bag over her shoulder, again thanking him. She had smiled and two large dimples appeared in her cheeks, her almond-shaped eyes slanting, giving her an exotic look.

He had run his glance over her as she'd eased her small frame against the wall of the elevator, her gaze leaving his as a fine blush stole over her creamy brown skin. Fascinated by the obvious blush, Max had continued to stare at her.

Beauty didn't really describe her.

Her flawless skin was the color of deep milk chocolate without a hint of cream, and was just as smooth in appearance. She had the type of skin that made a man want to reach out and touch her face just to verify if it was as soft as it looked.

Her slanted eyes, although a rich brown, had flecks of what appeared from his distance from her a lighter color. He had been tempted to draw closer to her to see exactly what shade they were, and barely restrained himself in time. Her nose was small, and set above a full set of sexy, plump lips.

His cock had stirred as his gaze lingered on her mouth.

He had forced his eyes away. If he hadn't, he'd been afraid he'd act on the inappropriate desire he had to go up to a woman he didn't know, lean down and kiss those delightfully full lips.

She had been dressed casually, in a formfitting black skirt, not too short, the hem flirting around her knees. She had worn a pink tank top beneath a billowy, long-sleeved white tunic, buttoned halfway and tucked neatly into her skirt.

Maybe a little bit on the bohemian side, but not outlandish. Nothing special, but on her it looked sexy as hell. The colors she had worn were a perfect foil for her dark skin, and the skirt was fitted enough that it showed off her small waist and tight butt. Perfectly, deliciously proportioned A.T.W.: ass to waist.

And what an ass she had. Perky, the round globes appeared firm, and he had felt his cock stir again at the thought of what they would feel like cupped in his hands. What it would feel like to slide his hands over their no-doubt silky-feeling perfection. She'd wake up the morning after from a night of hot sex with his handprints all over that butt of hers.

She had just enough overflow to...bounce.

His eyes had met hers, caught them on him, checking him out just as he'd been checking every fine inch of her out as well.

Good. She now knew he was interested, and as he prided himself on knowing women, he also knew he'd piqued her interest.

Max had known time was limited; the ride would only last so long.

"Which floor?" Max had asked, his voice low, guttural, his mind on what he would love to do to her even as his gaze locked and loaded on hers.

The offices of MagHard Interior Design were located in a building that the corporation owned and managed, leasing out the luxury suites in the high-rent district of downtown Austin at a premium price. His office as well as all of upper management resided on the top floor, with the two floors directly beneath for the rest of the company.

One floor was dedicated to the design team, the other for administration, including Human Resources.

Max had focused his gaze on the beautiful woman, her eyes downcast as she tried her best not to look at him.

So damn sexy, he had thought. And again his dick had reacted to the visual of the offbeat little beauty. A small smile had tugged the corner of his mouth upward when her tongue had sneaked out and swiped across her bottom lip.

When she had glanced up at him, he had dropped his lids low to hide his eyes. He knew his lust had to be shining brightly; there was no way he could hide his reaction.

She had that offbeat, backhanded, casual type of sex appeal. The type that came as naturally to her as breathing.

Max had been incredibly fascinated and headed toward clinical obsession the longer he stared at her.

The elevator had jerked slightly and she had been jostled, not enough to bring her to his side, but enough that it moved her closer. His eyes had been drawn to her breasts, which bounced right along with the elevator, and the jiggle…fuck. If he wasn't careful, Max knew he would be in trouble of accosting a woman he didn't even know.

His nostrils had flared as he dragged in a deep breath. He had felt the overwhelming need to close his eyes, take in her intoxicating essence. It reached out and ensnarled him, dragging him in. What the hell was going on with him? one part of his mind had questioned.

Although he'd had plenty of women, he'd never felt this immediate and damn-near feverish type of attraction before that day.

The thought had hit him that the woman was turning him on in ways he hadn't been turned on by anyone in a long time. Damn. And that was with her clothes on, in a public area…an elevator, no less.

What the hell would happen if he could get her alone?

He'd convince her to take off her clothes and see if that perfectly mounded butt of hers fit into his palms with a hint of hang time, the overflow spilling over his cupped palms like two deviously ripened small melons, like he thought it would.

Max had shaken his head. He was getting ahead of himself. At the rate his mind was racing, the images that were bombarding his heated libido, he'd have her up against the wall and be balls-deep before he could even find out who she was.

He'd never been this affected by someone he didn't know. Hadn't spoken to.

He had known that he only had a finite time before the elevator ride ended to find out who she was, whether she worked in the office building and where.

She had cleared her throat and Max had met her eyes.

"Could you press number fourteen for me?" She had asked, her soft voice like music, the end notes floating over his skin like a butterfly's caress.

He had frowned, the strength of her appeal unlike anything he'd ever felt.

Max had casually leaned forward to jab the button she'd requested, his gaze never leaving hers. Her eyes had broken contact, and again he caught the hint of a blush staining her pretty cocoa-brown skin.

His glance had raked over her again.

Max had learned a long time ago to go with his gut. It was what had allowed him to break away from the family and their fortune and earn his own way, and why to date he'd amassed a fortune through commercial real estate that was a force to be reckoned with, although it didn't exactly match the family holdings. Although he held an interest in the family business, he hadn't relied on his family to give him extra leverage.

Working for himself and *not* using the family name as
a way to get his foot in the door, Max prided himself on
the fact that he was a self-made man.

In doing so, he'd learned a valuable, sometimes painful
lesson, that when he didn't follow his hunches, his gut, it
was a surefire way of fucking up.

And he had no intention of fucking up this hunch. The
hunch that had told him that the woman occupying his
space was important to him.

And his gut had told him this chance encounter was…
going to be interesting. He didn't know in what way, but
he had felt it, deep within his core.

He had allowed the smile that had been lurking to break
free, fully aware that she'd caught him staring. But it was
her own fault for being so damn fine. So…intoxicating
to his senses.

He had drawn in a breath, his smile widening when he
saw her reaction. Her pupils had dilated. His glance had
dropped to the hollow of her throat, and the banging little
pulse that beckoned for his mouth to cover, caress and as-
sure that he wasn't going to hurt her…that he would take
good care of her. His dick was now painful within the con-
striction of his pants.

His eyes had suddenly narrowed as realization hit after
he had pushed the button. They worked for the same company. It was then he had noticed the messenger bag she
had slung over her shoulder that featured his family's crest.
Many of the new employees had been given a bag with
the emblem emblazoned on the front when they began to
work for the company.

"Thank you," she had said and ducked her head, but
Max had caught the flare of awareness, the look of admiration that crossed her beautiful face as she had been
sizing him up.

"No problem," Max had finally muttered, realizing that he'd been staring at the woman far too long.

He had waited for her to realize that he was headed toward the same company.

He had stuck out his hand. "Max Stele. I'm new," he had said, his voice low, his gaze fixed on hers.

Locked and loaded.

"Figured you worked for MagHard, too," he had said, indicating the button he'd just depressed and her bag with the corporate logo.

"Oh, okay...um, I'm Nikki. Nikki Danes. I, uh, work in Accounting," she had replied, and glanced down at his waiting, opened palm.

She had hesitated briefly before lightly placing her hand within his. Immediately Max's much larger one had clamped down firmly. He had bit down a groan; her hand was soft and felt...right held within his. He had held on longer than necessary, and when she had tugged, gently, he had allowed her to withdraw. For now.

"Do you like working there?" he had asked.

"Well, I think I do. Depends on how the dragon is feeling today."

He had barked out a surprised laugh at her response. As soon as the words left her pretty, full lips, her eyes had widened and she slammed a hand over her mouth, suppressing a groan. His libido and humor were at war with each other, both vying for dominance.

He had known who Nikki was referring to: Ms. Nadine Rockway, the accounting manager.

He also knew the woman had breath that could start a forest fire. But Nadine Rockway was a damn good accountant, one who had been handling the books for various Hardaway companies and working for and with his mother for years. The two were like sisters. Of a sort.

But her breath still stank to high heaven.

"Dragon lady, huh?" he had asked, staring down at her, keeping a straight face. "Is that because she's so...seasoned?" She bit her lip, but Max had seen the glint of humor in her pretty brown eyes and he had pressed on. "Or is it because her breath could scorch the fine hairs off a frog's back?"

"Well...that's an interesting way of putting it," she had stated, and they both had laughed.

"This is my floor," she had said, the giggles subsiding as the elevator came to a halt. "Maybe I'll see you around."

"No doubt about it, Ms. Danes," he had murmured.

After she'd left the elevator, her unique scent remained. Unconsciously, Max had adjusted himself in his pants, his shaft reacting again to the scent of the woman.

But as enticing as her unique scent had been, her casual beauty and the hint of her offbeat humor had snared his attention even more.

When the elevator had reached his floor, Max had stepped into the upper management offices with a new, upbeat feeling, suddenly looking forward to his stint. And all because of Nikki Danes.

Over the following weeks, he had gone out of his way to see her, finding any excuse to visit the administrative offices and catch glimpses of her. Yet for all the times he'd seen her, he'd become frustrated as hell, because he'd not once since that first moment had one damn moment alone with her.

Now nights were beginning to merge into one long pubescent wet dream, wherein he'd wake up with his shaft in his hand and sexy images of the pretty accounting assistant teasing his mind.

Despite his veiled excuses to visit the accounting department, he'd not had the opportunity to get her alone and talk to her. Not that Max hadn't tried his damnedest.

He'd found out her lunchtime, and although he'd gone to the cafeteria, he hadn't caught a glimpse of her. Further snooping and he'd found out she was a full-time grad student and often used her lunch periods to go and study.

Although his identity as a member of the Hardaway family was unknown, there were two people who knew who he really was: Nadine Rockway, Nikki's immediate supervisor and the head of the accounting department, and the chief of security and personnel, James Green.

Max knew that if he accessed the records and looked her up himself, it would be suspicious. There was no way in hell he was going to go to Nadine and ask. Without a doubt he knew that it would become a topic of conversation between the woman and his mother, something he could do without.

Which left James, a much better candidate for his mission to find out all he could about Nikki. The man had worked for the family business for years, just as Nadine had, but he was less inclined to gossip with Max's mother. Without asking questions—he was the chief of security, after all—he'd not only pulled her personal records from the files, but he'd also loaded her full dossier on a jump drive and placed it in a sealed envelope.

Max had, without shame, plugged the jump drive into his laptop, sat back and learned everything he could about her....

It was then he had decided a company party to celebrate the holidays was in order. And not just any type. For this holiday party, he had communicated to the staff the importance of attendance and dressing up.

He wanted to see her all dolled up, he had thought with a satisfied smile on his face.

Max felt a hot glide of awareness the minute she came into the room. He was snapped out of the memory, his glance colliding with hers.

Nikki Danes.

As those around him continued to speak—it was all background noise—his focus was all on her.

He moved his head to the side to try to catch a better look at her, and fought the urge to shove Larry from the design department to the side when the obese man blocked his view. When Larry finally moved aside to chase down one of the waiters carrying a platter of small sandwiches, Max finally caught a real good look at her.

Hot damn, he thought, his eyes on the gorgeous woman. He felt as though he'd been kicked in the chest the minute he got a good visual of her.

He'd had an idea she had a fine body, but no way did he know it looked like *that.* His cock thumped inside his shorts in response.

The dress she wore hugged every inch of her perfect curves like a custom-made glove.

The bold, deep red color of the wrap dress complemented her deep chocolate skin tone. Her legs seemed to go on forever and a day.... Again his cock stirred, thickening, elongating in response.

Even her shoes were sexy; they matched her dress in color, with strings that tied at her ankles and formed perfect bows. Bows he longed to unwrap. He loved a woman wearing stilettos, especially one with the kind of legs Nikki had.

He mumbled apologies as he began to move toward her, blindly ignoring those around him.

He only had eyes for her. And he intended to make her his....

Chapter 3

"I made it, chica!" Startled out of her deer-in-the-headlights stare with Max, Nikki nearly jumped out of her skin when Tony spoke directly behind her.

Turning, she was caught up in a hug filled with the mixed scent of True Star and jasmine, Tony's personal "signature" blend.

Although moments before she'd only had eyes for the man heading her way, the distraction of her friend's surprise appearance had her grinning ear to ear.

"I thought you weren't going to make it!" she said, pushing away and smiling up at Tony. She was used to having to look up at most people, but tonight, in the five-inch stilettos she was rocking, she was almost five foot nine, which would have put her closer to Tony's height of five foot eleven.

If he hadn't been wearing heels just as high. All in black except for the shiny silver vest and matching wedge-heeled shoes, he was…spectacular.

"Wow, you look great!" Nikki screamed.

"Oh, my God, no, chica, look at you! Hmm, mami, you look beautiful! A perfect ten!" he exclaimed, and Nikki gave him a fierce hug. A compliment like that from Tony was no easy thing, as he considered himself the guru of fashion. Around the office he had Nikki giggling constantly in his role as the self-proclaimed fashion police.

She spun around in a small circle for his full inspection, lightly curtsying and laughing. "So you like?"

Tony tilted his head to the side. A look entered his dark brown eyes, one that immediately told her he suspected something. "Uh-huh…and just who is this for?" he asked.

"This night is all about me," she said breezily.

Unable to resist, she glanced in the direction Max had been coming from, quelling the disappointment when she saw he had vanished. She barely refrained from slumping her shoulders and pouting like a little kid who couldn't find her favorite toy.

She quickly turned away, not wanting Tony and his discerning eyes to catch on.

Placing a purposeful smile on her face, she looped her arm thorough his and asked, "Can't a girl just wanna look good once in a while?"

He tsked at her. "Hmm. I guess. I'll let it go for now," he said. That moment, the band began to play a new song, one that was a perfect rendition of a current pop hit.

"Ooh, let's dance!" he continued, not missing a beat. "I told you this group was good, right?" he said, and before she could agree or disagree, Tony was dragging her onto the dance floor. As he did, she glanced over her shoulder in time to see Max, his gaze locked with hers as a woman she recognized from upper management touched his arm, speaking to him in earnest.

Nikki barely held on to the frustrated sigh. She knew she wasn't the only one who had her eyes on Max Stele.

"May I interrupt?"

Breathless from the exertion of dancing to not one but three back-to-back songs, Nikki turned and nearly collided with the hard wall of Max's chest.

"Oh, my," she said, her hands touching the granitelike wall of his chest, her fingers sinking into the soft, silk fabric of his shirt.

For the past two hours, between Tony keeping her busy talking—aka gossiping his damn head off—dancing, eating and drinking, and basically having the best time she'd had in years, she had been unable to continue her "mission," as she thought of it. That was probably a good thing, as after that first encounter Nikki hadn't been within ten feet of Max.

After the first dance, she'd begged off dancing again and had searched out Max, only to find him again surrounded by a bevy of women. All looking beautiful, all with one look on each of their faces: lust for Max Stele.

Refusing to let that ruin her good time, she'd allowed Tony to drag her onto the dance floor again and even accepted dance invites from some of her colleagues as well as men who'd come to the party as guests.

Occasionally she'd catch glimpses of him in the party throng, but as the night had worn on, folks had gotten bolder and more liquored up and the office party had acquired an all-out club vibe: dancing, singing, drinking… and many, many hookups, she noted.

"And I ain't mad at 'em…are you, boo?" Tony had asked her at one point when they'd caught several employees acting in a way she knew they'd be embarrassed as hell about come Monday morning.

But it wasn't Monday morning, and everyone was having a *goooood* time, she thought, giggling, the free-flowing alcohol and great music agreeing with her as she nodded her head at Tony, cosigning on his statement. Nope. She was definitely not mad at anyone for enjoying the event.

So when she bumped into him, spinning away from her current partner's arms and smack dab into his, she raised her eyes and her hands seemed to, of their own volition, come up and touch his chest. Her fingers widened, as did her eyes, when she felt the…strength of the hard wall.

Hmm.

The man was *fine,* she thought. And in the words of her friend, she most definitely wasn't mad at that fact, she thought, and giggled.

He smiled down at her. Placed a thick finger beneath her chin and raised her eyes to meet his. "Having a good time, baby?" he asked.

Any other time, a man calling her "baby," particularly one she didn't know, would immediately turn her off.

But when Max called her that… She kept her eyes on his, unable to look away as she held her breath, feeling a blush warm her face.

"I've been watching you all night. Dancing, having a good time."

"It's…it's been wonderful, all of this," she said, breaking eye contact to glance around.

At that moment, the bandleader grabbed the microphone and announced a small break, and immediately the sounds of a popular, bluesy R & B song filled the ballroom. Couples began to sway together to the music.

She swallowed, unable to look at him.

But he wasn't allowing her even that. He brought her face back around, locking his gaze with hers as he wrapped an arm around her waist, bringing her even tighter, more flush against his body as he began to sway them in unison to the music.

The lights had been dimmed even more and although she knew no one could see her expression, she felt as though her lust for this man was on display for all the world to see.

Her lust made her feel vulnerable. Exposed.

"And seeing you having a good time has made me quite excited," he murmured low, for her ears only.

Her eyes widened and she inhaled a sharp breath.

His shaft pressed hotly, thickly against her stomach while his hand moved up and down her back. She moaned, her eyes closing as she exhaled the long breath she'd been holding.

Damn.

He did this to her and they were both fully clothed. She was on fire for him....

"More," he whispered, bending his head down so that their foreheads nearly touched.

Startled, her eyes flew open and glanced up at him, their gazes locking.

A soft frown creased her brows. "Excuse me?"

"I want you more."

She gulped. It was as though he read her mind. There was no way she could hide from him.

She stared up into his beautiful emerald-green eyes, which blazed down at her. Watching her.... She read his need, one that matched her own.

She felt a rash of goose bumps feather down her legs, something that happened whenever she was sexually aroused.

It had been so long since that had happened, she'd forgotten the telling goose bumps appeared without fail when she was...wet.

She clenched her legs together, her core seeming to throb. Inhaling a deep breath, she broke eye contact with him, forcing herself to look away.

This is insane, she thought, her heartbeat racing out of control.

"It's okay," he breathed against her ear, again reading her mind. But it was as though he held some sort of key or magic wand, because as soon as he voiced the assuring words, she felt the tension begin to ease from her. When he hugged her tightly, she allowed her body to meld, once again, into his.

As they danced, their bodies moved as one, in perfect harmony, as though they'd practiced for years. They naturally seemed to catch the other's rhythm with the ease of seasoned pros.

This connection…whatever they had was unlike anything Nikki had ever felt. Maybe it was the wine making her feel this way, she thought. Maybe it was her desire to let loose and enjoy. To enjoy being a woman and all that meant. Maybe it was the fact that he was the most beautiful man she'd ever seen. Or maybe a combination of all of the above.

As she pressed her cheek against his chest, their bodies moving as one to the slow beat of the love song, she didn't care what it was. She knew one thing and one thing only. She wanted this man to sex her up six ways to Sunday. And she wanted him in the worst kind of way.

A smile kicked up the corner of her mouth.

She moved her head from his chest, suddenly aware, afraid someone was watching, that someone would see what he was doing to her, even though her desire was not overt.

"I want you so damn bad, Nikki Francine Danes. In the worst way."

And just like that, her desire and lust for him grew exponentially. His seductive pronouncement, whispered in her ear, made her glad she'd worn panties. If she hadn't, her cream would be running down her legs right about now, she thought. She bit back a groan and restrained herself from grinding her body against his.

"Come with me, Nikki. I have a room in the hotel," he said, and Nikki watched his sensual lips as they framed the words.

Without thinking, she lifted a finger to trace his mouth.

So sexy. Just like the rest of him.

He smiled. Her eyes were drawn to the sexy little dimple at the corner of his wickedly sensual mouth.

"Come play with me," he said, and she moaned at the immediate response of her body.

Why not? Why not…play? The thought rushed into her mind. A naughty thought. One that, had she had a little less champagne humming through her veins, she wouldn't dare to think. Taking him up on his offer would be unlike anything she'd ever done.

She was going to allow a man she didn't really know to take her to his room and, God willing, have the best sex of her life. She wanted him to spank her ass…and make her like it.

She nodded her head and without a thought to anyone looking, she allowed him to guide her from the dance floor and away from the party.

Chapter 4

The ride up the hotel elevator was mercifully empty and as Max ushered Nikki inside, his glance stole over her.

She was nervous, he could tell.

He refrained from hauling her sexy body close to his. Barely.

She was shy and lived with her grandmother, he thought, an unknown smile tugging the corners of his mouth as he recalled the many things he knew about Nikki Danes.

But right now, her excitement was the most relevant thing about her. Her excitement for him.

When he'd been unable to take any more of the hot glide of her sweet body against his, the subtle way she was grinding against his shaft, Max had known the time had come. He'd felt her reaction to him. She was as turned on as he was.

Her reaction had only confirmed what he'd felt from the moment he'd met her: she was shy yet there was…fire, untapped for sure, just below the surface.

He felt like a little boy in a candy shop, mentally rubbing his hands together at the thought of what it would feel like to have her beneath him, to be the man to blow across the embers of her sensuality and release the heat.

He wanted to be the man to do the job.

She kept her face down, shyly, away from his. Instinct was guiding him with her, as it did for everything.

Everything that mattered, he thought.

He shoved that thought aside, as for a moment the relevance she had for him was…new. Something he'd never experienced.

He'd examine that later. Right now it was all about having passionate sex with her.

Again he ignored the inner voice warning him it was more than just sex. He was marking his territory, an instinctual need to claim what his subconscious had marked as his three weeks ago.

He reached for her and brought her closer to his body. He knew that he needed to keep her grounded to him, that like the little hummingbird she appeared to be at the moment, it wouldn't take much for her to take to the air and fly away.

She was shy, he got that. She didn't seem to have much experience and there was no telling what was going on in her mind.

She seemed to have a war going on inside her, one he'd give any amount of money to get a true view of. He found that the more he was around her, the more…vested in her he was becoming.

But if he had his way about it, by the end of the night— the weekend, as he'd booked the room for Friday night through Monday morning—his little hummingbird's wings would be firmly and decidedly clipped.

Without thought he reached over and brought her close,

giving her no time to react. He wrapped his arms around her slight body, bringing their bodies into tight alignment, and slanted his mouth over hers.

Max couldn't deny himself the feeling of her lips, the softness of her touch, for another moment.

When she felt the smoothness of his firm lips against her mouth, Nikki melted against him.

Not sure what to expect after the suddenness of the kiss, she braced herself for the sensual assault he'd given her on the dance floor.

Her hands fisted the fine cloth of his shirt and she held her breath. He softly kissed her, feathery strokes teasing her mouth, his tongue snaking out to lick her lips.

As he kissed her, he kept a hand on the back of her head, keeping her steady, but without pressure. She moaned into his mouth, the gentleness of the kiss her undoing.

Soothing her. Guiding her. Like an animal in the wild stalking its prey...before it pounced.

The ghost of a warning rang in the back of her mind, but she forced it away.

When the elevator came to a halt, he pulled away, his hands still holding her. An enigmatic smile graced his sensual lips.

Again he held out a hand and wordlessly she placed hers in it, giving him silent permission to guide her into whatever the night had in store.

She followed him out of the elevator, her nerves taut. It wasn't until he stopped and turned to face her that she glanced around, surprised to find that they were inside the room.

"Is this what I think it is?" she asked, and felt foolish the minute she did, laughing lightly.

If she'd been in the right frame of mind, she would have

recognized that they were going to the top floor when he placed the key in the slot on the elevator panel that gave access to the top floor. The penthouse.

She glanced around, surprised, but trying her hardest to be the picture of cool sophistication as she took it all in.

"Wow," she blurted, and felt inadequate and gauche the minute the words left her mouth. *The very antithesis of cool sophistication,* she thought, and rolled her eyes at herself. But it was such a spectacular room, so vast, so elegant and beautiful that *wow* was the only word she could come up with.

She jumped when she felt his big hands land on her shoulders and felt slightly embarrassed by her nervous reaction. He turned her around to face him.

He smiled lightly, but in his eyes the fire from what they'd started, what was burning, lingered. Yet he tilted his head to the side, considering her.

She felt the nervousness that began in her gut bubble and churn, and she swallowed down the sudden anxiety.

What the hell was she doing with this man? She knew next to nothing about him and had simply decided that he would be the one to "clean out her cobwebs"? Her doubts about her mission began to war with the light buzz from the alcohol.

"I don't want you to do anything you aren't ready for, but I want you," he said, his deep voice sending shivers over her body. He brought her close so she could feel the evidence of his arousal. "But only if you want this." He brought his mouth down to touch hers lightly, his firm lips covering her mouth as he lightly bit down. Not hard enough to hurt, not at all. But enough that she felt the sting.

Her pussy began to throb.

"I know you enjoyed the party," he said when he released her, a small smile toying with the corners of his sensual mouth. "It's what I wanted, why I planned it. But again…I don't want you to do this if it's not what you want."

He brought his hand up and caressed the line of her jaw, the small smile still lurking in his deep green eyes.

It was as though he read her mind. Again.

Nikki knew she couldn't and wouldn't blame it on the alcohol.

She reached up and traced a finger down the line of his aquiline nose until her finger reached his lip, brushing over the hard yet sensual line of his mouth.

He took the tip into his mouth, sucked on the digit, eliciting a moan from her.

"I want you to want me as badly as I burn for you. As badly as I've wanted you from the first time I saw you in the elevator," he said, and tugged her toward him.

The tug was slightly…rough. Matching the tone in his voice. She knew he was holding on by a thread. Yet he wanted to make sure she was comfortable with her decision.

For whatever reason that calmed her, even as her passion for him grew.

"But…only if you want it," he said, and with that he took her hand in one of his while the other unzipped his slacks. Deftly, he brought his shaft out and he boldly used her hand to cover his hard, thick, long dick.

"Oh, God…yes," she moaned, closing her hand around him. He lifted her into his arms and carried her across the room toward the king-size bed. She reached a hand up and said softly, "It's been a while. Please be…careful with me."

She saw a flare of something flash in his beautiful green eyes before he nodded his head. He whispered softly against her mouth before covering it with his own, "As though my life depended on it."

Chapter 5

"Be careful with me," she'd whispered, her voice hesitant.

Those four words had nearly been his undoing. In them he heard more than the obvious. He heard her telling him something more, something his heart recognized as meaningful, deep and pure.

After placing her on the bed, he'd made quick work of his own clothes, shucking his slacks from his body, nearly ripping his shirt from his chest in his haste to feel her skin on his.

He watched her in the soft amber glow as she in turn kept her gaze on him.

Watching him undress.

His dick thumped against his shorts. He withdrew his wallet from his slacks and quickly, deftly, removed three of the tiny square foil wrappers. It would be enough to start.

"Do you like what you see?" he asked, his voice rough as he turned to face her. He saw her eyes widen at the three condoms. He kept their gazes locked as he drew his shorts down his legs.

She inhaled a swift breath, her eyes widening even more as she took all of him in.

His laugh was low and purely masculine.

"Yes," she breathed, her tongue coming out to snake across her full, beautiful lips. And just like that, she had his cock swelling in response. From just one glance at his cock.

If he wasn't careful, this would be over before he started.

His inclination had been to strip her clothes from her body and see just how beautiful she was, naked and exposed beneath him.

He'd forced himself to chill and try his damnedest to take it slow and not scare her. So he started at her feet, removing the sexy high heels after carefully untying the pretty ribbon tied in a loopy bow.

He brought her leg close to his after slipping the shoes from her feet, one by one, and ran his face along the silky skin, his eyes closing shut.

When he placed her dainty foot in his palm, he brought it instinctively to his mouth, his eyes seeking hers.

He ran his tongue over the top, up the length until he reached her ankle, his tongue stroking and licking the smooth skin.

When she moaned softly, he bit back a groan.

She was so responsive to his touch. His dick hardened painfully.

"God, your skin is so soft, so smooth," he said, and allowed his hands to run up the length of her thighs. She moaned as he found her panties and pulled them down, past her knees, her legs, until finally he tossed them to the floor.

"We won't be needing those." His voice was heavy with need.

He brought his mouth to her thighs, working upward,

his tongue leaving a hot, wet trail as he moved up her body. When he stopped at the junction of her thighs, he felt her body tremble.

Slowly, he lifted her dress, easing it up and away, releasing the front ties of the wraparound dress to reveal her beautiful naked body as she lay before him like an erotic offering.

He nearly came on the spot. He grabbed his cock unconsciously as he beheld her beauty.

He'd had an idea what she would look like naked, but no way in hell could he have imagined she'd look like this.

His hands came out to grasp her tiny waist loosely as he stared, transfixed with her magnificence. Her hips were full and jutted out enough to make a man salivate. He stared at her high, firm breasts and imagined the feel of them in his hands.

Slowly he traced up the length of her body to take the small, perfectly sculpted globes into his hands. Like her ass, her breasts had just the right amount of…overflow. He bounced them lightly, stroking a finger across the nipples, and groaned when the dark wine nubs hardened beneath his probing fingers.

Perfection.

She laughed softly, bringing him out of his dazed fascination. Her full mouth curved upward. Her feminine laughter mirrored his earlier one. It was the kind of soft laugh that let a man know his woman knew *exactly* what she was working with…and what she was doing to him.

Max's dick was hard as granite, yet he forced himself to go slowly. He ran an appreciative glance down her body.

She allowed her legs to drop to the side so that her pretty kitty was exposed. He brought a hand up to stroke across it.

Although her hair was cut low, she had a tiny tuft right above her lips. He ran a finger over the curls and a growl of need broke from his throat.

"So damn fine…even your pretty pussy is fine," he said roughly.

He brought his eyes to meet hers. There was an air of expectancy in the room. One they both knew would be fulfilled.…

He went down on her.

Placing his hands beneath the bend of her legs, he lifted her thighs, nudged them apart and lowered his head.

His tongue stroked one long caress across her pussy, end to end, from the back of her entry to the tip of her clit. He laved and sucked.

Her moans filled the room as she tossed on the bed.

He chuckled low, lightly against her pussy. He knew she loved his oral loving. Truth was, he loved giving it to her just as much.

Her scent, her taste were unique and different. Intoxicating.

He paused and heard her whimper. "Shh…I'll take care of you, baby. I just need time with this pretty kitty of yours," he said, his fingers coming out to separate her lips. "Is that okay?" he asked as she moaned, unable to answer him.

He separated her lips with his fingers and groaned at the sight of her glistening inner lips. It made his balls tingle when he noted that the inner skin of her lips was a slightly lighter shade of brown than her outer lips, the contrast sexy as hell to him. He dipped his fingers inside and gently skewered them in her body, withdrawing her moisture. He brought it to his lips and sucked her juices clean.

His nostrils flared as her heady, unique smell of arousal engulfed him, making his balls tighten and his cock thump, hard, painfully, against his thigh.

"Max…" she groaned, her feminine pleas for him to continue making his own breath catch.

"Okay, baby…I'll give you what you need," he said. "Do you trust me?" he asked. And as badly as he just wanted to do her, suck her and fuck her, her trust was…important. More important than his raging hard-on. More important than the fact that he didn't know if he'd ever felt like this about a woman he'd been around for such a short time. Much less not had communication with outside of one time.

He waited for her reply, as hard as it was to do that and not touch her. She nodded her head, her tongue coming out to lick her lower lip. "Please…make love to me."

That was all Max needed to hear.

He brought his face down again, to her entry.

He gloried in her pussy, suckling the clit deep into his mouth as his tongue came out and flicked rapid strokes over her lips. He couldn't get enough.

Her moans and cries filled the room as he continued laving her, his tongue doing to her what his cock would soon be doing, stroking, fucking…loving.

He knew she was close to the edge. Max's index finger came out to feather over her tuft as he continued stroking her, using his mouth, lips, tongue and fingers to bring her to screaming release.

He didn't stop suckling her until her cries stopped and her trembling body collapsed.

He moved his head, taking in her glistening pussy, the sexy way her legs were wide open, her dress not completely shed from her body as she lay on top of it.

Sexy as hell. He grabbed his shaft, running a finger over the top, feeling his own precome as he stared down at the woman who, for whatever reason, had become more important to him than any other woman had in all of his thirty-two years.

The thought should have scared the shit out of Max.

But it didn't. He reached over for the first condom of the night.…

"I'm not through with you yet…"

Her drowsy eyes flew open.

Chapter 6

In blissful contentment Nikki lay in the center of the king-size bed, her body melting into the soft mattress.

Satisfaction buzzed in every fiber of her being after being on the receiving end of Max's oral loving. Even as her body finally began to calm, her quivering thighs beginning to relax and her thudding heartbeat slowing to an even rhythm, every molecule was still alive with feeling, every nerve ending sensitive to the lightest touch.

She inhaled a deep breath. The breeze, coming from the lazy sway of the ceiling fan overhead, was like little erotic pricks to her overly sensitive skin.

It wasn't only the fan that was causing her hypersensitive nerve endings to jump. Most of *that* had to do with the slow, wickedly sensual flicks of a talented tongue and soft kisses from a pair of firm lips delivered to her clit as she came down from her high, from the hottest man she'd ever had between her thighs, she thought. She felt a small giggle bubbling forth out of sheer happiness.

She felt *sooo* good.

She inhaled a deep breath, but kept her eyes closed. No way could it get any better, she thought....

"I'm not through with you yet."

Her eyes flew open and she stared down at the dark head between her thighs.

"Max, wait, I—" The rest of her plea broke off when she gasped, her back arching high when he spread her legs wide and *blew* on her pussy.

Immediately her body reacted. As though she hadn't just had the best orgasm of her life—she'd never had the type of sexual satisfaction that she'd just experienced. But she wasn't tired or listless...that same satisfied body got energized in less than two-point-two seconds.

The minute she felt his warm breath on her kitty, she felt her clit engorge, as though in welcome of what was to come. What *more* sensual delights it was going to enjoy.

Her nipples hardened and those goose bumps returned with a vengeance when she heard his deep, masculine laugh. She opened her eyes and sought his gaze and her heart seemed to clench just the smallest bit when she caught the sexy little dimple that appeared in the corner of his cheek. And then she felt his cock, hard, thick...long, brush against her thighs as he raised his body.

With feline grace he leaned over and grasped the condom from the bedside table. Her heart began to thud, her nipples tight as she watched him tear it open with his teeth and discard the wrapper.

Her pussy clenched as though with a mind of its own as Nikki watched in helpless fascination when he grasped the base of his cock in one hand.

Even though his hand was large, he could barely circle it.

Her throat convulsed.

He kept her gaze locked on his when he began to roll the protection down the long…impossibly long and thick length of his rigid shaft. With the precision of a drill sergeant, he covered that beautiful monster.

She felt oddly mesmerized, almost dazed, watching the way he rolled the condom over his length, while at the same time her body was electrified. The effect was unexpectedly erotic.

And he hadn't even touched her with it.

"Ohhh," she moaned, barely aware she'd even made the sound, she was so caught up in the sensual web she found herself entangled in.

His eyes darkened in reaction to her response, a flush appearing on his lean face.

"Goddamn, you're fine. So damn sexy…so responsive," he growled, his voice now lower than she'd ever heard it. As he finished the task of placing condom on shaft, his voice was so low and guttural it was close to animalistic.

Nikki felt her feminine power rise in satisfaction. She knew that his voice became like that because he was close to the edge. A fine line for sure, but it was hot, wickedly hot, to know that she was the reason he was dangling so close to the edge.

She knew his need was riding him, hard.

She also knew she should be afraid and if she had any sense at all she would grab her clothes and run for the nearest exit, knowing good and well that what he had in store for her would be unlike anything she could imagine, much less had experienced.

Shoulda, woulda, coulda…it was all white noise to her.

He stopped and stared down at her, his hands falling down near his waist.

She had never seen a man so…vibrant. So alive. She inhaled a breath, her eyes darting down, taking in his massive manhood that proudly stood long and stiff away from the lighter-colored nest of curls surrounding it. His balls were heavy, perfectly rounded spheres.

She felt a yearning to place her tongue on them, softly lick them as he had licked her so intimately. To hold them in her mouth, see how they felt housed inside.

Oh, God, what was happening to her? What was he doing to her? she thought. She'd never felt so…alive. So sexual…

"You keep looking at my cock like that, my balls, and this won't last," he said bluntly. Instead of scaring her, his words empowered her even more.

Nikki leaned up enough that she could touch him. She ran a hand down over his stomach, the hard abs beneath bunching under her caress.

Growing bolder, she ran them down further until she reached the top of the sandy-colored, wavy hair surrounding his shaft.

She licked her dry lips.

"Do it." He bit off the demand, roughly.

Her eyes sought his.

She blew out a breath, a case of nerves halting her even as her hands lightly grazed his sac, heavy with need and come.

"I won't make you do anything. You have to tell me you want me, Nikki," he said. "You need to show me."

She swallowed down the nervousness, knowing that this was what she wanted, what *she* needed.

Her hands cupped his sac, her eyes widening at the weight. Although she'd made love before, it had never been so…intimate as it was with him.

She wanted to kiss it, lick it, but stopped.

She smiled shakily at him and felt relief when she saw

the same lust in his eyes as before, despite her inability to go through with touching him with her mouth.

He took her hands within his, kissed her open palms and laid her back down. "We will only do what you are ready to do, baby. I will never rush you for anything more."

That made her want him even more, if possible.

She drank him in as he poised above her, staring down at her from his emerald-colored eyes, his dark hair wavy and long, lightly resting on top of his wide shoulders, one thick, curly lock lying across one of his brows.

Her eyes roamed over his thick chest, heavy with muscle begging for her touch. He resembled a beautiful, dark fallen angel to her. Untamed. Wild… Hot.

With her heart racing, she opened her arms, inviting her fallen angel to come to her and give her whatever he wanted…in whatever way he wanted to give it to her.

She'd deal with regrets, if she had any, later…much later.

Chapter 7

The minute Nikki opened her arms to him, Max pressed her beautiful body down on the mattress, carefully covering her small body with his much bigger one.

He needed to feel her…

"Hmm. Damn, you feel so good against me," he whispered, his hands coming out to grab her waist before slipping down and grasping her hips.

He wanted to go slow, be gentle with her, but his need threatened to override his rational mind and he feared if he didn't get control ASAP, he'd lose it and go balls-deep inside her before she was ready for him.

He brought his forehead to rest against hers.

"Are you…are you all right?" She asked the question breathlessly and he cursed himself, believing she was faltering beneath his weight.

"I'm sorry, I didn't mean to crush you," he said, and began to shift his weight, stopping when he felt her small hand on his forearm.

"No, I'm fine! You're not heavy…" Her words stopped him and he remained where he was, only shifting her legs so that he lay between them.

"I just wanted to know if you were, you know, okay?" she asked, and he groaned painfully.

"I am. I just needed a moment so I didn't…hurt you. You're so small," he moaned into her neck, unable to re-sist the temptation.

She reached her hands up to wrap around his thick neck, replying, "I'm small, but I'm not fragile. I won't break," she said, and he dragged in a deep breath when he felt her turn her face into his neck, kissing the side with her full lips, her tongue boldly coming out to flick the lobe of his ear.

"Keep doing that, little girl, and you just might get what you're asking for."

"That's what your mouth is saying…"

It took a moment for her sexual teasing to register. When it did he was torn between being turned on even more—if that was even possible—to admiration for her cute wit.

His dick jumped and the war was over before it started.

He needed her, now.

"Let me test it first," he replied in a coarse voice. "I want to feel that pretty pussy of yours wrapped around me, trust me. But I won't hurt you," he said, and captured her lips with his before she could reply.

He shoved her legs farther apart, spreading her wide, and, placing his hand between them, sought her out. As he continued to kiss her, their mouths dueling as their sexual play grew heated, he inserted first one finger inside her clenching, tight heat.

"Oh, fuck!" he said, and slowly added another. Her walls came out to clench and tighten on his fingers, so tightly he knew he really had to prepare her.

He began to pump his fingers slowly into her vagina until she moaned against his mouth, grinding her hips as she sought more of him.

He slowly added one more finger, skewering it inside her even as she grew wetter with each drugging kiss, each twist of his fingers inside her body.

She whimpered against his mouth and he felt her need rising. But he had to make sure. She broke contact with his mouth, even as he continued his sensual assault. Panting, her chest heaving, she continued to work his fingers even as she pleaded, her voice barely above a hoarse whisper, "Max…oh, God, what are you doing to me?"

"I want that pussy juicy for me, baby." Max could barely respond; his need was now making thought and communication painful to attempt.

"I—I'm ready, please," she cried, keening and moaning when he continued.

He withdrew his fingers and brought them to his face, licking them clean as he'd done earlier, her essence flowing down the side of his hand.

His lips pulled back in a feral grin.

She was ready for him.

He leaned up and away from her, grasped his shaft at the midpoint and brought it to her entry. He leaned in and slowly began to feed her his cock. Slowly, carefully, inch by inch he gave her himself.

He felt the moment her feminine walls began to protest before the cry left her lips. He knew she was small and he was by no means even average. His dick was big, but he wasn't a brute. He'd go without before he'd hurt her. The thought of her being hurt by anyone, including himself, brought along with it a surge of unreasonable anger.

He tossed the thought of why that was to the side and waited for her.

"Baby…oh, my God, you're so big, I—" Her voice broke and soft whimpers tore at him.

He brought his mouth to hers and softly kissed her, whispering nonsensical shushing noises, seeking to give her solace.

He was only halfway in.

He brought his finger back out to play, this time focusing on her clit. Within seconds he felt the gush of liquid saturate the digit and relief made him tremble.

He slowly began to screw his hips and feed her more of himself until he'd given it all to her.

He captured her cry of pain and pleasure with his mouth, shoving his tongue deep.

"Nikki, baby, you are so hot…so tight and slick on my cock," he grunted as he slowly began to stroke in shallow, controlled movements. "Damn, you feel good on me!"

Slow, measured, slick kisses mimicked the way he dragged in and out of her heat. He repositioned her legs so that he hit her clit with each advance and retreat of his cock.

With each hot glide, each stroke, he felt the hair around his groin brush against her smooth pussy, making his cock damn near explode with the incredible dual sensation.

On every level she intoxicated him. Her scent, her body…the way she moved. She was the total sexual package.

He lifted her legs so that they lay over his arms and, grasping her hips, he began to ride her.

Jostling her body as he rotated his hips, knifing into her sweet pussy, he gave short, controlled thrusts as her cream came out and saturated his dick, running down the side of her leg as she loudly cried her pleasure.

With a shout he threw his head back, the muscles in

his neck straining, his arms shaking and sweat running freely down his face.

"Yes!" His roar filled the room as he ground into her moist warmth, his straining arms caging her within his embrace.

He felt her body tense and clench and knew she was ready to release. He thrust once, twice, and felt her body let go. When he felt her tightening walls and scream, he reached down and swallowed her cries with his mouth.

Within moments they went up in flames together, the orgasm intense, unlike anything he'd ever felt. It was as though a thousand butterflies were feathering his dick, toying with his balls.

Moments after they climaxed and lay back on the bed, spent, Max knew that his world would never be the same again. He thought of the file he'd had put together on her and the fact that he wasn't exactly who he said he was. How would she react when he told her about the latter? There was no way in hell he'd ever tell her about the former but he knew that he would have to tell her who he really was if he wanted any type of real relationship with her.

He turned to look at her. Her beautiful eyes were closed, a content look on her gorgeous face.

"Damn," he whispered, thinking, wondering how in hell he was going to tell her of his deceit.

Chapter 8

Monday morning found Nikki struggling to keep her mind on her work, and she forced herself not to check the clock again, for the twentieth time in as many minutes, to see when Ms. Rockway would emerge from her office and depart for her break. Then she would feel comfortable catching up with Max for their lunchtime tryst, one that they'd been meeting for every day at lunch for the last two weeks.

She hadn't seen him since he'd kissed her goodbye and left her house Saturday.

Even thinking of what they were doing, *where* he would decide to...do her this time, filled her with heady anticipation. She felt her face flush and her panties grow damp and drew in a shaky breath.

What he'd said in his panty-dropping voice on the phone to her earlier that morning, in the guise of asking her to get Ms. Rockway's signature on some made-up requisition, still made her blush.

It had been a struggle to think of anything else than how it felt when he ate her out, the way he carefully and with great attention to detail licked and laved every part of her body. And the fact that he let her know in no uncertain terms that their lunch ritual was as hot for him as it was for her meant even more to her.

The first surprise had been his unorthodox approach to lovemaking. She never knew what to expect.

Although they had only officially been seeing each other for two weeks, and their sexual trysts weren't exclusively lunchtime only, there was something about what they did during lunch that was not only sexy as hell to Nikki, but also strangely…sensual. As kinky as he got, as quick as some of their lunchtime trysts were, they were intimate, sensual and…fun.

She felt the smile grow. Just what the doctor ordered.

"I get off just looking at you, did you know that?"

The hotly voiced question whispered into the Bluetooth in her ear made Nikki jump. She'd picked up the call from her cell without looking to see who it was.

She would definitely have to give him his own ringtone, she thought, glad her supervisor wasn't around, knowing the blush she felt had to be showing on her face.

She glanced around to see if Max was near, disappointment surging when she noted her immediate area was free of anyone outside of the accounting department.

She sunk down lower in her chair, lowering her voice. In an attempt at nonchalance, she opened a document and pretended to work.

"Oh, yeah?" she asked, suppressing a giggle at the very schoolgirl way he was making her feel.

"Yes, baby. Those long legs of yours in that pretty skirt make me wonder if you are wearing any panties today. "

"Max." The soft sigh brushed from her lips at the unexpectedness of his intimate question.

"Yes, baby?"

She laughed, low, a lover's laugh. "Why do you say some of the stuff you do?" she replied, glancing around to see if anyone was near.

"I like to share things that make me wonder with my baby. Now…what color did you go with?"

"Black," she said, and bit the corner of her lip, her smile creasing her face.

"Sheer or lace? Bow or not?"

"Lace with a white bow. You haven't seen these. Yet."

"Hmm…yet, huh? I like the way you think. I will make it my mission to see every pair you own. And remove them from that pretty little ass of yours," he finished, his voice rough with a need she could hear through the phone. "There is a plumbing problem in one of the smaller conference rooms. I had maintenance lock it up until someone can come and fix it."

"And you're telling me this why?" she asked, but already knew the answer.

The backs of her thighs peppered with goose bumps, her nipples constricting.

"Come up to the management floor, room 1801. And put your panties in your pocket. You won't be needing them."

"Ooh," she breathed.

"I've got something special waiting for you, baby," he continued, and Nikki's eyes widened.

"Wha-what is it?"

"You'll just have to come up here and see. And remember…no panties."

He hung up and Nikki sank back in her chair.

"Oh, my God…is he serious?" she asked, but she knew the answer.

Her pussy quivered in anticipation and she could feel her own wetness in her panties.

Which was her answer to whether she was bold enough

to actually do what he was daring her: go up to management and have a sexual tryst in the middle of a working day.

She rose swiftly and called out that she was headed for lunch. Not waiting for Ms. Rockway to come out and stop her with a last-minute request, Nikki walked to the ladies' room and went into a stall to remove her panties.

Her face heated, she stuffed them into her purse and then walked briskly to the elevator and made her way up to meet Max.

She tested the door after glancing down the hallway to make sure no one saw her, then slipped inside. Immediately Max was on her, pulling her into his arms and locking the door behind her.

His warm, firm lips pressed against hers. His hands moved over her back, rubbing softly, then shifted to cup the globes of her butt, eliciting a moan from Nikki.

He released her ass and moved his hands around to the front and began to unbutton her blouse and deftly unsnap her bra. He tugged off her shirt, exposing her breasts, which bounded free. He lifted her and placed her on the conference table, coming to stand between her legs.

"We don't have a lot of time. But we have time for this," he said before kneeling in front of her.

"Max." She breathed the one-word plea.

He lifted her skirt and glanced up at her, approval in his eyes. "Good girl…you listened," he said, and winked. She laughed, then her breath caught when he began to stroke his tongue over her slick center.

She slammed her hand over her mouth to stop the shriek from emerging, afraid someone would hear and come running to her rescue.

He began to lick at her wet lips in earnest, the smooth yet rough touch of his tongue sending tremors through Nikki's body. She gripped the edges of the desk, holding on for dear life as his tongue continued its assault over the lips of her vagina in hot, languid glides. Glides of his tongue that left her…aching.

She moaned, her head hung low as she accepted his ministrations. When he stood, she barely suppressed the cry of denial, but was soon rewarded when he drew his slacks down his legs, revealing his thick, muscled thighs and beautifully sculpted cock.

Her low-lidded eyes observed his ritual way of sheathing his shaft and within moments he was deep inside of her.

As he stroked and rolled his hips, she held on for the ride, her head thrown back as she matched him stroke for stroke.

Just when she thought it couldn't get any better…

He picked her up, not losing the connection, his shaft still embedded deeply inside her warmth, and strode over to a big, oversized leather chair. It was different from the others, so she knew he'd brought this one in.

Just for this.

"Oh, baby," she moaned into his mouth when he sat them down, allowing her to straddle him, her legs dangling over the sides of the oversized chair.

"I thought you might like being in control," he said, giving her that one-of-a-kind, panty-dropping masculine laugh of his that she loved so much.

"Hmm…you know me so well," she purred as she began to ride him. Her walls clamped down on his length as his hands came up to hold onto her ass, allowing her natural bounce and his hard-driving thrusts to carry their bodies toward release. As they made love, their bodies quickly, easily caught the rhythm in a harmony that defied definition. Natural, symphonic, unique…as though they were made for each other.

Chapter 9

Back at her desk, a smile on her face, Nikki realized that she had to bring Tony into her confidence and with that she fessed up to what had happened at the ball and what was going on now. Tony was her friend and besides that, he was way *too* astute not to figure it out, when, ten times out of ten over the past couple of weeks she had returned from her lunch break with her hair in a different style and a glow in her cheeks that she couldn't begin to hide.

She opened up to him. While not giving the more intimate information, she told Tony that she and Max were seeing one another.

She'd expected Tony to go all gushy on her and completely over the top, but he surprised her, speaking with none of his normal flamboyance and theatrics, but instead sounding like a mix between a big brother who was concerned about her being taken advantage of by a supervisor—which technically Max was to her—and cautioning her against getting involved with someone from management, even if he was temporary.

She stored the caution in the back of her mind, but really, she had no intention of stopping the sensual train ride she found herself on...her new favorite motto was Toot Toot, All Aboard.

She sobered, thinking of Max and her newfound lust. The minute she thought it, she blushed. She shied away from calling it anything more than what it was. And whenever her mind took her there, she loudly hushed it.

While it might not be love, it was...new, exciting and different. She chuckled and put a hand over her mouth. Yeah, *different* was a way of putting it.

With Max she never knew what to expect.

They'd spent the weekend together that first time, and although she'd assumed it was going to be a one-time thing, and had actually convinced herself that she was perfectly okay with that, she knew that once was far from enough with Max Stele. He was intoxicating to her. Multifaceted. Mysterious.

She bit the corner of her mouth, thinking that he was a little too mysterious. He'd been gone from the office for the past few days and when she asked him where he was, what he was doing, he'd smiled and told her he had some business to conduct. Which to her mind was him telling her it was none of hers. Business, that was.

She shrugged it off, again telling herself that what they had was not a long-term affair. And that fact had been made more evident after she'd asked him how long he'd be at MagHard Interior Design, and what his plans were after they found a replacement for him.

They'd just finished making love, and were sitting at her kitchen table, naked and eating leftover pizza. She loved the spontaneity he'd brought to her world. What she didn't love so much was the mystery that seemed to be as much a part of the Max Stele package.

She'd started by asking him what he planned to do after...

"After?" he had asked, watching Nikki as she took a healthy bite of the gooey pizza he'd had delivered from her favorite neighborhood joint, Bosses Pizzeria.

As soon as she had swallowed, she had reached for a glass of sweet tea he'd poured for her and took a small sip, carefully gauging his reaction to her mild query about his future plans.

"Yes, after you leave the company. It is just a temp gig, right?" she had asked, knowing about as much today as she had less than two months ago when he'd started at the company. "And how did you get it anyway, the job?" she had asked. That was another thing that slightly bothered her. Although she was a new employee, she hadn't been aware that they hired temps in management. She'd asked Tony about it and he'd said that in his five years with them, they hadn't.

Max had taken a careful bite of the pizza, frowning slightly as though he was considering how to answer her question.

She had become aware of the small things he did, telling gestures to her that told her more than his words normally did.

While she had blabbed on and on about her life, about how she'd grown up with her grandparents and had a happy childhood, about the schools she'd attended, he'd told her... nothing.

Well, almost nothing. She'd been able to pry out of him that his mother had been a single mom, and that he was the youngest of three siblings. And the rebel.

She'd laughed. Yeah, she could totally see him as the rebel.

Small bits and pieces here and there: he had attended college, gotten a B.A. in architecture—which had surprised her—and later a master's in business and…that was about it, she thought with a frown.

Telling her that although he'd grown up in Texas, he'd lived the past few years in the Midwest. Which accounted for his lack of a tan, she'd said with a snicker, earning her a swipe on the butt from him.

But it was the things beyond the *what's your favorite color* and *what did you want to be when you grew up* that she began to want to know about him.

The longer she was around him, the more she wanted to *know him*. Beyond the superficial. She had sighed and shook her head.

"Forget it, it's not a biggie," she'd quipped. She had hopped up from the table, grabbed her dish and made for the sink.

He'd caught her, swinging her around, a frown on his face as he took the dish from her hand.

He had palmed both sides of her face, his look intense as he stared down at her.

He had opened his mouth to speak and shut it.

Making her want to smack him. She had known there was something he wasn't telling her, and the more he held on to it, the harder it was becoming for her to pretend like it wasn't there…that *something* between them.

Max needed to be prepared for anything Nikki threw at him. He thought back on that date with her, the mountain of questions she'd thrown at him.

That morning he'd gotten up and realized two things. One: that while he thought he'd been falling in love with her, he knew it was already a done deal; the woman had his heart on lockdown and the key hers to do with as she wanted.

Question was, would she throw away the key or store it within her own heart?

He'd left her sleeping and drove his car to the office. Wondering what the hell his next course of action was.

The answer had surprisingly come from his mother.

His cellphone had rang, indicating she was on the line. He had been in communication with his mother from the moment he'd taken over the office, and although the topic had stayed within the confines of business, i.e. a good replacement for Max, as she assumed he wanted out ASAP, it had, of course, gone to the personal.

"Mom, I've met someone..." he'd begun, and paused. "Someone I want you to meet." He stopped, waiting. A shout, scream, exclamation...something.

He knew it had to be significant for his mother. He'd not only never brought anyone home to meet her, he'd never even discussed a woman by name, much less told his mother he wanted her to *meet* the woman.

"Well, it is about damn time, Maxwell! I've been waiting for you to bring Nikki to me for the last week. Or at least to tell me about her, from your own mouth!"

"What? You knew?" Surprise left his mouth wide open and had he not been paying attention as he drove he would have wrecked his car. As it was he barely missed swiping another one as he swerved to miss.

"Well, of course I knew, darling. Nothing goes on in the company I don't know about," she had said, her cultured voice smug and eliciting a reluctant laugh from Max. He knew how his mother knew....

"So, old dragon breath knows about us, huh?" he had asked and they had both laughed.

Max sobered and paused.

His mother waited for a minute before she had said, "That's the reason I brought you to the company. You needed to meet someone special. But before you bring her to me, she has to know who you are, son." Her tone had been quiet and motherly.

He had sighed. "I know, Mom, but it's not that easy. There's more to it. I know information about her that I wouldn't know…shouldn't know, I guess," he had said, uneasily broaching the subject of how he'd used his influence with the chief of security to gather information about Nikki. "I'm not sure she's going to be keen on how I, uh… acquired it," he had said, not even comfortable with his mother knowing what he'd done. The way he'd invaded her personal life.

"The fact that you had James Green do a little digging into her past, Max?" she'd asked.

Why he was surprised was beyond him. As she had said…nothing went on that his mother didn't know about.

The rest of the ride into the office, he'd listened as his mother both fussed at and guided him on his next course of action.

"At the end of the day, it's your decision on how to go forward. Telling her who you really are…she'll understand that. She'll understand your reasons. They're valid, son. As a woman I feel confident telling you that," she'd begun and Max felt a semblance of relief.

Her next words snatched his security blanket away.

"But as for you digging into her past…go gently with that. You don't have to tell her, she'll never know…but tell her. If you want a real relationship, you have no other option."

And with that sage advice, Max had gone into his office and downloaded everything onto a jump drive, both his dossier…and the one he'd collected on Nikki.

After he loaded the documents, he knew what a man facing life in prison or freedom felt like when waiting for the jury's verdict.

Chapter 10

A few days later, Nikki woke up slowly, lazily from a night filled with restless sleep. She reflected on the past three weeks since she and Max had become involved. They had been filled with excitement and passion, and now uncertainty.

Her mind took her back to their last encounter.

It was the first time she'd spent the night at his place, and although she'd warned herself not to make too much of a big deal about it, a part of her knew that it was significant. Just as she knew there was much, much more to Max than met the eyes.

She'd known that as soon as he'd driven into the upperend neighborhood where he lived.

Tension had fairly radiated off of him, but she'd kept silent, not asking the burning question…how does a temp manager afford to live in the clearly affluent West Austin suburb? An area like this?

She nestled deeper into the down comforter and pulled

it up to her chin, not really ready to get out of bed, but knowing she had to. Her boss expected her staff to be in the office on time, and did not like to hear excuses.

Memories of the previous night still lingered. After each time they made love, their intimacy grew. But more than that, they had begun to share things with each other, things beyond the sexual.

She'd told him of her desire to be a designer at MagHard, hopefully soon as she received her master's degree at the end of the semester.

She'd lain in front of him, warm and satisfied from his latest lovemaking.

"And I know that with dedication and commitment, I can do it. I've already learned a lot from my time at MagHard," she'd confessed during their pillow talk.

He'd been silent before he spoke. "But you want more than just to be a designer at the firm, right? Don't you want to…branch out, start your own company?" he'd asked, and she'd sighed, nodding her head in the dark, running her fingers back and forth over the back of his hand that he had wrapped around her midsection as they spooned.

She smiled. It was as though he had read her mind. Sometimes the intuitive questions he asked seemed as though…he had a blueprint to her heart. The thought was as scary as it was enticing. No man had ever…gotten her, she'd always thought.

He'd kissed the back of her neck and asked, "What made you laugh?"

She snuggled back into his embrace and shook her head, a small smile playing around the corners of her mouth in the dark. "Nothing. Everything. I like you, Max Stele," had been her only reply, the region of her heart seeming to expand with the knowledge that she was falling in love with him.

After that night's marathon session they'd stayed up late, sharing their childhood stories.

She hadn't wanted to pry, but she wanted…yearned to learn more about Max.

"There's something that has been, well…on my mind," she had said, broaching one of the subjects that she had only recently been thinking about.

He'd brought her into his arms and held her close, his head on top of hers as he feathered it back and forth.

"What's that?" he had asked, his tone casual, yet she felt the tension that radiated from him the minute she spoke.

"Remember the night of the party?"

"Hmm, vaguely. Something comes to mind," he had said, pressing his shaft against her butt as she was spooned in front of him, one of his big arms loosely wrapped around her waist.

She had smacked the hand at her waist. "I'm being serious, pervert!" she had said with mock anger. Even when she was trying to be serious, he tried to bring levity to the moment.

"Hey, I resemble that remark," he had replied and she groaned before joining in his laughter.

She grew serious and plunged ahead. The question had been nagging at her all day as she recalled the evening that began their…affair.

"What's my middle name?" she had asked lightly and held her breath, waiting.

"Francine…why?" he had countered smoothly.

She paused, bit the corner of her mouth and jumped in. "How do you know that? Have you been spying on me?" she had asked.

There was only the briefest of pauses before he responded. "Why would I do that? Are you hiding something?" And for a moment Nikki had wished with all her might that she had the nerve to turn around and face him, to see his expression as he deflected her question with a question.

She felt her gut turn. "No, just wondering how you knew my middle name," she had asked, and waited.

"It's in your personal file, baby. How else would I know?" The answer had made her gut sink just the smallest bit. "Although I'm the temporary manager, I had to know about all key and essential personnel, so I read a few files. Yours was one," he had replied, his voice casual.

"Key and essential personnel? Me?" she had giggled, keeping it light.

"You're key and essential to me," he'd said and with that quip, he'd flipped her on her back and explained—or showed her—how key and essential she was to him.

She blushed at that memory of their lovemaking, but then grew reflective as more details unfolded from that night.

There was no way he'd gotten her middle name from the file, because she hadn't put it on her employment record. Not her full middle name. Most thought she was simply Nikki F. Danes. She only included her middle name on one social media site, but that was not a public profile.

But he'd called her Nikki Francine Dane.

She had forced herself to rise, and looked around the simple but beautiful furnished room. She'd been awestruck when he'd brought her into his home, the upper-end condo one of only a few in the affluent neighborhood.

She hadn't wanted to appear like a country bumpkin, but she was impressed and more than a little curious about how he could afford it.

"Which begs the question, who are you, really, Max Stele?" she said out loud. Not expecting an answer.

"I'm Maxwell Steele-Hardaway, Nikki…and I need to talk to you."

Nikki spun around and gaped, staring across at Max, her face losing color as the significance of his name, apparently his *true* name, sank in.

Her face scanned his, noting the grim lines bracketing his sensual mouth…her eyes going to a file in his hand. One he held out to her.

"People don't really use folders anymore. Everything is learned and created on disk. But I thought it would be easier for you to read this here and not on a computer. It seems so cold to read things from a computer. At least to me," he said, his deep voice, which normally turned her on, this time confusing her.

"What are you talking about?" she asked, frowning, pulling the ends of his robe closer around her body.

She felt dread coursing through her body as he walked toward her. He held out his hand, motioning for her to take the folder.

He wanted her to read it.

She looked from the folder in his outstretched hand back to his face, which was devoid of any real telling expression.

She knew the answers to some of the questions she'd been having about him were inside.

As much as she wanted to know, as much as she'd known he was hiding something from her, suddenly she found that she didn't want to know.

When she finally nodded her head, ready to accept it, whatever it was, he covered her hand with his.

She glanced up at him and he laughed, a slightly nervous-sounding laugh, and one that was completely unlike what she'd expect. Nervous and Max went together like oil and water. He was the most confident man she'd ever met. Her brows drew together.

"It's not earth-shattering, baby. What's inside," he said when her frown deepened. "It's just that…I want more with you." His words made her heart pause, hiccup a little and resume its normal beat.

"I want more than I ever thought I would. I didn't think I would feel the way I do, never thought I would…fall in love. But I have."

"Baby…" Her eyes flew to his, her gaze searching his out. She felt the sting of tears in her eyes. He loved her.

And she was crazy in love with him, and now…

"But before we went any further, before this amazing, beautiful thing we have could grow, I knew I had to come clean. So…" He paused and looked deeply into her eyes. In his she saw, clearly, his struggle. She drew in a breath.

"I need you to know this is only one part of me," he said, his eyes indicating the file. "And what I did was only because I wanted to get to know you. Even from the first moment I saw you on that elevator, I wanted to know you."

With that he handed her the file and turned, leaving the room and closing the door behind him.

All kinds of emotions were swirling around in Nikki's head, from high elation—the minute he'd said that he loved her, she had wanted to wrap her arms around his neck and kiss him until neither one of them could breathe—to fear and dread. As he'd said he loved her, his face had been so solemn, not happy at all, and she'd wanted to slap him and cry knowing that she wasn't going to like whatever he had to tell her.

She took the file and sat down on the bed, her eyes widening as she began to flip through the documents, her brow furrowing and her stomach hollowing out as she realized it appeared to be Max's résumé…and hers as well. But it wasn't the normal résumé she'd given to the company.

There were pictures of her, from the time she was young

to her most recent time as an employee of MagHard. The information went way beyond what she'd given to the company upon her employment.

He had her life in front of him. Everything she loved, liked to do, family life…hell, even her favorite nail polish was listed in the extensive folder.

He hadn't had to find out who she was. He had already known.

Which made her feel as though he was nothing more than a con. *Blueprint to my heart, my ass,* she thought, tears streaming down her face.

Max Stele…aka Maxwell Steele-Hardaway had had the blueprint for her heart at his fingertips all along.

Chapter 11

"Just take me home." Her demand was curt and to the point.

"Nikki, baby," Max began, reaching out to touch her. He had to touch his baby, had to bring her to his body and make her forgive him…make her understand.

"I was falling in love with you, goddamn it, and it was all just some kinda—" Nikki paused in her quiet anger, her voice little above a whisper, her face scrunched in anger and tears running down her face. "Some kinda game." She said the final word as though it were a curse word.

"God, no, baby! It wasn't a game. Look, I know it wasn't right, I should have told you who I was. I—"

"I don't give a shit about your name, Maxwell *Hardaway*…as much as it pisses me off that you didn't feel as though you could tell me that very important information…I get it. I get who your family is, and how you wanted distance from it." Her words had filled him with hope until she continued.

"I respect that you made your own way and didn't use your family name. All of that *I get!*" she continued, her voice beginning to rise as she faced him.

"What I don't get is how…why you felt you had the right to dig into my past like that. Why not just ask me. Unlike you, I had—have nothing to hide." She turned from him and wrapped her arms around her waist, the position defensive, angry…hurt.

He couldn't let her think that. He reached out and spun her around, forcing her to look at him.

"It wasn't like that, baby, please. I knew from the moment I first met you, the moment you walked into that elevator that I was sprung like an addict," he said, laughing harshly. "I didn't know how…what to do. I had never felt like that, had such a strong reaction like that, so immediately, for a woman. The more I saw glimpses of you around the office, I knew I had to learn more. I wanted some sort of…" He paused, running his hand through his hair, spiking it over his head, thinking of the right word. "Leverage…" he finished, finding the word inadequate the moment he said it.

He had known it was the wrong word when her dark complexion lost all color and appeared ashen.

Her mouth firmed and a small tic formed in the corner of her pretty, full lips.

Priding himself on his strong gut instincts, he shut his mouth, even though he had to fight to do it.

Her chest was still heaving, the tears drying on her pretty chocolate-colored skin. Her pain was his pain. But he knew she wouldn't want to hear that.

He felt the mist in his eyes turn to real tears, tears he'd never shed in his life for a woman, as he saw the response to the evidence of what he'd done to her, how he'd betrayed her. He knew there was nothing that would convince her that he'd had no intention of using the information for any other purpose but in his stupid, egomaniacal male way of finding out as much about her as he could.

Leverage.

The word hung between them in the silence, heavy and thick.

"I am not an acquisition in some kind of merger, Max. I am a woman. I *was* your woman.... Now take me home."

He stared at her, feeling like his heart was being ripped from his chest. Slowly he nodded his head and watched, his body and mind numb, as she slowly turned away and, with her head high, went into the bedroom to dress.

In silence he drove her home, both of them caught in their own thoughts. Both of them wondering why...how the other had become the focus of their life, how, when they were with each other, everything and nothing else seemed to matter.

Both of them torn. Angry tears continued to trickle down Nikki's face as she turned away and looked out the window. The beautiful cloudless, clear day going to waste; their world was dark, cloudy and...bleak.

In silence he wondered how to bridge the gap of deceit he had created, and wondered how to tell her he was madly, crazily in love with her.

In the end, he stayed silent.

Chapter 12

It had been less than two weeks since she'd spoken to Max, and although her office mates had no idea what had transpired between them, as none of them outside of Tony and Ms. Rockway knew of her...situation, Nikki still felt on display.

This was the only thing that seemed to be her saving grace, the only thing that allowed her to keep a shred of dignity.

She'd walked into Ms. Rockway's office and given her two weeks' notice succinctly, and without any outward emotion.

The woman had simply nodded her head, accepting Nikki's notice.

She began to think about what she wanted to do. Design. And although she loved the company, she felt she was ready to start on her own. Small, for sure. She shrugged. But why not? If she'd learned anything from Max, reading his dossier and then finding out all she had about him in the ensuing weeks, it was that starting her own company wouldn't be easy but it was something she knew she had the talent and drive to accomplish.

Max Hardaway. Even thinking of his name, his true name, was something that had been difficult for her to do.

And she couldn't have been more surprised when his mother, the owner and matriarch of the Hardaway empire, called her.

After she introduced herself, she hadn't given Nikki time to be terrified of the business tycoon...and mother of the man she was desperately in love with.

In no uncertain terms she'd said that no matter what had transpired between Nikki and her son, she was interested in seeing Nikki do well in business, and that Ms. Rockway had informed her of Nikki's resignation. Not sure what to expect, Nikki had listened, her admiration and respect for the woman growing as she'd outlined what she would like to do for Nikki.

Ms. Rockway had done nothing but sing Nikki's praises, something Nikki would never had suspected, as the woman was always so concise in her interactions. She listened as Naomi Steele-Hardaway explained that every good business needed a sound business plan and that every successful businesswoman needed a successful mentor.

She wanted to help Nikki with both. She'd told Nikki she would set up a time for them to meet and that her secretary would be contacting Nikki soon.

Nikki had hung up the phone, stunned, shaking her head at the turn of events.

She had grinned at the last tidbit of information Ms. Steele-Hardaway had given her concerning Max.

She sighed but continued on, clearing out the last of her things. To give him credit, he hadn't completely lied about who he was. But still...she shook her head.

"Give it time, chica," Tony said, and Nikki turned to face her friend.

"Yeah, I guess they say time heals all wounds and all that." She laughed without humor. "But I…hurt," she said simply and heard the catch in her voice.

"Give the man a chance, chica. You know that you care about him. And you know you love him," he said softly. "Now quit being a knucklehead about it, ain't nobody got time for all of *that*…we have a business to start!" he quipped, and she giggled even though she felt empty inside.

She'd told Tony what had happened, of course, and like the true friend he was, he first commiserated with her… then told her to stop being stupid and go after the man. She'd laughed and shaken her head.

When she'd told Tony of her resignation, he'd nearly cried. Haltingly, she then told him about her plans to start her own design firm, specializing in upper-end real estate, and he'd flung his arms around her and excitedly said he'd follow her. She'd thought he was joking until she saw that behind the joy in his eyes he was serious.

"Really? You want to do this with me?" she had asked and she caught a true glimpse of his character, one she'd always known was there. For all of his flamboyance, Tony had a sharp business mind and an eye for design.

"Here…I'm floundering. I can't really be…me, for a lack of a better word," he began, slightly self-conscious, and Nikki nodded, surprised but strangely pleased that he was showing her that side of himself. "It's a wonderful company, but I know that I can do better outside of the confines of the conservative way they do things. And to do that, to really be me…I need to believe in me. Take a chance. I want to do that with you. If you want me to…" His voice trailed off, uncertain.

She'd grinned and barely kept the tears at bay as they hugged and began to hatch their business plan.

"Just…give him the opportunity, chica…"

When Tony stopped speaking, she had turned to give him a rebuttal. He'd been saying what she already felt in her heart, but she wasn't sure how to go to Max. He hadn't exactly been beating down her door, she thought, sighing.

"I'm here on the clichéd bended knee."

At the sound of the deep voice coming from directly behind her, Nikki's heart lurched and her face bloomed with color.

"Max…" She breathed his name and spun around in her chair, nearly falling to the floor to see Max in front of her…on bended knee. She rose as though to go to him, but his words stopped her.

"I love you more than I thought possible," he began and stopped, his voice shaky.

In the back of her consciousness she was aware that the noise surrounding her cubicle, normal background office noise—conversations and the sound of fingers hitting keyboards—had become quiet.

But Nikki didn't really notice all of that. All her attention was on the man in front of her. On bended knee.

She felt tears hover.

"I know that I messed up, Nikki. I know that I should have trusted you earlier and told you who I was." He paused, his voice lowering, but kept his gaze on her. Honest and direct. "I know that I had no right to invade your privacy like I did." He reached inside his jacket and pulled out a small box.

Her heart felt like it stopped beating for a fraction of a second.

He continued, "I know that the way to your heart, to you, couldn't be found in a dossier or file."

He pulled out the ring.

The light bounced and danced off the large, square diamond within the velvet box.

"But if you accept this ring, I pledge to you that going forward, not only will I find out the hard way, like every other guy head over heels in love with a woman, what makes you tick, I will earn the right to say I have the key to your heart. Because you have the key to mine," he said and stopped, his voice thick with emotion.

"I love you, Nikki Francine Danes. Will you marry me?"

Simple. Honest. Direct...

Nikki jumped from her seat before he could finish and threw her arms around his neck.

The two kissed and embraced for long moments before she broke away. With tears running down her face, she grinned. Tilting her head to the side, she began to grin harder.

"Well?" he asked, again his voice breaking.

"You have the key to my heart already...and yes, I will marry you, Maxwell Marion Steele-Hardaway," she said and laughed outright at his expression.

"You're not the only who knows how to gather...intel," she quipped smugly before she was engulfed within his embrace.

"I am in for the ride of my life with you, I can tell," he groaned, but the humor in his eyes gleamed.

As the area around her cubicle exploded with cheers, catcalls and whistles, none of that mattered to Nikki as she became lost in Max's embrace.

Epilogue

"Hey, babe, do you know what we did with that new accounts file? I'm looking everywhere on the hard drive, jpeg, iPad, Mac...damn near everything and everywhere and I *still* can't find it! Please tell me—"

Max's irritated tirade was cut off short when Tony sailed past him—as much as a man could sail wearing stilettos—and slapped the small jump drive in his hand on his way through the office.

"And papi, it's not a jpeg, it's a jump drive," he threw over his shoulder as he made his way toward his small office, mumbling as he went, "How in the hell did that man make so much damn money and don't even know the difference between..." The rest was muffled as he went into his office.

Nikki saw the interaction between the two men and giggled softly before turning to glance back at her own monitor, where she was importing the latest software design program she'd bought.

"You think that's funny, huh?" A deep voice spoke directly behind her, right before firm, sensual lips captured her ear and sharp teeth lightly bit the lobe before suckling the injury.

"Hmm, baby...of course I'm not laughing at you! What kind of business partner would I be if I did that?"

"Oh, yeah?" Max asked, his voice a low, sexy purr. "I suppose it's just *that* partnership that keeps you on your toes, Nik?" he said and wrapped his arms around her expanding waist.

She jumped a little, shivered a whole lot when she felt his warm breath fan over her neck...and melted into his embrace, her heart doing that funny little flip it did whenever his big hands molded themselves over her stomach.

"No, baby, not even close," she replied, smiling softly.

"Hmm...that's what I like to hear," he said and continued grazing his face, nuzzling his nose on the sensitive skin on the back of her neck. An area that had only recently, since her pregnancy, been one of the many new hypersensitive sweet spots.

She smiled, tilting her head to the side to give him better access. Despite the madhouse of their lives, she had never been happier, more content on all levels, she thought with a giggle when he stroked the skin he'd been nosing.

"Are you happy, baby? Really happy? Have I earned the right to say I have the key to your heart?" he asked. And although he voiced the question lightly, she heard a slight rough quality in his voice.

"How could you question that?" she asked and looked around.

In the year and a half since they'd opened Danes and Steele Interior Design and Architecture, gotten married and were now months away from the birth of their son, life had been one amazing adventure for Nikki.

Although she'd appreciated the offer from Max's mother, now her mother-in-law, she'd declined. She never wanted anyone to think that she was relying on family for a leg up. Just like Max.

She grinned. Not that she'd allowed that same belief to dictate her merger with Max. Mixing business with personal had seemed the right thing to do. They'd formed their new business, one that combined their separate passions: architecture and design. With Tony as their third partner, acting as designer with Nikki and helping Max with the business end, the company was turning a significant profit in its first quarter.

And now their growth had allowed them to add more employees as the company grew.

Life didn't get any better. She turned within his embrace. Reached a hand up and smoothed away the frown there. She gazed up into his beautiful green eyes, so full of love for her that tears began to burn the backs of her eyes.

"Yes, baby," she replied simply. Honestly. "You have earned the blueprint of my heart."

He captured her mouth with his in a toe-curling, breath-stealing kiss. With a sigh of happiness, she allowed him to lift her, big belly and all, and stride from her office as he walked them toward their "special" room.

As Max walked with his bundle in his arms, past his office, Tony rolled his eyes, muttering, "There *they* go. Again…" and shook his head.

* * * * *

MISTLETOE IN MEMPHIS
Pamela Yaye

Special thanks to the team at
Harlequin Kimani Arabesque for their work on
A Very Merry Temptation, and my amazing editor,
Maria Ribas, for giving me the opportunity to write
for the Arabesque line, *and* for helping me get
Mistletoe in Memphis down to word count!
It wasn't easy, but we did it!!! :)

Dad, I appreciate your guidance, your wisdom,
your unwavering support and my snazzy
new laptop and desktop computer. I love them,
but I love you even more!!! :)

Chapter 1

"Where's your caterer friend?" Lincoln Davenport asked, addressing his petite, pencil-thin secretary, Naomi Kerr. Standing in the doorway of his office, he leaned against the door frame and folded his arms across his chest. Raising his eyebrows, he made a show of glancing at his gold Piaget wristwatch. "Our meeting was for nine o'clock. It's five after."

"Don't worry, Mr. Davenport. She'll be here." Naomi smiled, but worry lines creased her forehead, and her eyes were glued to the front window. The sky was covered with a sheet of somber, gray clouds, and snow flurries whirled in the crisp morning air. "It started snowing again, and you know how crazy some people drive when the weather goes south. Essence probably just got caught in traffic."

"I managed to get here on time, and so did you."

Naomi cleared her throat and toyed nervously with the buttons on her beige cardigan. "You're going to love Essence. Everyone always does. She's fun and outgoing and loves to have a good time."

"Sounds like my kind of girl," he deadpanned.

"She's also efficient and hardworking and—"

"That remains to be seen." Dropping his hands at his sides, Lincoln decided he'd waited long enough for the punctually challenged caterer. Normally, he left the hiring to his HR manager, but since she was out sick with the flu, he'd decided to fill in for her. Big mistake. "Call Ms. Sinclair and cancel our meeting. Memphis is full of great restaurants, and I can easily find another caterer who is professional *and* punctual."

A look of panic flashed across Naomi's face, but she slowly nodded her head.

Back in his office, Lincoln returned to his desk and continued watching the season finale of *So You Think You Can Cook* on his desktop. Unfamiliar with the reality show, he'd searched Google upon arriving at his office that morning and watched the season finale. Lincoln thought the show was silly, and the British host an obnoxious bore, but he enjoyed watching Essence Sinclair do her thing. She had a kick-ass sense of humor, easily charmed and wooed her competitors and freely spoke her mind. The thirty-two-year-old Memphis native did everything with flair, panache. It didn't matter if she was rolling crepes or sifting flour, she made it look damn sexy. And when the host crowned Essence the season two winner, she danced around the kitchen, hugging and kissing everyone on set— including the bearded cameraman and lanky prop guy. It made for great TV, and proved how warm and gregarious the caterer was.

Suddenly laughter filled the air, seeping through the olive-green walls of his office. The hairs on the back of his neck shot up. Lincoln could recognize that silky, sultry voice anywhere. Essence Sinclair was there, *finally*. She was twenty minutes late, and had wasted enough of his time already, but when he glanced at his computer screen and saw her striking face staring back at him, he decided it wouldn't hurt to meet her. Finding another caterer this late in the game would be a headache. One he didn't need, especially now. Lincoln hated Christmas, and if not for pressure from his board of directors to network with clients during the holiday season, he wouldn't be planning a damn thing. He'd rather spend the holidays—alone—catching up on sleep, listening to his favorite jazz records, or working in his home office. To keep his mind off his troubles, and the pain of his past, he had to stay busy.

Lincoln considered going out into the reception area and introducing himself to Essence, but quickly changed his mind. He was curious to meet the reality star, but didn't want to look too eager. Women like Essence were used to men tripping all over themselves in her presence, but Lincoln was determined not to embarrass himself. He'd be professional and all business during their meeting and, as long as he kept in mind that the caterer was an unconscionable flirt who got a kick out of teasing the opposite sex, he'd be fine.

The knock on his office door yanked Lincoln out of his thoughts. He grabbed one of the files stacked in the pile to his right, buried his nose in it and pretended to scrutinize the computer codes on the page. Lincoln didn't have any pressing business matters bedsides a conference call late that morning, but he didn't want Essence to think he was a slacker. Or that he was in fact waiting for her to show. Making a good impression mattered to him, and he wanted the caterer—just like the rest of the world—to think he was at the top of his game. Because he was.

"Sorry to bother you, sir, but Essence Sinclair is here."

A sweet, floral scent filled the air. It tickled his nose and roused his appetite. Lincoln glanced up from the file, and when his gaze landed on Essence he felt all the blood drain from his head. *Have mercy...* Desire walloped him, knocked him flat back on his leather executive chair. His tongue lay limp in his mouth, and for several moments he couldn't speak. Not that he wanted to. There were no words in the English language—or any language—to describe Essence Sinclair's staggering beauty, and Lincoln knew if he spoke he'd make a complete and utter fool of himself. He feared his legs would buckle from the weight of his desire, but he stood and strode confidently toward her.

Lincoln didn't have the power to look away, couldn't if someone paid him. Essence Sinclair was all that, and her brilliant, dazzling smile turned his brain to mincemeat. During her stint on *So You Think You Can Cook,* she always looked good, well put together, but this morning she was done up from head to toe. Big hair, crimson-red lips, makeup and nails done to perfection. The reality star had a classic Jackie O vibe about her, but with a sexy, seductive twist. Diamond hoop earrings dangled from her ears, a glitzy, oversized purse hung from her wrist and her black turtleneck dress kissed every sensuous curve on her shapely body. Her leopard-print pumps elongated her toned brown legs, and every time she moved her ankle bracelet tinkled. For as long as Lincoln could remember, he'd always had a weakness for sisters with an hourglass figure, and not only was Essence Sinclair stacked in all the right places, she was oozing with sexual confidence. At thirty-five, Lincoln had met his fair share of attractive women, but the titillating reality TV star was in a league of her own. *She's a modern-day femme fatale,* he thought, giving his eyes license to roam over her sinuous curves. *And if I were looking for a woman to share my bed with this holiday season, she'd be on the top of my Christmas wish list.*

"I'm so sorry I'm late. Traffic was horrible, and I got lost *twice,*" Essence said, resting her purse at her feet. "At one point, I got so frustrated I tossed my GPS out the window!"

Lincoln chuckled. Essence spoke to him in a friendly manner, as if they'd known each other for years. He liked that. It wasn't every day he met a bubbly, outgoing sister with a killer pair of legs. According to Naomi, her best friend was loved and admired by everyone, and now that Lincoln had met the drop-dead gorgeous caterer for himself, he could see why. Essence was a force, a woman of incredible presence, and as Lincoln listened to her, he decided she was the most beautiful woman he'd ever laid eyes on.

"I feel terrible about showing up late." Wearing an apologetic face, she tilted her head to the side and touched a hand to her chest. "Please forgive me. I promise it won't happen again."

"Don't sweat it. You're here now, and that's all that matters," Lincoln said, ignoring the wide-eyed expression on his secretary's face. A stickler for time, he was surprised to hear the words come out of his mouth next, but nodded and said, "Welcome to Global Technologies International, Ms. Sinclair. I'm Lincoln Davenport."

"Of course, yes—thanks for this, I mean, thanks for seeing me—" Essence broke off speaking when she realized she was starting to sound crazy. Her tongue suddenly felt too big for her mouth, and her stomach was overrun with hundreds of butterflies. *Get it together,* she chided herself, raking a hand through her wavy hair. *Cakes and Confessions by Essence is hanging on by a thread. You can't afford to screw this up.*

It took supreme effort, but Essence dragged her gaze away from Lincoln's delicious mouth and stared deep into his eyes. Wrong move. Now her heart was pounding in her chest. She'd walked into the office expecting to see a gray-haired man in tweed and polyester, but instead found a tall, dark hottie with an athletic physique sitting behind the circular glass desk. His eyes were dreamy, his build was lean and muscular and his skin was the deepest, warmest shade of brown there was. The computer software engineer was so damn good-looking, Essence felt light on her feet, as if she were going to pass out. But she wouldn't, of course. Not in front of this fine-ass man who reeked of money, class and power.

Eyebrows raised, Essence shot her friend a quizzical look. Naomi said her boss was a nerd, a work-obsessed executive who'd rather do sudoku puzzles than party, but the word *boring* didn't come to mind when Essence looked at Lincoln Davenport. However *suave, debonair* and *powerful* did. His designer eyeglasses give him a dapper, distinguished air and he was working the hell out of his tailored black suit. Add to that, he was well over six feet tall, had the whitest, brightest teeth she'd ever seen and a pair of sexy, thick lips she was dying to taste. If that weren't bad enough, his cologne was a rich, heady scent that aroused thoughts so sinful they'd shock the devil.

"It's great to meet you," Lincoln said, offering his right hand in greeting. "Naomi's told me wonderful things about you, and your catering company, Cakes and Confections by Essence."

Essence felt her temperature climb. Her attraction to Lincoln stunned her, and although she knew touching him was risky, she reached out and shook his hand. Big mistake. Her knees gave out, and the room swam out of focus. Lust infected her body. Every single inch. A hunger she'd never known filled her, consumed her. To the point where she was shaking and quivering like a drug addict experiencing symptoms of withdrawal.

"I'll leave you two alone," Naomi said. "Mr. Davenport, if you need anything just give me a buzz. I'll be at my desk typing up my notes from yesterday's staff meeting."

"Thanks, Naomi. Hold my calls, and push back my conference call to ten-thirty."

"Will do."

Alone now, Essence admired the hunky software developer in peace. She was in no rush to move. At least not yet. She liked being all up in his personal space and could easily stand there for the rest of the day admiring his rock-hard physique. Her eyes took in the hard slope of his chiseled jaw, the width of his shoulders and how delicious he looked in his double-breasted suit and burgundy silk tie. Essence had never felt such a strong connection to anyone, not even to her ex-boyfriend, and they'd dated off and on for years. Rashad Jones was a cocky, platinum-selling R & B singer worth millions, but he had nothing on Lincoln Davenport.

Essence heard the wall clock ticking, the incessant buzzing of Naomi's desk phone and male voices beyond the office door. All of the noise swirling around reminded Essence that Lincoln Davenport was a very busy man who had a successful software corporation to run. It was time to get down to business and discuss the upcoming holiday parties he wanted her to cater, but she didn't release his hand. Essence just stood there, without a care in the world, staring at Lincoln with stars in her eyes and a lopsided smile on her lips.

"Please, Ms. Sinclair, have a seat."

"Only if you call me Essence."

He moved closer, swallowed the space between them. "I can do that."

"Can I call you Lincoln?"

"I wouldn't have it any other way," he said smoothly. "Congratulations on winning season two of *So You Think You Can Cook.* You were amazing on the show."

"Thanks. It's been almost a year since I won, but it feels just like yesterday."

"Good, then it's not too late for me to buy you a celebratory drink."

Essence wore a cheeky smile. "Just say when."

"How does tomorrow sound?" he asked, his eyes lit with amusement. "We could have dinner at any restaurant of your choice, and then—"

Shake that booty, hoochie mama! C'mon, shake that booty...

Essence winced. At the sound of her ringtone, shame burned her cheeks and singed the tip of her ears. She'd forgotten to switch her cell phone to vibrate and because of her blunder Lincoln was scowling at her. His eyes were narrowed, and his grin was gone. He dropped her hand as if it were covered in cooties and took a giant step back.

"I am so sorry," Essence said, taking her cell phone out of her jacket pocket and turning it off. "I promise there won't be any more interruptions."

Lincoln stalked over to his desk. "Let's get down to business, shall we? I have a full day ahead of me and no time to waste."

Essence couldn't meet his gaze. She'd blown it. Screwed up. Made herself look incompetent and unprofessional in front of a prospective employer—a prospective employer she was ridiculously attracted to and intrigued by. His dinner invitation was off the table, and Essence feared if she messed up again she'd lose the catering contract, too.

Her eyes wandered, bounced aimlessly around the room. Glancing around Lincoln's office told Essence everything she needed to know about the hunk. Leather-bound volumes lined towering bookshelves, framed certificates and plaques beautified the olive-green walls and, unlike her cramped home office, everything was in order, in its rightful place. Lincoln Davenport was a perfectionist, a by-the-book type who liked to be in control. Knowing what made her clients tick was the key to her success, and Essence knew if she wanted Lincoln to hire her she'd have to let him call the shots. That would require talking less and listening more. Essence had never been good at biting her tongue or censoring her thoughts, but she was willing to do whatever it took to land the catering contract. Working for Lincoln Davenport would open a lot of doors for her and now more than ever, Essence needed to keep her wits about her. This used to be her busiest time of year, but the weakened economy had forced the rich and wealthy to scale back, and these days her cell phone hardly rang for catering jobs.

"I brought something for you." Essence reached inside the tote bag resting at her feet, pulled out a glass container and whipped off the cover. "I hope you're hungry, because I made you some of my most popular desserts."

Lincoln waved off her offer with a flick of his hand. "Thanks, but no thanks."

"Are you sure you don't want just a little taste?" she pressed, waving the container under his nose. "Go on, try one. I made caramel truffles, chocolate éclairs and coconut brownies."

"I don't like sweets."

"But I made them especially for you."

"Then you wasted your time." Lincoln sat down on his

chair and took a swig from his coffee mug. "Put that away. The smell of coconuts make me queasy."

Essence snapped the cover into place and returned the glass container back to her tote bag. Time for plan B. Adopting a professional tone, one she reserved for her most difficult clients, she took the seat across from Lincoln and said, "I understand that you're hosting several parties during the holiday season and would like my catering company to handle each event."

"That's why I suggested we meet. The sooner we finalize the details the better."

"Well, yes, of course. That's why I'm, um, here," Essence said, fumbling for her words. Shifting around in her chair, she ignored the fluttering sensation in her stomach and the sweat skating down the back of her turtleneck dress. *Great, now he thinks I'm a ditz.* Essence didn't know what was wrong with her. She loved talking and could never, ever get tired of hearing her own voice, but in Lincoln's presence she became nervous, unsure of herself, as flighty as a preteen girl meeting her idol. She couldn't sit still, couldn't stop fiddling with her watch or crossing and uncrossing her legs. "Why don't you tell me your vision for each event?"

"There's no need." Lincoln took a manila file folder out of his desk drawer and handed it to her. "Everything you need to know about each party is in there, and it goes without saying that I'd like my notes followed to a T."

For a moment, Essence just stared at the file. But when she saw the lines around Lincoln's eyes tighten, she reluctantly took the document from his outstretched hands. It was thick and heavy, and when she flipped it open and scanned the cover page, she groaned inwardly. She should have known this contract was too good to be true. No wonder Lincoln had hired her sight unseen. He probably couldn't find anyone else to meet his outrageous demands and ridiculous, detailed outline!

Making a mental note to kill Naomi once she left Lincoln's office, Essence quickly reviewed the contents of the manila file folder. "I've catered dozens of dessert parties over the years," she said, unable to resist speaking her mind, "but no one's ever given me twenty-five pages of notes before."

A frown covered his face. "What made you think I was having a dessert party?"

"You're not?"

"Eating crumpets and fondue is hardly my style."

Essence couldn't speak. Not because she didn't want to, but because her mind was racing a hundred miles an hour. Her thoughts were scrambled and the longer Lincoln glared at her—with his eyebrows furrowed and his lips stretched into a firm, hard line—the more self-conscious she felt.

"I think we got our wires crossed, so let me explain," he said, sneaking a glance at his gold wristwatch for the second time in minutes. "I'm having a holiday mixer here at the office, a dinner for some out-of-town associates at my home and a small, intimate brunch on New Year's Day for the university students I mentor."

"Have you considered menus or would you prefer I select the food?"

"Like I said, everything you need to know about each event is in the folder. Please refer to it. I don't want to have to repeat myself every day for the next six weeks."

Essence pressed her lips together to trap a curse word inside her mouth and continued flipping quietly through the bulging file folder. When she saw the sample menu for the holiday mixer on page six, she choked on her tongue. "You want caviar, escargot en croute and a cocktail station with chocolate martinis and frozen daiquiris at your office party?"

"That was my VP's idea. He said the staff would love it."

Essence wanted to cry. Could this meeting go any worse? All she needed now was to burst into tears and her humiliation would be complete. *What am I going to do now?* Her specialty was desserts, not caviar and escargot, but instead of telling Lincoln she didn't know how to make the items on the menu, Essence kept quiet. She badly needed the contract, *and* the handsome check that came with it. She'd just have to dust off her old cookbooks and call in reinforcements—namely her aunt Zizi—to give her a hand because she couldn't afford to screw up Lincoln Davenport's parties. Her reputation was on the line, and she was determined to prove to her competitors that she was more than just a pretty face who'd won a reality show.

"After Naomi suggested your catering company, I went online and checked out your website. Your sample menus didn't impress me, so I took the liberty of creating my own." Lincoln peered at her over the rim of his silver Armani eyeglasses. "You do know how to make other things besides pastries and truffles, right?"

"Of course," she said, annoyed by his condescending tone. Who did he think she was? Betty Crocker? Winning the top prize on *So You Think You Can Cook* proved that she was a talented chef, and Essence looked forward to making the software engineer eat his words. "International cuisine is my specialty and I can make a wide variety of foods from—"

"Great. I look forward to seeing you on the twenty-third."

"The twenty-third? That's the day after Thanksgiving."

"I'm well aware of that. The office mixer starts at five

o'clock sharp. Don't be late." Lincoln turned toward his keyboard and began typing furiously. "And, please, Ms. Sinclair, remember to put your cell phone on vibrate. I don't want it going off during the party."

This time Essence didn't ask Lincoln to call her by her first name. She didn't want him to. He was patronizing her, and Essence didn't like it one bit.

"Before I forget, here is your advance."

A smile filled her lips. One she didn't have to force. Essence took the envelope Lincoln offered and peeked inside. The smile slid off her face. "I charge twenty-five hundred dollars for small-scale parties," she explained calmly, though she wanted to grab him and shake the rest of her money out of his deep pockets. "My advance should be three thousand dollars, not five hundred."

He raised an eyebrow, but didn't speak. Essence knew her prices were steep—20 percent higher than her competitors'—but she knew she was worth every penny. And that's what she told clients who tried to nickel-and-dime her. She never dreamed Lincoln Davenport, an esteemed businessman who owned the largest software company in the state, would try to screw her over, but these days nothing the opposite sex did surprised her. It was a wonder she even dated anymore. Most of her girlfriends had resigned to being single and filled their homes with cats, junk food and sex toys, but Essence was still holding out hope of one day finding Mr. Right.

"The office mixer will be an audition of sorts." Steepling his hands, he settled back into his chair with the haughtiness of a king seated on a throne. "If everything goes well, I'll hire you to cater my other events and, possibly, other functions throughout the next year as well."

Essence wanted to demand the rest of her money, but her pride wouldn't let her. She didn't want anyone—

especially this gruff, surly businessman in the designer suit and fifty-thousand-dollar wristwatch—to know that her catering company was in trouble.

"I have a lot riding on this event, Ms. Sinclair. Don't let me down."

"I wouldn't dream of it."

Deciding she'd had all she could take of him for one day, Essence scooped up her purse and swung it over her shoulder. She had to go, had to leave before she did something stupid. Like toss the manila folder in Lincoln's face and stomp out of his lavish, art-filled office.

"I'll be in touch." Essence wore a sickly sweet smile, one that concealed the anger simmering below the surface. Lincoln Davenport was an esteemed businessman with perfect teeth and a ripped body, but he was working her last nerve. She didn't appreciate his tone or his attitude, but she didn't trip. She needed this contract, and couldn't afford to go off on her newest client. "Have a great day, Mr. Davenport."

"You do the same."

Head held high, shoulders pinned back in supreme confidence, she slipped on her oversized Gucci sunglasses and strode out of the office. She had nothing to worry about, no reason to stress or flip out. She could handle Lincoln Davenport. *I'd better,* Essence thought, releasing a deep, ragged breath. *Or I'll have to kiss my catering company goodbye.*

Chapter 2

Essence riffled through the white shopping bag, took out the pinecone wreath and climbed the metal step-ladder. That was no easy feat in stilettos and skinny jeans, but she was determined to finish the job she'd started. For the past hour, she'd been decorating Global Technologies International, and now that the office looked like a dazzling Christmas wonderland, she was ready to finish cooking for the holiday mixer. Five minutes ago she'd returned to the kitchen and popped a batch of gingerbread cookies into the oven, and now the scent of cinnamon was so heavy in the air her stomach groaned and grumbled. Eating would have to wait, she decided, securing the wreath on the door. She wanted everything to be set up by four, and she still had a ton of things to do before she could even *think* about having lunch.

Humming along with the Christmas CD playing on the office stereo put Essence in a festive mood. Tonight was going to be great, she could feel it. Lincoln Davenport

knew a lot of wealthy, influential people, and after tonight
so would she. Landing more corporate contracts could
help dig her out of the financial hole her business was in,
and Essence was keeping her fingers crossed that everything went smoothly at the mixer. It had to. Or she'd have
to close up shop. And that was the last thing she wanted to
do. Just the thought of firing her beloved staff and searching for a nine-to-five made Essence want to cry, and she
hadn't cried in years.

Instead of dwelling on her problems, Essence chose to
admire her handiwork. The reception area reeked of elegance and class, the colorful Christmas decorations bright-
ened the space and the chocolate fountain smelled so good
she was tempted to grab a spoon and dig in.

"What's all this?"

Essence yelped and rocked back on her high heels. Praying no one had heard her, she climbed down the stepladder, and turned to face Lincoln. He was scowling, but his
charcoal-gray suit made him look as distinguished as a
presidential candidate. Essence wanted to ask Lincoln if
he'd just returned from a *GQ* photo shoot or an audition
for *The Bachelor,* but sensed now was not the time to get
her flirt on. "Good afternoon, Mr. Davenport. It's great
seeing you again," she said brightly, trying not to stare at
his sexy mouth. "How was your Thanksgiving?"

"Quiet, and that's just the way I like it."

*I wonder what else you like, especially between the
sheets.* The thought made her body tingle all over. Essence slid her hands into the back pockets of her jeans, but
what she really wanted to do was slide her hands all over
Lincoln's broad, muscled chest. He filled out his suit like
no other and smelled as clean and as fresh as the Pacific
Ocean. His scent aroused her, brought images of stroll-
ing hand in hand along the beach, skinny-dipping in per-

fectly blue water and kissing under the night stars. *Knock it off,* she told herself, deleting the vision from her mind. *This isn't a romantic movie, and Lincoln Davenport isn't your leading man.*

"Why are you here so early? The mixer doesn't start for a couple of hours."

"I came to decorate," Essence said, spreading her hands at her side with more flair than a *Price Is Right* model. "What do you think?"

"I didn't hire you to decorate, Ms. Sinclair. I hired you to cook."

"I do more than just cook, Mr. Davenport."

He raised an eyebrow, but didn't speak. Just stood there staring at her with a puzzled expression on his handsome face.

"When you hired Cakes and Confections by Essence, you got it all. Exquisite food, elegant decor and courteous, professional service."

Essence watched Lincoln slowly examine the main floor. He glanced at the garland-draped windows, the twelve-foot Christmas tree adorned with lights, ornaments and dozens of candy canes, and the cinnamon-scented candles emitting a soft, red glow. Having catered dozens of corporate events in the past, Essence knew guests would get a kick out of the suit-clad snowman, and the NASDAQ-themed stockings hanging around the front desk. The white-and-gold color scheme created a cozy, relaxing feel throughout the main floor, but the decor obviously didn't have the desired effect on Lincoln. His arms were folded rigidly across his chest and a scowl covered the length of his face.

"Take everything down. *Now.* It's too loud and flashy. In case you haven't noticed, I'm a very simple, low-key guy." Lincoln gestured to the silver bells hanging from the ceiling.

Essence was disappointed, but she didn't argue. All afternoon, his employees had been walking by, commenting on how beautiful the reception area looked and Essence had to agree. Keeping her tone light, and her mood upbeat, she said, "What's a holiday mixer without a few office decorations to usher in the Christmas spirit?"

"A few decorations? There's enough tinsel in here to decorate the North Pole!"

"I know. Isn't it great!"

"I've never had a caterer decorate or rearrange the furniture before."

"Then you should be glad you hired me," she said, pointing at her chest, "because I'm going to ensure your guests have the time of their lives tonight!"

To her surprise, Lincoln cracked a smile. It was small, showed just a hint of his dimples, but a smile nonetheless. Determined to win his favor, Essence moved closer and rested a hand on his forearm. It was hard and firm, and as she stood there, gazing up at him, she fantasized about what it would be like to kiss him…to lick him…to love him until she sweat out her perm.

Essence dropped her hands at her sides, but the damage had been done. Her heart was thundering loudly in her ears, and thoughts of sexing him—right there in the middle of the reception area—consumed her. Essence was so hot and bothered she could feel her nipples harden under her purple sweater and a tingling sensation shooting between her lips.

She worried she was coming down with something. Had to be. She felt feverish, like a patient on her deathbed, and was shaking so hard she could hear her chandelier earrings swinging back and forth.

To chase the butterflies in her stomach away, Essence took a long, deep breath. Seconds passed before her mind cleared and her heartbeat quit drumming in her ears. Back in control, she straightened her shoulders and raised her gaze back up to his face. "Why don't you come into the staff kitchen and let me fix you something to eat?" she asked, hoping to score some points with the surly software engineer. "You've had a very busy morning. I bet you're starving."

Lincoln shook his head. "I can't. I have a four-thirty conference call to prepare for."

"No worries. I'll put something aside for you. It will be there whenever you're ready."

"Thanks, Essence. I appreciate it."

"I'm glad we're back on a first-name basis. I was starting to think you hated me."

They shared a laugh, one that lasted for several seconds. Sensing a shift in Lincoln's mood, Essence decided it was time to put her foot down. Taking down the decorations would cut into her set-up time, and she still had appetizers to make and silverware to buff to a shine. "The decorations are staying up." When he didn't argue, she forged on. "Your guests will love snapping pictures in front of the tree, and the chocolate mistletoe is a hit every year!"

"Really? People actually like all this holiday crap?"

"Trust me, they love it," Essence said. "But so do I. Christmas is a wonderful, magical time of year filled with love and compassion for our fellow man, and I can't get enough of it."

"You sound like a hopeless romantic."

"It's not my fault," she argued, shrugging a shoulder. "My parents have been happily married for over forty years and still act like gushing newlyweds."

"That's hard to believe in this day and age of the seventy-two-day marriage and quickie divorce."

"If you find the right person, anything's possible." Essence couldn't believe she was standing in the reception area, shooting the breeze with Lincoln, as if he were an old friend. They'd met only once, and although their meeting was memorable for all the wrong reasons, she was enjoying their conversation immensely. All while staring into his dreamy brown eyes.

"Your boyfriend must be very romantic."

"I'm single, and my ex didn't have a romantic bone in his body," she blurted out. "His idea of a romantic evening was Mexican takeout, a six-pack of Bud Light and Jackie Chan movies. Needless to say, I was *not* impressed."

Lincoln threw his head back and chuckled. Essence loved the sound, loved how warm and giddy it made her feel inside. He had a way of doing that to her, of stirring emotions she'd never experienced before. It had to be something in the air, because one look at Lincoln Davenport made every bone in her body horny as hell. "If you think that's funny," she quipped, propping her hands on her hips, "wait until I tell you about the guy who brought his mother on our first date." She paused.

Lincoln laughed so loud, he attracted the attention of everyone in the reception area. His employees gawked and stared. Several had the deer-in-headlights look, and the Hispanic man standing beside the water cooler spilled his coffee on his penny loafers when his foam cup slipped out of his hand and fell to the floor.

"Naomi was right. You're hilarious, *and* beautiful."

Essence smiled in return. "So, can I keep my decorations up for the mixer?"

"Okay, but at the end of the night everything comes down. Deal?"

"You're the boss," she said with a nod. "And what the boss wants, the boss gets."

His gaze slid down her face, and lingered on her lips. "Is that right?"

Essence stumbled over her words. "I, ah, better, um, get back to the kitchen. I have a million things to do before the party starts."

"That makes two of us." Straightening his tie, he flicked his gaze around the reception area. "I know you're trying to get everyone in the Christmas spirit, but please turn down the music. This is a place of business, not a rap concert."

"What do *you* know about Memphis rap?"

Lincoln wore a smile. "I mean, I do listen to the radio from time to time."

"So, you're a fan of Eight Ball and Three 6 Mafia, huh?" Essence knew good and well that Lincoln didn't listen to rap music, but she enjoyed teasing him anyway.

"Of course, I'm a fan. They're good ole Memphis boys." He winked and put a finger to his lips. "Don't tell anyone, but I also love car shows, WWE wrestling and Snoop Dogg movies, but keep that between us. If my VP finds out, he'll never let me live it down," he said.

Essence laughed. "Wow, I'm surprised. Looks like I pegged you all wrong."

"I make it a point to know what's hot in pop culture, so I can bond with the students I teach at the U of M." Lincoln didn't move, didn't touch her, but the look in his eyes made her skin flush with desire. "Do you know what I think is really hot?"

"The new playboy calendar?"

His lips held a grin, one that lit his eyes and warmed his sable-brown skin. Angling his body toward her, he lowered his mouth to her ear as if he were about to share his deepest, darkest secret. "I think women who know how to take control are incredibly sexy."

Fear and lust shot through her veins. Sliding behind the stepladder, Essence gripped the handle for dear life. Keeping her distance from Lincoln was definitely the way to go. It didn't matter that she was attracted to him, didn't matter that they shared an undeniable chemistry. Mixing business with pleasure would be career suicide, and Essence had worked too hard and too long to blow her reputation for a tawdry holiday fling. Besides, she wasn't in the market for a lover—she was in the market for a husband. Essence was looking for the real thing, her soul mate, and a forever type of love that would stand the test of time. She wanted it all—the house with the white picket fence, three adorable kids and family vacations to outrageously priced theme parks. After the stress her ex had put her through over the years, she deserved a loving, committed relationship, and refused to settle for anything less. "I better go finish cooking."

"I'll see you at six." His gaze bore into her, making her feel vulnerable and exposed. "And don't be late. I'm looking forward to tasting your cooking."

Just my cooking? Her cheeks were burning, flushed hot with desire, but it was the fire simmering below the surface that worried her. How much longer could she play this little cat-and-mouse game with Lincoln? And what would happen if she threw caution to the wind and surrendered to her fantasies?

Essence cast her thoughts aside. It was time to quit shooting the breeze with Lincoln and undressing him with her eyes. It was time to get back to work—and not a moment too soon. She turned down the stereo, swiped her shopping bags off the floor and rushed through the reception area as fast as her high heels could take her. Essence knew Lincoln was watching her, she could feel the heat of his piercing gaze, and each step she took made her heart beat wilder and faster.

Continuing down the hallway, Essence mentally reviewed what was left on her to-do list. Everything was running smoothly, on schedule. But when she opened the door and saw Naomi hunched over one of the serving trays, popping truffles into her mouth, her good mood fizzled.

"Those aren't for you! They're for the party!" Racing over to the table, Essence smacked Naomi's hands away and whisked the tray away to safety. "I should have known you were in here stuffing your face. When it comes to chocolate, you have absolutely no self-control."

"I'm here to help. How will you know what tastes good if I don't sample the food?"

Essence pointed at the door. "Nice try, Naomi. Now get out."

"I'm not going anywhere." She hopped up on the kitchen counter and swiped a cream puff from the ceramic bowl. "I'm on a break, and if I go back to my desk, Mr. Davenport will think I'm slacking and find more work for me to do."

Essence wore a mock frown. "The tyrant! Who does he think you are? His VP?"

"I know! Everyone deserves a break, and I deserve an *extra* coffee break because I work harder than anyone else in the company," she said with a fervent nod of her head.

While Essence cooked, Naomi kept up a steady stream of loud, animated conversation. The only time she stopped talking was when she was stuffing her face, but Essence didn't mind her friend hanging out in the kitchen. If not for Naomi, she wouldn't be catering the holiday office mixer or have scored Lincoln Davenport as a client.

A smile kissed her lips, but Essence wiped it clean off

her face. Thinking about Lincoln was a waste of time. They had nothing in common, and she was looking for a serious long-term relationship, not a booty-call arrangement with her new boss.

Essence checked her watch and was surprised to see that it was already four o'clock. What was taking the delivery guy so long? She thought of calling the Williams-Sonoma store to inquire about her shipment of wine and champagne, but decided to cool her heels. The party didn't start for another hour, and she had a feeling the delivery guy would put in an appearance before she finished icing her famous red-velvet Santa cupcakes.

"So, what do you think of my boss?"

The question caught Essence off guard, and in her haste to speak she stumbled over her words. "Y-Your boss? Who, Lincoln?"

"No, my *other* boss, Channing Tatum!"

Naomi snorted a laugh. Her girlfriend was styling in her animal-print dress and leather boots, but every time she giggled, it was hard to believe she was an educated thirty-year-old woman who had dreams of one day working for the United Nations.

"I think Lincoln likes you. This morning, while I was giving him a rundown about his day, he kept asking me personal questions about you."

"Sure he was."

"I'm serious. He was trying to be all cool about it, but I could see right through him. He was quizzing me about you because he's interested. I know it. I can feel it.…"

Glancing up from her cupcakes, she searched her friend's face for the truth. Essence didn't believe a word Naomi was saying. Not because her best friend had a penchant for stretching the truth, but because Lincoln Davenport wasn't marriage material. He was a workaholic, a man obsessed with making money and closing deals and Essence didn't want anything to do with him. At least not romantically.

"You're perfect for Mr. Davenport. You're strong and intelligent and you have your own successful business. See, you guys have a lot in common."

Essence started to ask Naomi if Lincoln was dating anyone, but stopped herself before the question left her mouth. She had a party to get ready for and no time to waste. Discussing a man who was completely wrong for her *was* a waste of time.

"Something smells good," Naomi said, licking her lips. "Real good."

Opening the stove, she took out the baking dish and set it on the counter. Pride filled her. Her hard work had paid off. The escargot looked great, just like the recipe her Aunt Zizi had given her last week, and as Essence sprinkled some spices over the appetizer, she felt her mouth water and her stomach rumble for the second, unruly time. "Girl, come over here and try this."

"See! I told you that you needed my help." Naomi leaped off the counter and rushed over to the stove. Making a disgusted face, she propped one hand on her hip and pointed at the oversized white dish with the other. "What the hell is *that?*"

"Escargot en croute." Essence grabbed a fork and picked up one of the creamy white pastries. "It's delicious. Give it a taste. I'm sure you'll love it."

"Do I have to?"

"Yes."

"But I don't want to," she argued, shaking her head. "It smells good but it looks—"

Essence stuck the fork in Naomi's mouth. The color drained from her friend's face, and her eyes bulged out of her head. Chewing furiously, she flapped her hands wildly in the air and shuffled her feet. Watching Naomi hop around on one foot as if she had to use the bathroom made Essence want to laugh, but there was nothing funny about her friend's reaction to her food. "Yuck, it tastes bitter!" she complained, swiping a water glass off the counter and downing it in one big gulp. "No offense, girl, but that's nasty."

Convinced her best friend was exaggerating, Essence grabbed a fork off the counter, scooped up a pastry and took a big bite. The first thing she noticed was the dish had no taste, and was tough. Wishing she'd added another garlic clove to the recipe, she slumped against the counter. Her jaw hurt from chewing and if not for Naomi watching her, she would have tossed the appetizer into the garbage.

Essence closed her eyes and massaged her temples with her fingertips. This was a nightmare. Her worst fear had come true. She didn't have enough time to whip up another batch of escargot and worried that if she did, it wouldn't taste good anyway. Add to that, her champagne still hadn't arrived, and her servers were late. Sure, only by five minutes, but every second that ticked off the clock only increased her anxiety. "Damn, what am I going to do now?"

"Beats me, but you better think of something quick, because Mr. Davenport is expecting you to deliver."

"I know, I know—don't remind me," Essence mumbled, feeling defeated. She had to do something now, but what? Standing in the middle of the kitchen, wallowing in self-pity wasn't going to get the job done, that Essence knew for sure.

"I'm still hungry," Naomi announced, snatching a meatball out of the ceramic dish and popping it into her mouth. She chewed slowly, a look of sheer contentment on her face. "Now this is good. Way better than that nasty, rubbery escargot thing you forced me to try."

Essence swiped her purse off the counter, stuffed her arms into her tweed button-down coat and tore across the staff room at the speed of light. "I'll be back."

"Are you going home to change into your party dress?"

"No," she said, tossing a sad smile over her shoulder. "I'm going to go save my neck!"

Chapter 3

"Lincoln, this is the best office mixer you've ever had, and the food is off the chain!"

Smiling his thanks, Lincoln shook hands with the owner of the fusion restaurant on the top floor. The party was in full swing, and everywhere Lincoln turned guests were laughing, eating and dancing. But no one was having more fun than Jared Mays. The twentysomething bachelor was standing beside the bar cheesing like a Mega Millions winner. Every year he got ridiculously drunk to the point where he stumbled and staggered around, but tonight the slim, jet-setting playboy looked as sober as a circuit-court judge. "How have you been?" Lincoln asked. "The last time I was at Skyline Grill the hostess said you were on vacation."

"I was in Zurich. Had such a good time, I want to permanently relocate. You ever been?"

"No. I only travel for work, not pleasure. And besides, I don't have time."

"Make time. It's one of the coolest places I've ever been to, and I get around!"

Three doctors who worked at the Wellness Center on the first floor joined them at the bar, and the group launched into a spirited discussion about Wall Street. Once a week Lincoln joined the guys for drinks and a game of pool upstairs in Jared's restaurant, and although he loved discussing business he didn't feel like talking shop tonight.

While the men argued, Lincoln perused the large serving table covered in appetizers and desserts. He looked high and low for the caviar and braised chestnuts, but couldn't find them anywhere. Starving, but leery of trying something new, Lincoln searched for something he recognized, something that wasn't sweet or packed with thousands of calories.

"These bourbon chicken wings are finger-lickin' good," the pediatrician said, stuffing one into his mouth. He chewed slowly, as if savoring each bite. "I could eat the whole platter!"

"I hear you, man." The allergist nodded his shiny bald head. "I feel like a kid again, enjoying Christmas dinner at Big Mama's house!"

Jared joked, "Is that why you're eating like it's the last supper?"

The men chuckled.

"Mercy! Check out the legs on that sexy Southern belle," the chiropractor said, his eyes big, brown golf balls. "Who is that stunning creature in the tight red dress, and who do I have to bribe to get her number?"

"Back off, Baldwin! I saw her first."

"Keep dreaming, Doc. That sister is *way* out of your league." Jared popped the collar on his navy blue dress shirt. "You can't handle a woman like that, but *I* sure can."

Lincoln didn't have to look up from the table to know

who the men were arguing over, but he did anyway. He had to. Couldn't go five minutes without searching the room for Essence. Since the holiday mixer had started, she'd been flittering around the main floor serving cocktails, appetizers and an eyeful of cleavage. Her knee-length, zipper-front dress was classy and chic, but every time she laughed—which seemed to be every ten seconds—her big, bountiful breasts mashed together. And it was turning him on in the worst way.

Watching her on the sly, Lincoln admired her mesmerizing strut, the fine, delicious slope of her hips and how her dazzling, thousand-watt smile lit up the entire room. Lincoln was intrigued by her, couldn't help it. There wasn't a man in the world who wouldn't find Essence Sinclair appealing. He wasn't interested in finding that one special woman, or ever settling down, but if he were, she would have to look like Essence Sinclair. The caterer was a firecracker, a sister who excited him in every way, but Lincoln was too smart to fall for her. He didn't know much about her—just what he'd read online—but what he did know was that they were opposites in every sense of the word. Lincoln wasn't interested in getting played by another red-hot woman that treated flirting like a professional sport.

"That sister has more curves than a winding road," the pediatrician praised, his tone dripping with lust. "Lincoln, do you know who she is?"

"Of course he does. It's his party." Jared gestured to the Christmas tree with his tumbler.

"What's her name and, most importantly, is she a good lay?"

At the thought of making love to Essence, his erection rose and stabbed the zipper of his Armani dress pants. His head was spinning, crammed full with naked images of the reality star, and when Lincoln finally spoke he heard the raw, thick hunger in his voice. "Her name is Essence Sinclair. Her catering company, Cakes and Confections by Essence, prepared the food and drinks tonight."

"Essence Sinclair?" Frowning, the chiropractor slanted his head to the right and stroked his long, square chin. "I've heard her name before, but I can't remember where."

Jared snapped his fingers. "I knew she looked familiar!"

"Who is she, man? Inquiring minds want to know."

"Essence Sinclair won season two of *So You Think You Can Cook,* a two-page spread in *Cuisine at Home* magazine and the twenty-five-thousand-dollar cash prize," Jared explained. "I caught the show only a couple of times, but a man never forgets a sister with a booty like that."

Tell me about it, Lincoln thought miserably, grabbing a glass of fruit punch and tasting the ice-cold drink. It quenched his thirst, but didn't lower his sweltering body temperature. Lincoln couldn't stop staring at Essence and, as he glanced around the room, he noticed he wasn't the only one. Every eye in the room was glued to her. It had been like that all night, from the moment she'd stepped out of the kitchen and into the reception area. The caterer was the life of the party, and everyone—from his business associates to his friends—was raving about how witty and vivacious she was. Lincoln wouldn't know. Essence was so busy working the room that he hadn't had a chance to talk to her. He didn't like it. Not one bit. Essence should be behind the scenes whipping up appetizers in the kitchen, not wooing and charming his guests.

His gaze zeroed in on her, and when Essence caught him in the act, she stared right back. In that brief, mind-numbing second, Lincoln felt as if they were the only two people in the room.

Tray in hand, posture perfect, Essence glided through the reception area with the grace of a beauty-pageant contestant walking the stage. Her floral-scented perfume sweetened the air, and when their eyes met for a second time, a smile blossomed on her plump, red lips. Lips he wanted to kiss, and suck and feel pressed hard against his mouth. Lincoln's burn for her grew so hot he feared he'd collapse on the tinsel-scattered floor. He was embarrassed by how helpless he felt, how weak. He'd never felt this way before, never, ever met a woman who held this kind of power over him. *I don't even know how I lost control, so how the hell am I supposed to get it back?*

"Here she comes, fellas. Play it cool, and watch this bad boy do his thing."

"Wyatt, what are you talking about?" Lincoln asked, cranking his head in the pediatrician's direction. "You're not a bad boy. You're one of the nicest guys I know."

"Not anymore. I'm turning over a new leaf. Now I'm bad to the bone."

Jared snorted a laugh. "I hate to burst your bubble, bro, but bad boys don't own poodles or do tai chi."

"Keep it down. Someone might hear you." Wyatt gave a nervous glance around the room. "Women don't want nice, guys. They want thugs and drama, and from now on that's exactly what I'm going to give them. I'm going to make Russell Brand look like a Boy Scout!"

Lincoln sympathized with his friend. Unfortunately, he knew exactly how the single, middle-aged physician felt. How many times, over the years, had women told him that he was too nice? Too serious? Boring, even. His ex-girlfriend, who had dumped him last year on Christmas Eve via text, labeled him a commitment-phobe. She flung other words around such as *dull, distant* and *distracted,* and once even accused him of being preoccupied in bed. That stung, still to this day. Lincoln was single by choice, and although he hadn't been on a date in months, it didn't bother him. Why should it? He had it all. A successful career, the respect and admiration of his colleagues, an impressive home and a stock portfolio that could rival The Donald's. He didn't need a woman. All his life, the opposite sex had given him nothing but trouble and heartache. He was better off without them—especially sisters who looked and acted like Essence—but that didn't stop Lincoln from lusting after her. He was cynical about relationships, and jaded for sure, but he wasn't blind.

"Good evening. Can I interest you gentlemen in some peppermint eggnog?"

"You interest me very much," Jared said smoothly, licking his lips. "I'm Jared Mays. Congratulations on winning *So You Think You Can Cook*."

"Thank you. Is that a no on the eggnog, sir?"

He picked up one of the offered cocktail glasses and downed it in five seconds flat. "Yum."

"Anyone else?" Essence asked, her smile bright. "I guarantee you'll like it."

Lincoln wasn't thirsty, and he hated thick, sweet drinks, but for some strange reason he took a glass. And so did his friends. He tasted the drink and was surprised by how smooth it was. Before he knew it, his glass was empty and he was reaching for another one.

"You've been working hard all night. You deserve a break."

Essence protested, but her words fell on deaf ears. Jared took the silver tray out of her hands, rested it on the nearest table and boldly stepped to her. "I'd love to dance with you."

"And," she quipped, leaning heavily on the word, "I'd love the new Cartier necklace that was unveiled in Paris last week, but we can't always get what we want, can we?"

"I can afford to buy you a different necklace for every day of the week."

Her eyes narrowed, but her sickly, sweet smile stayed in place. "I can afford to buy it myself. I was just making an observation."

Lincoln hid a grin. Listening to Essence and Jared go at it was better than watching the Fight Network any day. On and on they went, sparring like heavyweights, and after several minutes of riveting verbal banter Jared looked winded, as if he'd just finished doing a hundred one-arm pushups.

"Just one dance," Jared pressed. "Come on. This is my favorite Christmas song."

"I'd love to but I can't. I'm working."

Jared clapped Lincoln on the back. "You don't mind if Essence takes a break, do you?"

Lincoln did mind. He hated the thought of Jared touching her, but he damn sure wasn't going to tell his friend that. "Of course not," he lied, forcing the words up out of his dry mouth. "Essence is free to do what she wants."

Her smile froze, and surprise flickered across her face. Her eyes combed his, and the sheer strength of her gaze knocked the very breath out of him.

Lincoln tasted his drink, waited for the moment to pass. But it didn't. His limbs felt heavy, his vision was blurry and he was burning up. He felt as if he'd just taken a shot to his ribs and leaned against the bar to keep from toppling over.

"You heard the boss. Now let's get out there and get it off and poppin'!"

Essence straightened and looped her hand around the arm Jared offered. "It has to be a quick dance, Mr. Mays. I have to replenish the candy station and mix more cocktails...."

Lincoln blinked hard, forced his eyes to focus. He eyed

the attractive twosome as they weaved their way through the crowd and found a vacant spot to move and groove. And groove they did. Not for one song, or two, but so many that Lincoln lost count. Unlike him, Jared moved fluidly, like a trained dancer, and looked confident out on the dance floor. He'd bet the Bahamian playboy was exactly her type—a slick, smooth bad boy to the core who was wild and spontaneous—and when his friends echoed his thoughts Lincoln felt his spirits plummet.

"Jared is the man!" Baldwin praised, his voice one of awe and wonder. "Bet he has that sexy reality star in his bed by the end of the night."

"The kid's young, but he's as smooth as Billy Dee in *Lady Sings the Blues*."

Lincoln cocked an eyebrow. "That's a bit of a stretch, don't you think, Wyatt?"

"No, look at them. She is smiling and laughing at all his jokes. Shoot, I wouldn't be surprised if they started sexin' on the dance floor."

Baldwin chuckled. "Get out of here, man. That stuff only happens on the adult channel!"

The physicians moved on, setting out in search of their own willing and eager dance partners, but Lincoln remained at the bar, watching Essence on the sly. He told himself he didn't care what she did, or who she danced with, but if that were true, why did seeing her in the arms of Jared Mays rile him up? Why were the veins in his neck twitching and his blood boiling? Because she was supposed to be in the kitchen, not dirty dancing, he decided, raking a hand over his head. *What game is she playing?* he wondered. *Is she here to cater my office party or here to make a love connection with one of my wealthy, successful clients?* Lincoln didn't know the answer to any of the questions circling his mind, but he intended to find out before the night was over.

Essence swiped a cocktail off the tray on the conference room table, put it to her lips and downed the berry-flavored drink in one swig. She had reason to celebrate, to let go and finally cut loose. Her Christmas-themed menu for Lincoln's office mixer was a hit, and guests had scooped up her pretty pink business cards as though they were hotcakes.

On cloud nine, she floated around the room, collecting garbage and tearing down Christmas decorations. High off the success of the party, she'd sent her employees home, opting instead to clean up the office by herself. Essence needed time alone to process her thoughts and all the wonderful, unexpected things that had happened at the office mixer. She'd been fighting all her life to make something of herself, and impressing Lincoln's well-heeled clients proved how far she'd come. Schmoozing with his guests had paid off big-time. She'd been booked to cater a bachelorette party, an anniversary brunch and a Valentine's Day Quinceañera. The contracts weren't quite enough to take her business to the next level, but it was a start.

"I've been looking for you."

At the sound of Lincoln's voice, Essence snapped to attention. She'd been so busy thinking about all the highlights of the office mixer, she hadn't heard Lincoln enter the conference room. He closed the door behind him, and then strode over to her.

"We need to talk."

It's about time, she thought, hiding a smile. All night she'd wanted to talk to him, to find out what he thought about the food and drinks, but every time she saw him he was chatting with a guest or posing for pictures. He didn't smile for the camera, and every time she saw him scowl, she thought, *This man is a modern-day scrooge.* "Debriefing with clients is one of my favorite parts of my job," she said, ditching the garbage bag and gesturing to the conference room table. "Take a seat, and I'll go grab us a snack. While we eat, we can discuss what worked tonight and what didn't."

"Nothing worked."

Essence didn't get the joke. *Was that supposed to be funny?*

"The menu I gave you wasn't a wish list. I wanted it followed to a T."

"I made everything you requested—"

"Except the escargot en croute." His tone was as sharp as his gaze. "Let me guess. You were so busy dancing with Jared Mays that you forgot it was in the oven and it burned to a crisp, didn't it?"

Essence pursed her lips. It wasn't in her nature to complain and she never, ever argued with clients, but she refused to let Lincoln Davenport disrespect her. Not after she'd busted her butt catering to his guests, and went above and beyond her job description. "I wasn't satisfied with how the escargot turned out, so I bought some from Williams-Sonoma. It's the best specialty store in the city, and the manager is a personal friend."

"I never saw it on the serving table."

"Guests complained about the smell, so I put it back in the kitchen. If you had asked, I would have showed you where it was."

Lincoln frowned and crossed his arms over his chest. Again. Every time she saw him, he was either glaring at her or copping an attitude, and Essence was getting sick of it. He had a thriving business, a Bill Gates amount of money and probably a bevy of gorgeous young women sitting by the phone waiting for his call. What did he have to be surly about? And what was with the menacing expression on his face? Was he trying to intimidate her? It was hard to believe a few hours ago they'd stood in the lobby, flirting and shooting the breeze. *I must have imagined it,* she decided, raking a hand through her hair and expelling a deep breath.

"I wanted Dom Pérignon Rosé served tonight, not Salon 1995."

"Yes, I know, and I apologize. My supplier delivered the wrong champagne, and by the time I noticed the error they were already closed for the night."

"I won't be using you for my other events," Lincoln announced. "Jared Mays is back in town, and his restaurant specializes in catering large-scale events and parties."

Her face fell. "But the party was a hit, and everyone had a great time."

"No," he corrected. "*You* had a great time. I hired you to cater the party, not to sashay around the room looking for your next sugar daddy."

Stunned, Essence stood there, her eyes wide, her mouth ajar. She tried to make sense of what Lincoln said, but the more she thought about it, the more convinced she was that the cocktail she'd downed earlier was making her thoughts fuzzy and her brain hazy.

"I know your type, Ms. Sinclair. You can't fool me."

"Excuse me?" Hearing the bite in her tone, she paused, and took a deep breath. Essence counted backward from ten and recited the Serenity Prayer in the hopes that it would calm her spirit, but as she listened to Lincoln judge her, her temper took a nosedive.

"You're a sexy, provocative woman who uses her looks to get ahead. That's why you spent all night charming my wealthy male guests, and shaking your ass with Jared Mays."

In her haste to defend herself, Essence stumbled and tripped over her tongue. Good thing, too, because she would have gone up and down both sides of Lincoln in English, *and* Spanish. It took supreme effort to keep her cool, to not go off on him, but when Essence spoke she couldn't contain her anger. Each word sounded like a shout, and her voice was three octaves higher than usual. "I would have been perfectly happy spending the night in the kitchen, but one of my servers called in sick at the last minute, and I had no choice but to help serve," she explained, spitting the words out through clenched teeth. "But you know what, Lincoln, you're right. I *did* have a great time tonight. I love meeting new people, and hearing how much guests enjoy the food I prepared is the most rewarding part of my job."

His nose twitched, as if he were trying not to laugh, but when he spoke his tone was filled with sarcasm. "Of course, my bad. You and Jared were discussing the gingerbread house while you were out on the dance floor bumping and grinding."

"Bumping and grinding? Are you kidding me? I didn't want to dance with Mr. Mays, but you put me on the spot," she shot back, good and angry now. "What was I supposed to do? Turn him down *after* you offered me up like a sacrificial lamb!"

A chuckle exploded out of Lincoln's mouth. He threw his head back and laughed long and hard. Watching him bust a gut annoyed the hell out of Essence. As angry as she was, though, she couldn't help but admire his chiseled features and his smokin' hot physique. Lincoln Davenport had a remarkable air, that unique quality that celebrities reeked of, that filled every room they entered. It was easy to recognize, difficult to define, and impossible to ignore, and every time their eyes met, Essence couldn't breathe. The CEO was irresistible. And, he was staring at her. Hard. Intently. As if he were trying to read her mind.

Lincoln slid his hands into his pockets. His scowl was gone, his shoulders were relaxed and for the first time tonight he looked perfectly calm. "So, you're not interested in Jared Mays?"

"Not in the least," Essence said. "He's a spoiled rich kid looking for a good time."

"Aren't you?"

"I'll be thirty-three in a few weeks."

Lincoln shrugged his shoulders. "What does that mean?"

"It means I'm looking for a serious, long-term relationship, not a part-time lover."

Pausing, as if considering her words, he stroked the length of his jaw.

Her heart rate pounded, beat in double time. His eyes bore into her, pierced her flesh.

"It looks as if I owe you an apology."

Essence released a sigh of relief. He believed her. Finally. To lighten the mood, she joked, "You do, Mr. Davenport, and I'm patiently waiting."

Another chuckle, this one louder and sexier than the last. "I like your fire."

And I like your lips...and your mouth...and how sexy you look in that Armani suit....

"I lost my cool. It won't happen again." Lincoln sounded sincere, and if his smile was any wider it could power the entire office with light. "I received countless compliments about the food and decor tonight. Thanks for all your hard work, Essence. Job well done."

Lincoln reached out and touched her bare shoulder, ran his hands along her hot flesh.

Essence felt a rush, a tremor that shook her body. Something told her to move. To hightail it back to the kitchen as fast as her stiletto-clad feet could take her. Inching closer to the table, she discreetly scooped up her cell phone and palmed it in her left hand. She couldn't remember ever feeling this anxious around a man, but had the butterflies and clammy skin to prove just how uneasy she was. It was time to leave before she did something crazy, like pounce on this dreamy, dark-chocolate brother who reeked of power and class.

The air held an array of sweet aromas, dizzying scents that were as intoxicating as his piercing gaze. Essence felt woozy, light on her feet, as if she'd just polished off a bottle of Sambuca. The last time she'd felt this way was…was… Nothing came to mind. That's when it hit her. She'd *never* felt this way. Never felt the urge to run, to hide, to scamper off to safety. Tearing out of a room because she was scared of being alone with a guy? Essence could hardly believe it, but that's exactly what she was doing. Running away from Lincoln, her feelings and the lustful urges attacking her brain and body.

"I'm glad we cleared the air," Essence said, faking a confident, it's-all-good voice. The truth was that she was scared. She didn't know how they ended up this close, but there they were, standing chest to chest. Needing to put some distance between them, she inched back slowly so Lincoln wouldn't notice. He did, of course, and closed in on her again. "I'm going back to the kitchen. I have to clean the, ah, stove before I can call it a night."

Essence stepped past him and reached for the door handle.

In a moment of sheer madness, Lincoln seized her

around the waist and spun her back around. Straight into his arms. Right where he needed her to be. "Not so fast. We're not finished talking." He held her tightly, pressed her warm body to his chest. It was a bold move, one he'd never done to a woman before, but one he felt compelled to do. The truth was that Lincoln didn't feel like himself, wasn't acting like himself, either. From the day he met Essence, from the exact moment he'd laid eyes on her, he'd been battling a case of spine-tingling, mind-numbing lust. He hadn't been able to concentrate on work all week. Every second of the day he thought about kissing her, touching her, branding her big, beautiful lips with his mouth. Never had a woman held this much power over him. He couldn't do anything without imagining Essence naked, flat on her back, her long, chocolate-brown legs clamped around his waist. Desire reigned supreme, the strongest, most intense emotion powering through his veins, and as he stood there, staring into her eyes, he could feel himself falling deeper under her spell.

And that, like roller coasters and relationships, scared the hell out of him.

Chapter 4

"Do you have any idea how incredibly stunning you look tonight?" Wetting his lips with his tongue, Lincoln fixed his hungry gaze on her mouth—her moist, inviting lips that looked poised to turn him out in a million different ways. "This dress was made for a woman with your grace and beauty, and I noticed you the second you stepped into the room."

Essence rolled her eyes to the white conference room ceiling. She'd had enough. One minute Lincoln blew hot, the next he blew cold. He was playing mind games with her, toying with her emotions, and she didn't appreciate it. "Ten minutes ago you called me a tease looking for my next sugar daddy," she pointed out, "and now you think I'm classy and sophisticated. Make up your mind, Lincoln. Which one is it?"

He winced, wore a contrite face. "The things I said earlier were way out of line."

"You could say that again." Essence lowered her gaze to his hands. "Still are."

There was a breathy, sultry quality to her voice. He heard it—desire—felt it radiating off her flesh, bouncing off the walls, sucking all the air out of the conference room. That's why he didn't release his hold, why he wouldn't let her go. Lincoln couldn't fight his feelings anymore. He was going to deal with his attraction to Essence once and for all. Right here, right now. She was nothing more than a distraction, just another sexy, provocative woman who lived to turn heads, and once he got her out of his system he could get back to doing what he did best— brokering million-dollar software deals.

"What are you doing?" she demanded, struggling to free herself. "What do you want?"

"You, in my bed, tonight."

Essence inhaled a sharp breath. His deep, rich tone gave her chills from her ears to her toes and everywhere in between. His eyes smoldered, simmered with a passion and a hunger so raw, her mouth dried. The room was spinning, the walls closing in. It took a moment for Essence to recover from his bold confession, to actually come to terms with the bombshell he'd just dropped. Parting her lips, she said the only thing she could—"I work for you and I don't believe in mixing business with pleasure."

"Then, in that case, you're fired." Without breaking eye contact, he drew his hands up from her hips to her shoulders. But his hands weren't still for long.

"You'll soon learn that I always get what I want, and right now, I want you."

Essence didn't see the kiss coming. If she had, she would have dove under the conference table or took cover behind the coatrack. Or, at least that's what she told herself as she sank into his arms and swathed her hands around his neck. The kiss exceeded her wildest dreams. It was fraught with passion, laced with desire and sweeter than a hundred candy canes. Waves of pleasure flowed through her, filled every inch of her clammy, quivering body. His lips were a strong, potent, sensuous drug Essence just couldn't get enough of.

Essence heard music playing, birds chirping, felt the warmth of the sun on her face, but she knew it was just a figment of her imagination. She was lost, so far gone, her mind was playing tricks on her. They were knee-deep, in the thick of it, so entrenched in the throes of lust that nothing else mattered. She craved more, needed more. Wanted him more than she'd ever wanted anyone before.

"I want you bad, Essence. More than I've wanted anyone."

He wore a seductive gaze, one so strong and intense, her nipples hardened under her designer dress. Essence didn't know what to say, and worse, was shaking so hard she feared her words would come out in a stutter. Lincoln pressed his lips against hers, expertly sliding his tongue into her mouth. Essence did the only thing she could. What she'd been itching to do from the moment she first saw him. She kissed him back. Hard on the lips. With everything she had. With all the lust and passion coursing through her veins. Hungry didn't begin to describe how she felt. Pleasure consumed her body, made it impossible to think straight, to act like a mature, responsible human being. Stroking his shoulders, his neck and his smooth, textured hair was her undoing. Desire drove her, filled her with a sense of urgency, a wild, out-of-control hunger that could rival a movie set overrun with adult film stars.

The air in the conference room was electric, saturated with the scent of their desire. Essence was ready. Ready to ride him, to possess him, to do all the naughty, raunchy things she'd been fantasizing about all week. She ached for him, longed for him, yearned for him to touch her most intimate and private parts.

Caught up in the moment and the intensity of her feelings, she closed her eyes and blocked out the voices in her head. The ones that told her to grab her stuff and leave. But leaving was out of the question. Not when Lincoln was nibbling her ear, tweaking her nipples and talking dirty to her. He said things that made her body flush with heat, that drove her temperature up another hundred, unbearable degrees. Essence was dizzy, overwhelmed in the best possible way and anxious to please.

Essence touched Lincoln's chest, stroked and caressed him through his dress shirt. Her hands were shaking so hard and she was so flustered, she couldn't undo the buttons. That's when she ripped the shirt from his chest. Parting her lips, she slid her hands around his waist and closed her mouth around his nipple. She kissed from one nipple to the next, and down his lean torso. Fine, thin hair covered his chest, and when Essence ran her fingers through it, Lincoln roughly cupped her butt. Both hands gripped her, held her in place. His hold didn't prevent Essence from unbuckling his pants and sliding her hand into his boxer briefs.

Her mouth dried. *Now, this is a magic Mike,* she thought, marveling at the width and length of his erection. It was beautiful—long, thick and erect—and holding his shaft in her hands made Essence so hot and bothered she couldn't wait to feel Lincoln inside her.

"Get out of this dress," he growled. His voice was husky, his words an order and his gaze fixed on her mouth.

She touched the zipper, but he covered her hands with his own.

"Allow me."

Lincoln unzipped her dress, and when it fell to the floor in a heap, kicked it aside. He'd replace it, buy her five or ten more designer dresses just like it if she desired, but tonight he didn't care about being a gentleman or doing things by the book. He wanted Essence, and he was going to have her. Tonight. Now. Right on top of the conference room table. The only thing on his mind was having his fill of her.

Lincoln stuck a hand into his back pocket and fumbled with his wallet. He felt the condom packet between his fingers and breathed a sigh of relief. Within seconds he was protected.

Her body was perfect, sexier than he could have ever imagined, and when she pressed her chest against his, he almost came right then and there.

Using his tongue, he traced the soft fullness of her lips. She tasted sweet, a heady mix of fruit and wine, and the rich blend gave him a shot of pure adrenaline. Needing more, he crushed his lips against hers, ravished and explored her pretty red mouth. She was hungry, too, as crazed and overcome as he was. He could feel it in her kiss, in each urgent, passionate caress. He wanted to bend her over the table and plunge so deep inside of her that she would cry out in ecstasy. But before Lincoln could make his dream a reality, Essence pushed him down on one of the leather chairs around the table, climbed on top of him and closed her thick thighs around his waist.

Essence threw her head back and arched her spine. Just like that. Lincoln was inside her.

Moving, thrusting, filling her with his incredible width and length. Pleasure stole her breath. Made her head spin, her body tingle and her clit throb. Essence wanted to stop Lincoln, but her brain didn't send the message to her mouth.

Now, for the first time ever, she sympathized with her

girlfriends who explained away a one-night stand by saying, "We got carried away," and "It just happened." Finally,
Essence understood. Because there she was—a smart, responsible thirty-two-year-old woman—having a one-night
stand for the first time in her life. And dammit, it felt good.

Gripping his shoulder blades, she rocked and rolled her
hips to the pace of his quick, powerful thrusts. Essence
closed her eyes, soaked it all in. The chocolate-scented
air, the taste of his kiss, the pleasure of his silky, sensuous touch. If someone had told her an hour ago that she'd
be having sex with Lincoln Davenport in the conference
room of Global Technologies International, she would have
suggested they see a shrink. But there she was, straddling
his lap, riding him like a possessed woman. Being naked
under the harsh, bright lights should have terrified Essence, but it didn't. Her physical imperfections were on
display, but Lincoln made her feel beautiful, as desirable
as a Victoria's Secret model strutting the catwalk in white
angel wings. His words, his kisses and his groans intensi-
fied her need. Her body was on fire, a raging inferno that
burned out of control, and each thrust drew her closer to
the brink, to the edge of delirium.

Cupping the back of his head, she playfully urged him
forward. Lincoln came willingly and drew his lips slowly
up the front of her neck.

He devoured her. Kiss by kiss. Stroke by stroke. Thrust
by powerful, urgent thrust. Desperately, she clung to him.
To keep from screaming out and filling the entire building
with her moans, Essence sank her teeth into his shoulders.
Just like a crazed, sex-deprived woman. Which is exactly
what she was. She hadn't had sex in a year, and although
Essence had a battery-operated friend she affectionately
called "The Big Dipper," nothing compared to making
love to Lincoln Davenport. He was a buttoned-up execu-

tive, an articulate, well-spoken brother with a plethora of university degrees and business awards, but he was also an expert and exquisite lover. A muscled six-foot beast between the sheets who was down for whatever. And Essence was loving every wild, torrid minute of their late-night encounter.

"Faster, Lincoln. Harder…harder…harder…" she cooed, licking the inside of his ear. "That's just the way I like it… how I want it…how I need it…"

Essence rammed her hips against his groin, rocking so hard the chair went flying into the back wall. She was losing it, coming apart at the seams, living out her wildest, most outrageous fantasy with a man she'd known for a week. That should have scared her, should have sent her crashing through the nearest exit, but instead, the thought increased her desire, sent it shooting though the roof. Up and down, back and forth, she pumped her legs with all her might. Watching his length move expertly inside her thrilled Essence more than hanging upside down on a roller coaster. Lincoln knew what she needed and gave it to her over and over again.

"Oh, God, I love when you touch me there, when you lick me there," she purred.

Eyes closed, head back, she relished in the beauty of the moment. Swimming in a sea of pleasure, a pool of head-spinning euphoria and bliss, made it impossible for Essence to think clearly, rationally. All she could do was feel, enjoy and relish the moment. This was the kind of loving the greats crooned about. Loving that spurned songwriters to pen chart-topping hits that resonated with lovers around the globe. Essence had never been loved like this. She'd never been with a man who gave as good as he got, who was this eager to please, but so damn cool about it. He could give pointers to every man in America. If sex were a sport, Lincoln Davenport would be the league MVP. Without question, he was the best lover she'd ever had, the only man to ever connect with her emotionally and physically while making love.

Lincoln locked his hands around her waist, held her tight. Essence cupped her breasts and shoved them into his mouth. Desire shot through him at a thousand mind-blowing miles an hour. That's what he loved. That's what he couldn't get enough of. Confidence was sexy, and Essence Sinclair was swimming in it. She knew what she wanted, how she wanted it and wasn't afraid to tell him what she liked. That was a turn-on. Downright erotic. Lincoln loved being with a sister who was vocal and passionate about her feelings. He got a kick out of the cursing and groaning and moaning she did, too. Lincoln couldn't get enough of it. He wanted more, in fact.

Feeling her lips on his ears sent shivers ripping down his spine. Sensations he'd never experienced before. Lincoln felt wobbly, outside of himself, and wondered if someone had slipped a roofie into his cognac. It was a ludicrous thought, but there was no other explanation for why he was screwing the hell out of Essence Sinclair. This wasn't him. He wasn't spontaneous, he didn't do anything that wasn't penciled into his weekly agenda, and he'd never— not once—had sex outside of the bedroom. No one had ever asked, and he'd never felt the desire to. Then Essence had sashayed into his office like a walking wet dream and flipped his world upside down.

Essence moaned over and over again, shouted his name so many times his ego inflated like a hot-air balloon. He watched her raise her arms in the air and tip farther and farther. And just when he thought she was going to fall and send them both crashing to the cold, hard ground, Essence braced her hands on the floor and locked her elbows.

Lincoln felt his eyes widen, and his mouth gape open. It was the sexiest, most erotic move he'd ever seen a woman perform and shocking enough to trigger his orgasm. His body quivered, shook and throbbed. Lincoln didn't want Essence to think he was a two-minute brother, one of those trifling, selfish men who didn't care about pleasing their lover, but he couldn't stop the tremors that overtook his body, or the tingles stabbing his spine.

Losing the battle with his flesh, Lincoln gripped her hips, gave a quick, powerful thrust and released. Goose bumps pricked his skin, tickled and pierced his back. This was heaven. The ultimate high. Nothing compared to it. Nothing surpassed it. It had no equal, no match. Sinking a hole in one made Lincoln puff out his chest in pride, but making love to Essence made him feel like "the man," a bona fide stud, which was a welcome change from how his ex-girlfriend used to make him feel. And he would never, for as long as he lived, forget how incredible it felt being buried deep inside her.

Lincoln blew out a breath, raked a hand over his head. The realization shocked him, made his head spin and his brain throb. He didn't believe in love at first sight, and enjoyed being a bachelor, but he recognized, right then and there, what a remarkable woman Essence was.

Essence struggled to sit up, but Lincoln tightened his grip around her waist. He didn't want to let her go. At least not yet. He wanted to know more about her, wanted to know what her story was, and feared if he released her she'd make a break for the conference room door.

Lincoln heard a low, muffled buzzing sound in the distance, and knew it was his iPhone going off. He didn't know where it was, or even what time it was, but there was one thing he knew for sure—his life had just changed forever. That thought in mind, he kissed Essence softly on the lips and held her that much tighter.

"I can't believe we just had sex," Essence said, her voice a throaty whisper. "I've done a lot of crazy things in my life, but I've never done anything like this before."

"That makes two of us."

Essence sat up straight, a quizzical expression on her face. She looked sleepy and her hair was tousled, but her skin was glowing. Smiling sheepishly like a kid caught with her hand in the cookie jar, she snatched her dress off the back of the chair and swathed it around her waist. "You've never had a one-night stand? Really?"

"Yeah, why are you so surprised?"

"Because you're handsome, and wealthy and smart as hell," she said, her head cocked and her brows raised. "Guys like you, who can have any woman you want, usually do."

Her words blew Lincoln away, but he guarded his features, kept his expression blank. The part about him being wealthy was true, nothing he hadn't heard before, but he wasn't a ladies' man. Not in the least. Unlike his friends and the Jared Mays of the world, he didn't have it in him to hurt or mistreat women, and avoided drama of any kind. All his life, females had passed him over for bad boys, for guys who didn't have a faithful, honest bone in their bodies, and although Essence had given him the best sex of his life, Lincoln had a sneaking suspicion she was no different than any of the other women he'd dated in the past.

"Do you have a girlfriend?"

"If I did, I wouldn't be here with you."

"Just checking. You'd be surprised what some men do when their girl isn't around."

"I'm not the average man."

"You can say that again." Essence slid her gaze from

his face to his lap, and then lingered there for a long moment. Raking a hand through her hair, she gave her head a shake and wore a shy smile. "I better go before I... Never mind.... I've embarrassed myself enough for one night."

Lincoln touched a hand to her cheek, stroked her smooth, chocolate-brown skin. "Come to my place," he proposed, dropping a kiss on her delicate, bare shoulder. "We can share a bottle of wine, have something to eat and talk."

"What are we going to do after said 'talk'?"

A grin stroked his lips. "Take a wild guess?"

Her body tensed, stiffened. "Lincoln, I like you a lot, and I think you're a great guy, but this was just a one-time thing. I work for you and I have a reputation to uphold."

"I fired you, remember?"

"I—I—I thought you were joking," she stammered, sliding off his lap and standing. "I want to cater your other events, but I'm not going to keep sleeping with you just to keep—"

Narrowing her eyes, she broke off speaking and glanced over her shoulder.

Light bounced off the window and circled the length of the conference room.

"Oh, no! Someone's outside in the hall!"

"Don't worry. It's just security doing their hourly checks." Lincoln shrugged on his damaged Kenneth Cole dress shirt and slid on his pants. "Relax. I'll get rid of them."

Essence released a sigh of relief. Zipping her dress up quickly, she stuffed her feet back into her heels and swiped her cell phone up off the floor. "I guess this is good night, then. I'll talk to you...tomorrow...or maybe—"

"No, don't go. I want you to stay." Cupping her chin, he lowered his mouth and kissed her gently on the lips.

One kiss wasn't enough, but Lincoln knew if he fell victim again to his desire, they'd be right back at square one. Back to kissing, caressing and stroking each other, and he didn't want to risk anyone catching them in the act. Essence wasn't just any girl, she was special, and he didn't want anyone seeing her naked, mouthwatering shape. "Wait for me in my office. I'm right behind you."

Lincoln watched Essence slip through the adjoining side door, and then turned to the front of the conference room. Just as he passed the coatrack, the knob turned. To prevent the guards from barging in, Lincoln threw his shoulder into the door and braced his weight against it. "What's up, fellas?"

"Is everything okay, Mr. Davenport?" the pudgy, over-weight one asked, stealing a peek inside the conference room. "The janitor said he heard a woman scream."

"I hope Willie didn't help himself to the leftover food from the holiday mixer," he joked. "The last time he had rum cake he passed out in the ladies' room!"

The guards chuckled.

"You guys deserve a break." Lincoln pointed down the hall at the staff kitchen. "Go take a load off, and have something to eat and drink while you're at it."

The bearded guard checked his weathered brown watch. "Are you sure, Mr. Davenport? We're only an hour into our shift, and we haven't finished checking the other offices."

"I'm positive. If anyone gives you a hard time, send them to me."

"Thanks, Mr. Davenport. That's mighty kind of you.…"

Out of the corner of his eye, Lincoln saw Essence rush through the sliding glass doors and dash over to the shiny black car parked under the lamppost. Disappointment over-whelmed him. It bruised his ego and crushed his pride. His plans were going up in smoke, right before his very eyes. This wasn't how the night was supposed to end. They should be in his new Audi, headed to his Collierville home, listening to cool jazz and stealing kisses. Instead, Essence was speeding out of the parking lot as if Five-O was hot on her trail.

Lincoln told himself to chill out, to quit stressing. All wasn't lost. Once he got rid of the security guards and found his cell phone, he'd give Essence a call and suggest they meet up for drinks at one of the quiet nearby cafés on Beale Street. But then Lincoln remembered that he didn't have her cell phone number, and his shoulders sagged for the second time.

Chapter 5

"Earth to Essence! Earth to Essence! Hello? Wake up!"
At the sound of Naomi's high-pitched drawl, Essence blinked and straightened in her chair. Snapping out of her daydream—the one with her and Lincoln making love on a satin-draped bed covered with red rose petals—she snatched up her ballpoint pen and ruffled the papers on her desk. She was supposed to be planning a *Fifty Shades of Grey*-themed bachelorette party, but from the moment she'd stepped into her home office that morning, she'd been consumed with thoughts of Lincoln. And when she wasn't fantasizing about him and all the deliciously wicked things they'd done last night in the conference room, she was staring at her cell phone, willing the stupid thing to ring. Lincoln hadn't called or texted her, and Essence couldn't help but wonder what his silence meant. "Sorry, girl," she said, pushing all thoughts of Lincoln to the back of her mind. "I was so busy working I didn't hear you come in."

"Busy working, my ass. You're sitting there daydreaming about that louse, Rashad."

"No, I'm not. We're done for good."

"Then why won't you go out with Jared Mays?"

"Because he's arrogant and cocky and spent the whole night staring at my boobs." Essence wore a disgusted face. "I'm not interested in him—"

"You should be," Naomi insisted, plopping down on the velvet wing-backed chair and crossing her thin, sweatpants-clad legs. "He's fine, crazy rich and apparently good in bed."

Yeah, but Lincoln's amazing, she thought, unable to wipe the smile off her face. Not that it mattered. He hadn't called and likely wasn't going to. They'd had their fun—an incredible night of sex—and now he was on to the next girl. Essence wanted to confide in Naomi about what happened with Lincoln, but she was scared her roommate would judge her. And with good reason. Last night Essence had thrown her own dating rules out the window. Even now, hours after leaving Global Technologies International, Essence still couldn't explain why she'd tossed her inhibitions aside and had sex with Lincoln. That morning, she'd woken up convinced that their encounter was nothing more than an erotic wet dream, but when she slipped out of bed, reality struck. The tender ache between her legs and her sore, tender limbs were a telltale sign of vigorous lovemaking, signs she just couldn't ignore or explain away.

Essence opened her mouth, the truth on the tip of her tongue, but couldn't get the words out. Fear of being judged prevented her from telling Naomi the truth. And since last night was a one-time thing that she had no intention of ever repeating, no one needed to know. Now, if she could just stop reliving every second of her encounter with Lincoln and finalize the menu for the bachelorette party she was catering next Saturday, life would be normal, perfect.

"Jared Mays is a popular, well-connected businessman and hooking up with him could open a lot of doors for you...." Frowning, Naomi broke off speaking, and glanced around the small colorful office overrun with cookbooks and paintings. "Who's that?"

Essence listened for a moment, and smiled when she heard Dr. Rashondra Brown's crisp, authoritative voice. She reached across the desk and lowered the volume on the computer speakers. "I'm listening to Dr. Rashondra Brown's new book, *Why Your Ass is Still Single.*" Essence picked up the audio book and handed it to her best friend. "I've only listened to the first disk, but so far I really like it. I love how Dr. Rashondra tells it like it is!"

"I wish I'd read this book *before* I broke my lease and moved in with Cash." Sighing, Naomi raked a hand through her short, thick twists. "Thanks again for letting me crash here, Essence. I could stay with my mom, but I'm too embarrassed to face her. She told me Cash would play me, and unfortunately she was right."

"Don't sweat it. I love having you here," Essence said, meaning every word. "You're great company, and you clean like nobody's business!"

Naomi wore a soft smile, but the sadness in her eyes remained. "Did you make an offer on that house in Collierville you were telling me about yesterday? The one with the huge gourmet kitchen and fenced backyard?"

"The asking price is steep, so my Realtor suggested we keep looking."

"Why don't you just use your winnings from *So You Think You Can Cook?*"

Essence stared down at her hands, fidgeted with the strap on her gold wristwatch. The one she'd spent an arm and a leg on. "There's nothing left," she confessed. "It's all gone."

"What! You blew twenty-five thousand dollars in six months?" Naomi's words came out in a blast that shook the office windows. "Girl, that's crazy! What were you thinking?"

"I didn't blow twenty-five thousand dollars, Naomi. After taxes, I got eighteen grand."

"And…" she prompted, leaning forward in her chair.

"I bought my used late-model Lexus and did a little shopping."

Naomi's scowl deepened, covered the length of her heart-shaped face. "That should still leave you with a nice chunk of change in the bank for a rainy day."

"It did, but my parents asked for a loan and I didn't have the heart to say no."

"But you loaned them money last year when their house was facing foreclosure, and they still haven't paid you back."

"I know, but they're my parents," Essence argued, her voice louder than she intended. "What do you expect me to do? Sit back and watch them lose everything they've worked for?"

"Of course not, but if you keep giving them money, you'll always be in the hole. And, trust me, there's nothing fun about living paycheck to paycheck."

Essence released a deep sigh. Her girlfriend was right, but there was nothing she could do about it now. She'd given her parents the last of her winnings—nine thousand dollars and some change—and seriously doubted she'd ever see a dime of it again. The thought saddened her, but she pushed back her feelings, pretended they weren't there. *Don't worry,* she told herself, *if I cater Lincoln's other holiday events, I'll have the money I need for the down payment.*

"From now on, I'm only dating white-collar guys," Naomi announced. "A broke man can't do nothing for me!"

"Then, *you* should date Jared Mays. He's exactly your type."

"He's too loud and way too short." Standing up on her tiptoes, a cheeky grin on her thin lips, she sliced a hand in the air. "A brother has to be at *least* six feet tall to enjoy this ride!"

For the first time all day, Essence laughed. But then she remembered Lincoln hadn't called her, and her giggles dried up. "Yesterday you were pushing Lincoln Davenport at me, and today you're all for me hooking up with Jared Mays. What gives?"

"I was just teasing you about Lincoln," Naomi replied, wearing a smirk. "He's too wrapped up in his work to date, and besides, you guys have nothing in common."

You're wrong. We have amazing chemistry, and we can't keep our hands off each other!

"Girl, you killed at that party last night."

"You think so?" Essence beamed with pride as Naomi recounted how guests had gushed over the food, the decor and the festive party favors. As they discussed the highlights of the holiday mixer, her thoughts strayed. To Lincoln. To the time they shared together—caressing, stroking and kissing each other with reckless abandon. It didn't surprise her that that he hadn't called. Why would he? To seduce her, he'd said and done all the right things, and once she gave up the goods, he was gone. *Am I ever going to meet a good guy? Someone who isn't going to play me, and who loves me for me?*

"What are you wearing tonight?"

Essence shook off her troubling thoughts. "I'm not going."

"Quit playing. You live for salsa night at the Rumba

Room," Naomi said. "Last Saturday you danced until the bar closed, then shimmied all the way to the car!"

Essence stared at her desk. Her eyes strayed to her cell phone. She didn't tell Naomi the truth—that she was hoping Lincoln would call—and instead faked a yawn. "I just don't have it in me tonight to dance and schmooze. I'm beat."

"All right, suit yourself," she said with a shrug. "I'm going to the store. Need anything?"

"I'd love a box of Krispy Kreme doughnuts."

"But they're full of empty calories and loaded with sugar."

"Everyone can't be a stick figure like you, Naomi. I'm proud of my curves, and if a man doesn't love me for me, then it's *his* loss, because I love my body just the way it is."

And so does Lincoln, she added silently. *Last night he loved me in ways I've never dreamed of, in ways no one has ever loved me before.*

"Fine, fine, I'll get your doughnuts." A wave and Naomi was gone.

The phone rang, and Essence snatched it up on the second ring. It was probably her aunt Zizi calling to find out how the escargot en croute turned out, but she put the receiver to her ear and spoke in a crisp, professional tone. Deep down, she secretly hoped it was Lincoln, finally calling to check in on her, and smiled at the thought of his handsome face with bedroom eyes. "Good morning, Cakes and Confections by Essence."

"What's up, sweet cheeks? Miss me?"

Her smile fizzled. "Rashad, what do you want? I'm busy."

"Too busy to talk to your man?"

Essence faked a laugh. "I'm hanging up now. Bye."

"I call from Seattle to see how you're doing and all I

get is attitude. What's up with that?" he asked. "Aren't you even going to ask how my West Coast tour is going?"

"I don't have time for this. I have work to do."

"Really? I heard your catering company is struggling and…"

The lump in her throat was too big to swallow. To keep from cursing him out, Essence breathed deeply through her nose and channeled positive thoughts. It didn't help. In fact, the more she thought about what Rashad said, the angrier she got. They'd dated long before fame and fortune and groupies came calling, and if not for Essence posting Rashad's talent show performances on YouTube, he'd still be hanging out on the street corner playing dominoes with his friends. But just because they shared a past and their families were close didn't mean Essence had to like him. She didn't. At least not anymore. He wasn't the kind, sweet guy she'd fallen for her freshman year in college. Success had gone straight to Rashad's head, and these days Essence couldn't stand to be around him. The R & B singer treated his handlers like crap, had an ego that could rival any popular performer and thought if he plied her with gifts she'd take him back. It wasn't going to happen. Not today. Not ever.

"I have a proposition for you," he said smoothly. "Come with me to the Christmas Gala, and I'll give you five Gs. No games. No strings. Just cold, hard cash."

"No, thanks."

"Ten."

Convinced she'd misheard him, she gave her head a hard shake and pressed the phone closer to her ear. Essence could hear loud, boisterous laughter, and male and female voices in the background. Rashad was in his hotel room, doing what he did best—partying and blowing money on his enormous, no-good entourage.

"I'm not playing, sweet cheeks. I'm being straight up."

"Quit calling me that, Rashad. I don't like it."

"You used to. Used to like everything I said and did."

Essence didn't want to rehash all the highs and lows of their tumultuous on-and-off-again relationship, or encourage his useless trip down memory lane, so she changed the subject. "Are you performing at the Gala, or just going to show off some new bling?"

"Both. And I need you on my arm."

"And you're willing to pay me to be your date?"

"What's ten grand?" he argued. "That's chump change to a baller like me."

Essence considered his offer. It was too good to be true. He was up to something, but what? Then it hit her—the real reason for Rashad's long-distance call and all the sweet talk about her being his girl. Men always wanted what they couldn't have, and now that she'd finally moved on with her life, he wanted her back. Go figure. "It doesn't matter what you say or do, Rashad. I'm not going to sleep with you."

"You will, but not because I paid you," he said with all the confidence in the world. "I want you to look like a million bucks when I meet the VP of Urban Beats Records, so I'll throw in an extra couple thousand for a dress. It needs to be tight and short and revealing. I want every man in the room to wish you were their girl, got it?"

Essence reasoned with her conscience, with that still, small voice who told her to hang up the phone. Ten thousand dollars was enough to put a down payment on her dream house, that cozy three-bedroom ranch-style house she'd been pining after for the last three months. Essence loved living in the inner city, and her neighbors treated her like family, but crime was on the rise and when she was out after dark she often feared for her safety. It was time to move on. "Why do you want *me* to go with you to the party?" she asked, her curiosity getting the best of her. "Why don't you take one of your model girlfriends?"

"Because I want you."

"Cut the crap, Rashad, and tell me what's really going on."

"The VP at Urban Beats Records is from Memphis, and a huge fan of *So You Think You Can Cook,* and when I told him you were my girl, he got all hyped up and excited," he explained. "Old boy has the hots for you, and with you on my arm, I'm guaranteed a fair shake."

"Now I'm really *not* interested in attending the Christmas Gala," she grumbled.

"But I need you. You have a great feel for people and you're one of the few people I trust wholeheartedly. You'll tell me if the VP is jerking me around, or giving it to me straight. My agent is a decent guy, but at the end of the day all he cares about is his thirty percent."

"It sounds like you need a better team."

"If Ramiyah was alive she would've come with me, no questions asked...." His voice broke, and he trailed off speaking. Rashad coughed, and then cleared his throat several times.

Essence felt an ache in her chest and a pang in her heart. To calm herself, she took a deep breath and pressed her eyes shut. This happened every time someone said Ramiyah's name, and Essence wondered if she'd ever be able to think about her childhood friend without tearing up.

"Please, Essence. I'm begging you. This is the big break I've been waiting for."

Rap music blasted over the phone line, and then a door slammed.

"Give me your account number," Rashad said, shouting his words, "and I'll have my business manager deposit the money into your account later today."

I wonder what Lincoln would think about this deal. It didn't matter, she told herself, glancing at the wall clock above her desk. They weren't a couple, and he thought so little of her he hadn't even called. Probably wasn't going to. Lincoln claimed he'd never had a one-night stand, but Essence knew that was a lie. She was sure Lincoln had the protocol down to a science. She'd fallen for him hook, line and sinker, and now her catering contract held in the balance. Had he hired someone else? One of her larger, more experienced competitors?

"Sorry, Rashad, I can't." He couldn't see her, but she wore a sad smile and shook her head. "I hope the rest of your West Coast tour goes well. Take care of yourself."

"Sweet cheeks, wait!—"

Essence dropped the phone back in the cradle. Glad to be rid of Rashad, she hit Play on the stereo and jacked up the volume on the Christmas CD. She had to do something to get her mind off Lincoln, her rejected mortgage application and Rashad's outrageous offer. Work was the perfect distraction, and soon all her troubles faded to the back of her mind. The rest of the morning was quiet and uneventful, and by the time Essence turned off her computer and called it quits for the day, the sun had begun its descent.

In the kitchen, she fixed herself a turkey sandwich and read her newest text messages. Still nothing from Lincoln. Sadness filled her, overwhelmed her heart. Essence told herself not to sweat it, but there was nothing she could say or do to change how she felt inside.

Essence pushed away from the table and left her untouched sandwich on the plate. She'd eat later, after she had a long, luxurious bubble bath. As she exited the kitchen, she heard the doorbell chime. For a second, Essence considered ignoring it. What if it was Rashad popping up unannounced again? What if he'd come to sweeten his previous deal?

Essence stamped out the thought. Rashad couldn't be in Seattle and in Memphis at the same time. The R & B singer was slick, but not *that* slick. Remembering Naomi went

grocery shopping and had Krispy Kreme doughnuts with
her made Essence sprint into the foyer. She needed something to take her mind off Lincoln, something to make
her feel better, and eating her favorite treat while watching *Modern Family* was sure to cheer her up.

Sure it will, jeered her inner voice. *You have a better chance of winning the lottery than forgetting all the
wicked, delicious things Lincoln can do with his tongue.*

Essence opened the door, saw the elves standing on
her holiday welcome mat and blinked hard. She had to
be dreaming, because elves didn't exist, and they damn
sure didn't pop up on her doorstep on a cold, frigid December afternoon. Delivery men didn't wear green tunic-
style costumes, complete with velvet hats, belts and shoes,
so Essence knew the young men had either lost a bet, or
their minds.

"Are you Essence Sinclair?" the short, stocky elf asked.

Tongue-tied, all Essence could do was nod.

"Then this is for you." The ringleader stomped his foot,
and his band of merry men clapped, hooted and rocked out
like an eighties punk band. "Jingle bell, jingle bell, jingle
bell rock…" they sang, their dance moves as smooth and
as captivating as their voices.

Their rousing, lively rendition of her favorite holiday
songs blew Essence away, and when they finished the two-
minute medley and bowed graciously at the waist, she
cheered.

"That was amazing! You guys are amazing!"

Grinning from ear to ear, the elves spun around, lifted a
wide, enormous package covered in shiny, metallic wrapping paper off the ground and marched into the living
room. They rested it on the coffee table, and then dashed
out the door singing "Feliz Navidad" as they left.

Wow, Rashad must really miss me, Essence thought,
grabbing the heart-shaped envelope stuck to the front of the

package. *He's never, ever done anything this romantic!* On the front of the card, two children holding hands played in the snow. The image brought back fond memories, made Essence reflect on the happiest days of her childhood. Wearing a wistful smile, she read the note written inside. Her eyes popped straight out of her head. The gift wasn't from Rashad...it was from Lincoln!

It's the holidays. The most magical time of the year. That's why I'm taking you out on a romantic, fun-filled date you won't ever forget. Be prepared to be swept up in the joy and excitement of the season....

Essence melted like a slab of ice in the Arabian Desert. Yesterday, after Lincoln had ordered her to take down the decorations, she'd rambled on and on about how special Christmas was, about how it was a magical time of year, and now, less than twenty-four hours later, he was quoting her. *Talk about smooth,* she thought, rereading the sweet, thoughtful note. Essence liked the card, and appreciated the gift, no matter what it was. But she could smell chocolate and cinnamon and knew she was going to love what was inside the package.

Humming a jingle, she ripped off the wrapping paper and tossed it to the ground. Essence instantly recognized the red-and-gold sleigh. Yesterday, when she'd popped into the Williams-Sonoma store to buy the escargot en croute, she'd noticed it sitting beside the cash register. She also noticed the staggering price. Essence couldn't believe Lincoln had bought the holiday gift package for her. After all, they hardly knew each other. The sleigh was huge, twice the size of the stuffed Santa she had standing in her front window, and chock-full of sugar cookies, dried fruit, multicolored candy canes and bottles of wine. The ceramic jar held magazines, Christmas CDs and the largest assortment of Italian cheeses Essence had ever seen. And when she saw the chocolate high-heeled shoe peeking out from behind the tin of caramel popcorn, she threw her head back and had a good laugh.

It's too bad Lincoln's my boss, she thought, tearing open the bag of chocolate rum balls and tossing a sweet, chewy morsel into her mouth. *He has great taste in gifts, and is a sexy, passionate lover, too!*

Essence had mixed feelings. She liked Lincoln and wanted to get to know him better, but was scared of falling for another guy who was scared of commitment. And it was obvious Lincoln Davenport was looking for a good time, not a wife. Essence refused to be the CEO's plaything, and just because they'd slept together once didn't mean they had to do it again.

Entering the main floor bathroom, Essence told herself not to get excited about tonight, to play it cool when Lincoln showed up. Because she'd been disappointed so many times before, she had few expectations. As she stripped off her clothes and stepped into the shower, Essence wondered if Lincoln was taking her out just to get her into bed, or because he felt a real, genuine connection with her.

Lathering her bath sponge with kiwi-scented body wash, she spread it across her face and down the length of her neck. Essence felt her body relax, felt the cares and stresses of the day recede and the voices in her head go quiet. Closing her eyes, she imagined her hands were Lincoln's hands, her touch, his touch, each caress, his urgent caress. That's what made her shower, without a doubt, the most sensuous one of her life.

Chapter 6

At six o'clock sharp, Lincoln knocked on the front door of apartment 1A. Sliding his gloved hands into the pockets of his wool coat, he admired the colored lights swathed around the wreath, the Christmas banner hanging in the front window and the plastic frost-covered Santa poking out of the grass. It was chilly outside, the air so thick with cold his teeth were chattering, but Essence was worth the wait. *Don't come on too strong or you'll scare her,* warned the voice inside his head. *Be cool, man. You've got this.*

As he stood at her doorstep, he reviewed the plans he'd made for their date and the tips he'd read in a *Maxim* magazine. He'd popped into the gas station to fill up that morning, and while waiting in line, his gaze had landed on the popular men's magazine. Not the bra-clad model in the pink trench coat, but the bold, black headline on the cover. After making sure no one was looking, he picked up the magazine and flipped to page sixty-nine. The article, "Romance 101," was a short read, and after committing

the Romance Commandments to memory, he flipped to
the next page and read "Master her G-Spot" for good measure. Last night, Essence had made him feel like a stud,
as if he could do no wrong, but Lincoln knew it couldn't
hurt to see what the female panel of experts had to say.

Lincoln glanced down the street, surprised to see all
the activity going on in the working-class neighborhood.
Power walkers chugged down the block, three school-aged
girls played in the snow and the teenage boys standing on
the corner eyed the silver sports car parked at the curb. Lincoln did, too. He'd rented it that afternoon, but still wasn't
used to driving around a car that garnered enormous attention. His Audi was nice, a top-of-the-line ride with all the
fixings, but it wasn't as tricked-out as the Aston Martin.
According to the *Maxim* magazine article, women craved
spontaneity and grand, over-the-top gestures and cruising
around town in an expensive sports car was sure to give
Essence a thrill. At least he hoped so. Lincoln wanted to
impress her, wanted to show her that last night was more
than just about sex, and hoped by the end of their date Essence would know that he was feeling her in a big way. He
had everything a man could want—wealth, prestige and
money—and liked his quiet, drama-free life just the way it
was, but there was something so appealing about Essence
he couldn't get her out of his mind. And making love to
her last night surely hadn't helped his cause. If anything,
it had made him need her even more.

Lincoln had first-day-of-school jitters, and was so anxious to see Essence he knocked on the door again. This
time louder and longer. His impatience paid off. The door
swung open, and when Lincoln saw Essence standing in
the hallway in a deep purple off-the-shoulder sweater, tight
black leggings and suede boots, he did what he'd promised
himself he wouldn't do.

He rushed her.

Pulling her into his arms, he backed her against the door and crushed his mouth against her soft, plump lips. He kissed and caressed and stroked her until his skin was drenched with sweat. His feelings for Essence bordered on obsession, and the emotions that flooded his brain and body created the perfect storm. Lincoln recognized he was losing it, acting completely out of character, but his lips and hands had a mind of their own, and there was nothing he could do to control them. It took supreme effort, but he broke off the kiss and slid his hands around her waist. "Hey," he said, trying to sound chill, unaffected by her smile. "I never thought it was possible, but you look more beautiful than you did yesterday."

"You know just what to say to make me melt." Essence cringed at the sound of her thick, breathless tone. Her voice sounded squeaky, like a tween girl talking on a bullhorn, and when Lincoln teasingly nibbled on her bottom lip, the fluttery sensation in her stomach shot straight to her core. "How are you?"

"I'm great. Never felt better."

"Lincoln, we need to talk."

The light in his eyes dimmed, and the grin slid off his face. "What's on your mind?"

"Last night was a...a..." Essence stumbled over her words. She couldn't bring herself to lie, couldn't bring herself to say the most thrilling and exciting night of her life was a mistake. "I'm catering your holiday parties and I don't want things to get awkward between us, so—"

"They won't." His tone was thick and husky as hell. "You don't work for me anymore."

"You can't do that," she argued. "We signed a contract."

"Contracts were meant to be broken. Happens every day in the business world."

Essence swallowed hard. "So, you found someone else?"

"I don't want anyone else." Lincoln recognized his words were loaded, filled with meaning and truth, but played it off. Had to. He didn't want to mislead Essence, or make her think he was sweating her.

Right, buddy, his conscience jeered. *You're off to a real fine start, then!*

"I'm looking for something long-term," she blurted out. "Not a holiday fling or a friends-with-benefits arrangement, either."

Lincoln nodded, but didn't speak for a long moment. What could he say? *I know we just met, but I think you could be the one?* Essence would laugh in his face or—worse—call him a delusional, sex-starved businessman looking for someone to keep his bed warm. Lincoln was going to play it cool, just like the *Maxim* article advised, and wait to see if his feelings were clouded by lust, or the real, genuine thing. "Does that mean we can't go out tonight?"

"No. I just wanted you to know where I stand."

"Thanks, Essence. I appreciate that. And the catering job is still yours if you want it."

"Good, because I've finished planning your dinner party!" Animated, she talked with her hands and passionately shared her ideas. "I'll admit, the theme is a little out there, but I think guests will get a kick out of the ugliest sweater contest and playing pin the tail on the Santa...."

Lincoln listened to Essence, but he didn't understand a word she said. He was too busy staring at her mouth, at her sexy, pouty red lips. Lincoln recognized he had a serious problem. One a cold shower couldn't cure, and he wondered how the hell he was going to make it through dinner without pouncing on her like a dog in heat. It was easy to be around Essence, a guaranteed good time, and her laugh was so infectious it brought a grin to his lips every time. "It's going to be impossible for me to keep my hands off you tonight," he confessed, touching a hand to her cheek. "You're wearing my favorite color and your perfume is driving me wild."

Now you know how I feel every time you look at me.

Essence stared at Lincoln. Her body hummed with desire as she admired how debonair he looked in his wool coat, black suit and leather shoes. Contrary to what Lincoln said, she knew a wardrobe change was definitely in order. Her outfit was too casual, not "va-va-voom" enough, but she had a leather, skin-tight dress hanging in her closet that was sure to knock his socks off. "I'm going to go change. You're wearing a suit, and I feel frumpy in this outfit—"

"You and the word *frumpy* have no business being in the same sentence." Lincoln wore a stern face, but his voice held a note of amusement. "Essence, it doesn't matter what you wear. You're gorgeous. Hell, you'd look good in a burka and combat boots!"

Essence laughed until tears filled her eyes.

"An outfit should be tight enough to show you're a woman, and loose enough to prove you're a lady." He lowered his mouth and brushed his lips so tenderly against her ear she shivered. "And tonight you look like a million bucks."

"Are you sure? I'm just not feeling this outfit."

"Essence, you don't have to flaunt your body to get my attention. You already have it." Spotting her coat laying across the sofa, Lincoln scooped it up and draped it over her shoulders. He leaned in to kiss her neck, saw the tiny, scripted tattoo at the edge of her hairline and pulled back. He opened his mouth to ask who the initials R.J. belonged to, but swallowed the question. Lincoln suspected the initials belonged to an old flame, and didn't want to hear all the sordid details about her past relationship. He couldn't stomach it, couldn't handle hearing Essence talk about another man.

Taking her hand in his, he led her out the front door, locked it behind him and continued down the slick, ice-covered walkway. "Did you get the package?"

"Oh, how rude of me. I loved it, Lincoln. Thanks so much," she said, smiling up at him. "It was a thoughtful, wonderful surprise. The elves were the best part!"

He gave a loud, hearty chuckle. "I'm glad you enjoyed them."

"I did, and all the yummy treats in the basket, too. How did you know I loved sweets as much as I like to make them?"

"Lucky guess. I don't know anyone who loves Christmas as much as you do, and I had a feeling you'd be all over the pistachio cookies and peppermint chocolate syrup!"

"You guessed right." The expression on her face was coy, and her eyes shone with mischief. "Maybe later we can play with the body paint."

Lincoln leaned over and dropped a kiss on her lips. "It's a date." He held Essence tight, close to his side. His affection toward her shocked him and he knew if his ex-girlfriend saw him now she'd keel over in the freshly fallen snow. Not because she wanted him back—she was happily married and expecting her first child—but because he'd never been affectionate toward her. From the beginning, she'd accused him of holding back, of being closed off from his feelings. It was true. He was. When his mother died, his father had shipped him off to live with relatives, and as a teen he'd witnessed the ugly side of love. The lying, the cheating, all the games women played to get one over on men not only turned him off from relationships, but love as well. That's what made his feelings for Essence Sinclair all the more shocking.

Lincoln clicked the key fob, and the engine purred to life.

"You have an Aston Martin?" Essence let out a squeal that could wake every sleeping baby on the block. "I've dreamed of driving this car ever since I saw *Tomorrow Never Dies*."

"Then go ahead. Get behind the wheel."

Lincoln opened the driver's-side door and watched Essence slide in. He all but exploded in his pants when she gripped the stick shift and playfully winked at him. The whole scene was terribly erotic, and the ultimate turn-on. That was no surprise. Everything about Essence Sinclair made him hot. Her smile, her juicy red lips, the way she flipped her hair over her shoulders.

Lincoln gave her a quick rundown of the controls, and then they were off.

"This car is amazing," she said, gripping the steering wheel and settling back comfortably into her leather seat. "Driving it makes me feel like one of those badass Bond chicks!"

Essence wanted to pinch herself. She couldn't remember that last time she'd felt this giddy, this excited to be out on a date. As they cruised down the street, past the community center and elementary school, Essence noticed all the envious, wide-eyed expressions on random pedestrians' faces.

A grin overwhelmed her mouth. Ten minutes ago she'd been wearing the exact same expression. It shocked her that Lincoln drove a sports car. He wasn't flashy, but the Aston Martin sure was and sitting in the comfortable, plush seat aroused her.

"You better tell me where we're going before we end

up in Arkansas!" Essence joked, stealing a glance at him. Keeping her hands on the wheel and off Lincoln was a challenge. He looked unbearably handsome in his black fedora, dark suit and wool coat, and when he rested a hand on her thigh, Essence imagined herself climbing on his lap and driving *him* instead of the expensive sports car.

Once parked on East McLemore Avenue, Lincoln strode over to the driver's side door, helped her out of her seat and slipped a hand around her waist.

"Welcome to the Stax Museum," greeted the heavy-set woman standing at the entrance of the old historic building twinkling with lights. Her flaming-red wig, printed baby-doll dress and platform heels looked cheap, but her smile was warm. "I'm your tour guide, Jessie Pearl."

"It's great to meet you," Essence said with a small wave of her hand. "I didn't know the museum offered private evening tours."

"We don't, but Mr. Davenport is quite persuasive and made me an offer I just couldn't refuse!" She belted out a laugh, one as loud as her tacky seventies getup. "Have either of you ever visited us here at the Stax Museum before?"

Lincoln and Essence shook their heads.

"Well, why not?" Eyebrows raised, she stuck a hand to her wide, plump hip. "This building was once the home of the legendary Stax Records studio, and music pioneers like Otis Redding and Booker T recorded here for many years...."

As she spoke, she beckoned them to follow her through the clean, rose-scented lobby. It was a bright, colorful space filled with framed photographs, information plaques and musical instruments encased in gold-rimmed glass.

"Stax Records was ahead of its time, and the most successful black-owned record label to ever come out of the state of Tennessee," she explained, beaming. "Our artists are so influential and relevant today, they've been covered by Aerosmith and the Rolling Stones."

Essence admired the display full of shiny, glittery awards. "Being here reminds me of all the Saturday mornings I spent baking with my mom. She always had the Staple Singers playing, and I'd dance around the kitchen using the wooden spoon as a microphone."

Jessie Pearl pointed a finger at her chest. "Me, too, chil'. Me, too!"

For the next hour, Lincoln and Essence explored the main floor exhibits. Walking hand in hand, they talked and joked with their flamboyant tour guide, and snapped pictures of their favorite displays *and* of each other. They checked out the control room, strolled through the hall of records and listened to the first album ever recorded at the studio. But for Essence, the highlight of the tour was seeing Isaac Hayes's old Cadillac. Outfitted with shag carpeting, leather seats and a twenty-four-karat-gold exterior trim, it was easily the sexiest car Essence had ever seen.

"This is one hot ride," Essence said, drawing a hand absently across the hood of the sleek black car. A torrid image filled her mind. She saw herself in the backseat with Lincoln, living out her sexiest, raunchiest fantasy, and when she caught Lincoln staring at her, she knew they shared the same thought.

The last stop on the tour was Studio A, and when Essence stepped through the gold curtain her stomach growled. The air held a strong, tantalizing aroma, and as she strode through the studio the scent got stronger, and her stomach grumbled louder.

Frowning, Essence glanced from Lincoln to the tour guide. In the middle of the dance floor was a large round table dressed with flowers, fine china and scented candles that filled the space with their rich, heady fragrance. The lights were low, jazz music was playing and the short, dark-haired waiter standing beside the table was wearing a wide, welcoming smile.

"I bet all that walking made you hungry," Lincoln said, pulling out one of the wooden chairs and sweeping a hand graciously toward the table. "Care to join me?"

"I'd love to." Before taking her seat, Essence leaned over and gave Lincoln a peck on the cheek. "Thanks for tonight, Lincoln. I'm having a really great time."

At her words, his chest puffed out with pride.

"I think it's cool that you guys have a restaurant here," Essence said, draping her Christmas-themed silk napkin over her lap. "I never would have guessed it."

"We don't. This dinner was all your boyfriend's doing." Jessie Pearl whipped her bright curly hair over her shoulders. "You're lucky I'm not ten years younger, or I'd fight you for him!"

Everyone in the room cracked up.

"Have a great evening, you two. And come back again to see us real soon, ya hear?"

The tour guide departed, and the waiter poured the wine. "My name is Elliot, and it will be my pleasure to serve you tonight," he said with a smile. "I have prepared minestrone soup, braised lamb chops with mushroom Wellington and chocolate pistachio torte for dessert."

"Chocolate pistachio torte?" Essence repeated, slowly licking her lips. "We have to start off with dessert. I haven't had a good torte in years."

"We can't eat dessert first," Lincoln argued, shaking his head. "It'll ruin our meal."

"Says who? Come on. Live a little."

He turned to the waiter and shrugged a shoulder. "I guess we're starting with dessert."

"Smart move, sir."

"Just one dessert. Nothing for me, thanks."

Essence waited for the waiter to leave before she spoke. "If I didn't know better I'd think you were on a diet," she teased. "But that would be insane, because the only men I know who obsess over their figures are either drag queens or hairdressers!"

"I don't diet, but I am conscious about what I eat. In high school I was a shy, overweight teen, and if not for my gym teacher taking pity on me and showing me some weightlifting techniques and teaching me about proper nutrition, I'd still be forty pounds heavier."

Essence felt her jaw drop, but quickly closed it. Her gaze roved down his body, and lingered at her favorite parts. Last night, she'd boldly licked his abs, stroked his pecs and sucked his nipples. Actually just thinking about the rest of his trim, athletic physique turned her on. "It's hard to imagine you ever being out of shape. You have such a gorgeous body."

"Thank you. So do you."

Essence flashed him a wink. "I know, and don't you forget it!"

The waiter returned carrying a white ceramic bowl topped with vanilla ice cream, chocolate syrup and strawberries. Essence scooped up her spoon, scooted forward on her chair and dug in. The first bite made her eyes flutter closed, the second made her purr like a kitten and the third caused a dreamy, lopsided smile to kiss her lips. "I think I've died and gone to dessert heaven," she cooed, touching a hand to her chest. "Lincoln, you've got to try this. It's the creamiest, sexiest cake I've ever had, and the caramel filling is to die for."

"I didn't know cake could be sexy."

Essence wet her lips with her tongue, and smiled inwardly when she saw his eyes widen. Desire showed on his face, and for a long moment, he just sat there, staring at her. "I know you don't like sweets or eating dessert before dinner, but take a walk on the wild side just this once."

Lincoln didn't have the heart to disappoint her, so he parted his lips as Essence slid her fork into his mouth. He chewed slowly, savored the rich, tasty dessert. To his surprise, he liked the cake. It was soft, and moist and reminded him of his mother's chocolate pound cake. "You're right, Essence. This is good."

"I told you!"

Wearing a cheeky smile, she sliced another piece of the cake and fed it to Lincoln. On and on they went, flirting and feeding each other until there was nothing left in the bowl. The waiter returned, retrieved the empty bowl and placed their entrees in front of them. During the second course, they chatted about their plans for the Christmas holidays, movies they were dying to see and their love of miniature golf and arcade games.

"I feel like I've been monopolizing the conversation," Essence said, her smile apologetic. "Tell me more about you."

Lincoln did. He told Essence about his days at Morehouse College, how he started his own software company and why his last relationship failed. Lincoln didn't hold back, he couldn't. He spoke freely, told Essence things he'd never shared with anyone before, and plied her with dozens of personal questions as well. He loved her energy, her joie de vivre, how she appreciated the little things, and talking with her was so easy, so comfortable.

"You grew up in Atlanta, right?" Essence asked, reaching for her wineglass. "I just love it there. The people, the energy, all of the great shopping!"

Lincoln paused, took a moment to gather his thoughts. Normally, when people asked him this question, he lied, but for some inexplicable reason he wanted to tell Essence the truth. "I'm not from Atlanta. I'm from Climax, Georgia."

A grin warmed her lips. "Right, and I'm from Foreplay, Tennessee!"

"I'm serious."

"I'm sorry. I thought you were joking." Essence wore a sheepish smile, lowered her face to her plate. "I've never heard of Climax, Georgia, before. What's it like?"

"It's a small, quiet town that has the kindest country folk you'll ever meet. They love their families, their community and a good, hearty meal, in that order."

"They sound like my kind of people."

"You'd probably love the annual Swine Time Festival." Amusement touched his face and echoed in his tone. "People come from far and wide to watch the great greased pig chase, but the hog calling contest is my personal favorite!"

"Quit making me laugh," she said, dabbing her eyes with the back of her hand. "I'm ruining my makeup!"

The waiter popped up beside the table and flashed his pearly whites at Essence. "How was your meal, Ms. Sinclair? I trust that everything was to your liking."

"The food was divine. I especially liked the braised lamb. Well done."

"That means a lot coming from you," he said, stars shining in his greenish-blue eyes. "I loved watching you every week on *So You Think I can Cook,* and I wanted you to win so bad I developed carpal tunnel syndrome from dialing repeatedly!"

Essence laughed, and Lincoln did, too.

"I thought we could burn off some of these calories by taking a short stroll." Lincoln helped Essence to her feet and back into her winter jacket. "Is that okay with you?"

"Sounds great. It's a gorgeous night, and besides, I could use the exercise."

Outside, the block was overrun with college students, starry-eyed couples walking hand in hand and fashionably dressed singles out looking for a good time. Christmas music played from store windows, the scent of freshly brewed coffee wafted out of the street corner café and the cheery, festive mood in the air made Essence feel like dancing in the streets.

"Did you go to university or culinary school?" Lincoln asked, guiding her past the group of teens standing in front of the bus shed.

"I went to the University of Memphis, but dropped out my freshman year." Sadness touched her eyes and covered the length of her beautiful heart-shaped face. Her voice was so low, so painfully quiet, Lincoln had to lean in close to hear her. "I was overwhelmed by the course load and too embarrassed to ask for help, and before I knew it, failing poorly. To this day, I still regret dropping out of school. It was the biggest mistake I ever made."

Lincoln wore a sympathetic smile. "Ever think of going back to finish up your degree?"

"All the time, but I'll be thirty-three in a couple of weeks."

"And?" he prompted. "What does your age have to do with you returning to college?"

"Promise you won't laugh?"

He squeezed her hand. "I'd never laugh at you, Essence. I'm not that kind of guy."

Rashad sure is, she thought, remembering all the times her ex had made fun of her in front of his family and friends. Essence sucked at Scrabble, and couldn't find Kazakhstan on a world map if her life depended on it, but she wasn't the ditz her ex had made her out to be.

"Knowing I'll be the oldest person in Microeconomics makes me feel insecure, as if I've somehow already failed even before I got started," she confessed, avoiding his gaze.

"Essence, times have changed. There isn't a negative stigma attached to adult learners anymore, and I see mature students on the U of M campus every day," he said, squeezing her hand. "Completing your business degree will be a cinch. You're smart, and one of the most creative, passionate people I've ever met."

His words touched her deeply. Essence knew she wasn't in Lincoln's league, but she appreciated him not making fun of her. Unlike the men she'd dated in the past, he seemed genuinely interested in what she had to say, and the way he stared deep into her eyes made Essence feel special, as if he truly cared about her. "No one's ever called me smart before," she confessed. "Pretty, yes, but never smart."

"You are all those things and more."

"I am?"

"Of course you are. You won season two of *So You Think You Can Cook,* and started a successful catering company. Not bad for a saucy, round-the-way girl from Memphis, huh?"

Lincoln wore a teasing smile, one that should have made Essence laugh, but instead it made her body flush with a scorching, devastating heat. It was hard—no, damn near impossible—to act normal around him when all she could think about was last night. Sensual, erotic images that were too hot for TV sprung up in her mind. Pictures of her riding him, licking him, shoving her aching breasts into his mouth, filled her thoughts, and Essence was so overcome with lust, so crazed with desire she yearned to make sweet love to him again, right then and there in one of the bus shacks.

"Earning a university degree will not only open a lot of doors for you, it will take your business to the next level and afford you access to a whole new world."

They walked for a few minutes in silence.

"I don't know if I'm ready to return to school, but it would be nice to finally get my parents off my back. They paid for my courses the first time around and remind me every chance I get that I wasted their hard-earned money."

"Imagine how happy they'd be watching you cross the stage on graduation day."

"I bet your mother brags about you to perfect strangers, and still carries your grade-school pictures in her wallet," she teased, pushing all thoughts of sexing him to the back of her mind. "You have two graduate degrees, own a successful software business and teach at an esteemed university, as well. She has a lot to be proud of."

"I don't have parents." His smile faded and his face hardened like stone.

Essence had a ton of questions, but before she could open her mouth to ask a single one, Lincoln continued. As she listened to him speak, her heart broke for him. The sadness in his voice was real, his grief palpable, and his hurt as visible as the stars splashed across the sky.

"I've been on my own since I was eighteen, and I've had to struggle and fight for everything I have."

"That's so sad—"

"Not to me." His eyes were bright, beaming with unspoken pride, but his voice was as cold as ice. "I did it. I made good and fulfilled every single one of my dreams despite my troubled upbringing. I have everything a man could want, and more."

"I wish I could say the same."

"You have a great career, a ton of friends, and from what I gather a fairly good relationship with your family. What more could you want?" Lincoln questioned, raising an eyebrow. "And don't say that new Cartier necklace unveiled in Paris last week. It's a quarter of a million dollars, and under heavy security!"

Essence laughed. She didn't want to tell Lincoln the truth, that she was desperate to be a mother, but when she parted her lips those words tumbled out of her mouth. "I want to be a wife and mother more than anything in this world. I know that sounds corny, but all I've ever wanted was a husband and kids and a house with a white picket fence."

"You're an incredible woman, Essence. You'll find the right guy."

Why not you? Why am I good enough to sleep with, but not to marry?

"Thanks, Lincoln," she said, ignoring the question that rose in her thoughts. "Maybe I should get *you* to rewrite my online dating profile, because the last guy who contacted me on FindYourSomeone.com was an inmate on death row!"

As they crossed the intersection, their laughter carried on the crisp, winter breeze. "I wish tonight wasn't a school night," Essence joked as they reached the car. "I'm having such a good time I don't want the night to end."

"Who says it has to?"

"You did! On the drive over here, you mentioned having a six o'clock breakfast meeting tomorrow with an out-of-town client."

He shook his head, studied her closely. "I'm starting to think you slipped something into my food, because whenever you're around I come down with a serious case of amnesia!"

Chuckling, he unlocked the car and held open the passenger-side door for her.

"This was nice, Lincoln. We should do it again soon."

"What are you doing tomorrow?"

"Baking sugar cookies, cleaning my apartment and catching up on my reality TV time." Essence giggled.

"Maybe after you get your reality fix, we can do dinner and a movie."

"Dinner and a movie? That's cliché, don't you think?" Essence acted aloof, wore a bored, tired face, but deep down she didn't care where they went. Being with Lincoln was enough, but Essence knew if she wanted to stand out from all the other women the software engineer was dating, she had to make him work, had to make him put effort into planning their dates. "Surprise me," she said, sliding into the car and crossing her legs. "And make it good!"

Lincoln fixed his eyes on her. His gaze was filled with fire and heat, and when he brushed a finger against her cheek, she shivered something fierce. "Be careful what you wish for this holiday season," he warned, his deep, raspy drawl rife with lust. "You just might get it, *and* more."

Chapter 7

"I think someone put a root on my boss!"

Carrot juice spewed out of Essence's mouth. Her girl-friends, who were sitting with her in the corner booth in the Blues City Café, cracked up. They giggled so loud and snickered so long, they attracted the attention of everyone in the crowded café. Shooting Naomi a what-the-hell-are-you-talking-about look, Essence grabbed a napkin and cleaned her mouth. "I met with Lincoln last night to…to discuss his, um, dinner party on Saturday and he seemed perfectly fine to me."

"That's because you don't know him like I do," Naomi said, dismissing her words with a flick of her hand. "I'm not kidding, ya'll. My boss is acting all kinds of crazy. Smiling for no reason, whistling Christmas songs and leaving work early. I've seen Mr. Davenport in expensive designer suits before, but now he's dressing *just* like Diddy!"

"Wow, girl, you're right, this *is* serious." Chandra Rivers struggled to keep a straight face. "You better find a voodoo priestess quick!"

Their ear-splitting shrieks drowned out the country music song playing on the rusted old jukebox. The waiter returned, cleared their empty lunch dishes from the table and took off. The café was jam-packed, and the line that stretched out the front door snaked around the corner of Beale Street. Known for putting a little "South in Your Mouth," the popular restaurant not only attracted tourists from all over the country but A-list stars, pro athletes and local entertainers. The staff treated patrons like family and the tin ceiling and eclectic decor only enhanced the establishment's down-home Southern vibe.

"Maybe your boss is having a midlife crisis." Avery Moreau took her cell phone out of her tan clutch purse and checked it for missed calls. "The same thing happened to my ex when he turned forty, except he wasn't *acting.* He's just crazy, ya'll."

Essence patted back a yawn, one that filled her eyes with tears. *This is what I get for staying up late with Lincoln,* she thought, suddenly overwhelmed with fatigue. *I'm so worn out from our all-night lovemaking session, I can hardly keep my eyes open, and it's only six o'clock.*

"Essence, can you give me a lift to Meineke?" Chandra asked. "My car's getting fixed, and since the shop is near your place, I figured you wouldn't mind giving me a ride."

"I'm not going home," she said. "I have a date, I mean, an appointment."

Her girlfriends exchanged a curious glance.

"Which one is it?" Avery questioned, raising an eyebrow. "A date or an appointment?"

Essence grabbed her glass of carrot juice and stuck the straw in her mouth. As she sipped what was left of her drink, she carefully weighed her options. She hated keeping secrets from her girlfriends, but she didn't want them to interrogate her about Lincoln. Or read too much into their relationship. Just because they'd seen each other every day for the past three weeks, and made love more than newlyweds, didn't mean they were going to ride off into the sunset. They weren't. They were just hanging out, just having fun.

And lots of great sex, too.

Essence felt her pulse quicken and her heart beat wild and fast. Images of last night rose in her thoughts, and brought a dreamy smile to her red, glossy lips. Lincoln was a sensitive, passionate lover who made the Energizer Bunny look like a slacker, but what Essence admired most about him was his honesty. He didn't play mind games, and was open and straight-up about everything. Lincoln challenged her way of thinking, but made her feel worthy of his affection, and smart, too. No one had ever done that before. Not her mom, not her dad and certainly none of her trifling ex-boyfriends. Essence was still struggling to keep her catering company afloat but Lincoln's encouragement made her feel more confident about her business and her future.

"Stop holding out on us," Chandra said, dropping her cell phone back into her bejeweled designer purse. "Tell us what's going on with you."

"If you must know, I'm meeting Lincoln at seven for drinks."

"My Lincoln?" Naomi touched a hand to her chest.

Everyone stared at Naomi, but before Essence could respond, her girlfriend fired off a storm of personal questions at her. "How long has this been going on? Have you been to his house? Are you guys sleeping together? Oh, no! *You're* the chick he's been running around with for the past three weeks!"

"We're not running around," Essence argued. "In the process of planning his holiday parties we've gotten to know each other and discovered we have a lot in common. We like going out for dinner and enjoy late-night walks. Is that a crime?"

Naomi narrowed her eyes, made a face that could bring a WWE wrestler to his knees. "Why keep it from me?"

"Because it's not that serious. We're just hanging out."

"Hanging out, my ass," Naomi quipped, folding her arms. "You've fallen for him, Essence. Just admit it."

"What's with the attitude?" Chandra asked, jabbing Naomi in the side with her elbow. "Why are you giving Essence a hard time for kicking it with your boss? Do *you* want him?"

"Of course not. I just don't want to see her get hurt."

"I'm not going to get hurt. I know what I'm doing."

And tonight, I'm doing Lincoln! Essence thought, but didn't say. She loved her girlfriends, and appreciated their concern, but she wasn't going to let anyone stop her from seeing Lincoln. Not when he had come to mean so much to her. It was hard to believe they'd only known each other for a few short weeks. Essence felt close to him, as if she'd known him all her life. When they were together, nothing else mattered. For hours, they'd talk and drink and laugh, completely oblivious to the world around them, and when they were alone at his place, Essence felt like the luckiest woman alive. "Lincoln puts all my ex-boyfriends to shame. He's warm and affectionate and does sweet, thoughtful things to brighten my day—"

"Really?" Naomi said, her eyes wide. "Like what?"

Essence raised her voice so she could be heard above the noise in the dining room, and spoke with a smile. One she couldn't get rid of no matter how hard she tried. "It snowed last Saturday, but when I went outside I noticed the walkway had been shoveled and my car was clean. On my windshield was a note from Lincoln inviting me to Paulette's for brunch."

"Shut up! No way!" Avery hollered, eyes wide. "There isn't a man on this earth who'd drive across town on football Sunday to shovel snow on a wickedly cold day."

"Lincoln did, and that's not all..." Essence knew she was gushing, could feel the wide, toothy smile on her face, but didn't temper her excitement. Finally, after all these weeks of seeing Lincoln, she could confide in her closest friends and Essence didn't hold back. She told them about every wonderful thing Lincoln had done for her—the time he'd made her breakfast in bed, the afternoon he'd showed up on her doorstep with two dozen red roses and the night they'd taken a romantic carriage ride through downtown— but wisely kept all their juicy bedroom secrets to herself. "I wore my new Prada pumps to dinner last night and, when I complained about getting snow on them, Lincoln picked me up and carried me all the way back to the car!"

Naomi waved her hands frantically back and forth. "Now I *know* you're lying. Mr. Davenport would never do something like that. He's not the type and he doesn't believe in public displays of affection, either. That's why his ex-girlfriend dumped him last year. She said he treated her more like a sister than his girlfriend."

"Well, believe it—because he did it," Essence said, her tone cheeky.

"This Lincoln guy sounds incredibly romantic." Chandra clapped and danced in her seat. "I bet he's planning something amazing for your birthday next weekend!"

"I hope so. My birthday sucked last year, and it would be great to do something fun."

"Mr. Davenport won't be here. He'll be in Washington."

"He will?" Essence cranked her head in Naomi's direction. "Are you sure?"

"Positive. He's delivering the keynote address at the Entrepreneurs Business Conference this weekend, then heading to Georgia to spend Christmas with his grandparents."

Disappointment overwhelmed her, sat on her chest like a slab of concrete. But she hid her feelings, played it cool. "It's no biggie," Essence said with a shrug of her shoulder. "It's not like Lincoln's my man or anything. He's free to do whoever he wants, and so am I."

Naomi sighed in relief, and wiped imaginary sweat off her forehead. "I'm *so* glad you said that. I was worried you'd fallen in love with him."

"Me? No. Never." Essence faked shock and gave her head a hard shake. "We're just having fun. It's nothing serious."

The waiter returned, carrying red Christmas-themed bowls topped with ice cream and sprinkles, and the conversation around the table came to a screeching halt.

"How come you didn't order dessert?" Avery asked, licking sprinkles off her spoon.

Because I like to lick my dessert off my man, Essence thought, a grin pinching her lips. Deciding now was the perfect time to escape, she stuffed her arms into her leather jacket, grabbed her purse off the floor and slid out of the booth. "I have to run," she said, putting a fifty-dollar bill inside the leather billet. "See you guys later."

Waving goodbye, Essence strode through the restaurant and out the front doors. Outside, the winter breeze was cool and light and the sky was free of clouds. The streets were filled with people, some wearing Santa hats, others in formal clothes, and Essence could hear Christmas music playing loudly in the distance.

As Essence walked across the street, thoughts of Lincoln were heavy on her mind. Lincoln Davenport was all that, and more. He was a gentleman in every sense of the word, one of the smartest men she'd ever met and more romantic than the hero in any chick flick. Last night he'd gone all out, and twenty-four hours later Essence was still thinking about their romantic marathon date. They'd had dinner at the best French restaurant in the city, watched the hilarious animated play *Santa vs The Snowman* at the Pink Palace Museum and then capped off the evening by taking a moonlit carriage ride through the streets of downtown Memphis.

Her phone rang, curtailing her trip down memory lane. Essence took her cell out of her jacket pocket, saw Rashad's phone number on the screen and groaned out loud. When he wasn't blowing up her phone, he was emailing her, and she was sick and tired of reading his long, weepy messages. Her first impulse was to ignore the call, but she decided she had to put an end to his harassment once and for all, and put her cell phone to her ear.

"Rashad, quit calling me. We're over, and I'm not taking you back."

"Yes, you will. You always do."

"Not this time. I've moved on and you should, too."

"Whatever, sweet cheeks, just be ready to party on Saturday night by eight," he told her, his tone full of bravado. "I fulfilled my end of the deal, and now it's your turn."

"We never made a deal, and I'm not going anywhere with you."

"It's too late to back out now. I already deposited the money into your account and…"

Her mind reeling, she opened her car door and dropped into the driver's seat. Essence switched on the light, put Rashad on speaker phone and peeled off her black leather gloves. While he droned on and on about his upcoming meeting with the vice president at Urban Beats Records on Saturday night, she logged on to the internet and signed into her bank account.

Her jaw dropped. Essence blinked, couldn't believe her eyes. Her business account, which had been in the red three days earlier, now held twelve thousand, five hundred dollars. Seeing all those zeroes in her bank account should have excited her, but instead of feeling elated about the unexpected funds, she felt as vulnerable as a woman standing on a street corner in fishnet stockings. "Who gave you my bank account number?"

"It doesn't matter. You got some loot. Just say thanks and keep it moving."

"Rashad, I don't need your money."

"Fine, then donate it to charity," he snapped, his voice gruff. "I don't care what you do with the money as long as you don't stand me up on Saturday night."

For the first time in Essence's life, she was absolutely and completely speechless. Twelve thousand dollars was enough to put a down payment on her dream house, but Essence knew the money came with strings, and that didn't sit well with her. She wasn't that kind of girl, but her ex was *definitely* that kind of guy.

"Sweet cheeks, you'd be a fool not to be my date for the Christmas Gala. There'll be a ton of big names there," Rashad said. "People with money and connections who love throwing large, lavish *catered* events. Think of all the wealthy, influential people you'll meet…."

Essence imagined the scene in her mind's eye. Meeting the mayor, the governor and other prominent Memphians was the big break she'd been waiting for. Winning season two of *So You Think You Can Cook* hadn't catapulted her to fame and fortune, and Essence knew if she wanted to take her catering company to the next level she had to step out of the box, had to take risks. That's why she'd sat down with Lincoln last Friday and filled out the University of Memphis application packet. And why she spent so many hours picking his brain about financial matters. This was her chance to drum up some business, to become a household name in the catering world, so why was she stalling?

Because the only man I want is Lincoln. I don't want to go out with Rashad, Jared Mays or that NBA player who asked for my number back in the café. I want Lincoln. Only Lincoln and no one else.

The realization stunned her, threw her for a loop. But as shocking as it was, Essence knew it was true. Every word of it. And that sucked, because from the very beginning Lincoln had made it perfectly clear that he didn't do relationships. Essence felt a rush of emotion, of despair. Once again, she'd fallen head over heels for a man who'd never commit to her, a man who wanted a warm body in his bed and nothing more. This time things were worse because she loved Lincoln with her whole heart. It was more than just the way he treated her, and far greater than their insane attraction and sizzling chemistry. It was easy to be around him. They laughed a lot, touched and kissed even more. With Lincoln, Essence was free to be herself—her loud, outrageous self. When she was with him, all was right in the world. She wanted to be with him, all the time, every day, and spent her free time thinking up ways to make him happy. That's why she treated Lincoln to home-cooked meals, why she stayed up late into the night talking with him and why she'd quit hitting the nightclubs with her girlfriends. Why would she go to a dark, crowded bar, when she already had Mr. Right?

"Sweet cheeks, this meeting with Urban Beats Records could make or break my career."

Essence blinked hard and returned to the present. Talk-

ing to Rashad was impossible when she had Lincoln on
the brain, but she forced herself to listen to what her ex
was saying.

"If you do this for me, I swear I'll never ask you for
anything ever again...."

As he spoke, Essence warmed to the idea of attending
the Christmas Gala. It was a business deal, she told herself.
A business deal and nothing more. And besides, going to
the Christmas Gala with Rashad was a hell of a lot better than spending her birthday alone. If it were up to her,
she'd spend the day with Lincoln, but he was going out of
town and hadn't even told her about his upcoming business trip. "Okay, I'll be your date to the Christmas Gala,
but if you step out of line or do anything crazy on Saturday night, I'm going home."

"Don't worry, I'll be on my best behavior."

"I'm not kidding, Rashad. Disrespect me in any way,
and I'm out the door—"

He cut her off. "I got it. Quit nagging."

"I just want to make sure everything is crystal clear."

"It is, and don't forget to buy a tight, little black dress
that shows off your curves and that big, fat badonkadonk!"

Essence clicked off her cell phone and chucked it into
her purse. Her ex was never, ever going to change. Just
when she thought they were cool and back on good terms,
he said something juvenile and idiotic to piss her off. *What
have I gotten myself into?* she wondered, staring out her
car windshield. *And why do I have a feeling that by the
time Saturday night rolls around, I'm going to end up regretting this?*

Chapter 8

Lincoln's house makes my apartment look like a shack with carpeting, Essence thought, pulling up in front of his three-story Collierville mansion. As she parked, she admired all of the unique touches surrounding the enormous ranch-style home. The stone structures, the marble fountain, the fully landscaped yard and the garden overflowing with seasonal plants and herbs. The picture-perfect house was every woman's dream, and as Essence strode up the walkway, holding her six grocery bags, she wondered if Lincoln liked living in the large, lavish mansion alone.

The afternoon breeze was fierce, and snow flurries were drifting down from the sky, but the sun was surprisingly warm and bright. Essence squinted, thinking hard. She couldn't remember Lincoln's housekeeper's name and feared she'd look like a fool when the thin, stiff-lipped Polish woman answered the front door. Lincoln was still at work, likely knee-deep in software programs and computer codes, but had encouraged her to come to the house whenever she was ready to set up. The dinner party didn't start for hours, but Essence had a million and one things to do before his friends and business associates arrived at six o'clock.

As she stepped onto the porch, the blue sensor lights flashed and the front door swung open. When Essence saw Lincoln standing in the doorway in a hideous multi-colored sweater covered in tinsel, she burst out laughing. Laughed so hard tears spilled down her cheeks.

"Think I have a chance of winning the ugliest sweater contest tonight?" he asked, a grin playing on his lips. "The woman at the thrift store said I looked like a hot mess, but I could use a second opinion."

"That's the ugliest, tackiest sweater I've ever seen," Essence said, unable to control her giggles. "Trust me, you've got the contest in the bag!"

"Hey, quit laughing at my sweater. The contest was *your* brilliant idea."

"I know, but I never expected you to actually go along with it."

"I had no choice. You told me if I didn't, I couldn't come to the party—and I'm the host!"

Chuckling, he dropped a kiss on her cheek and took the grocery bags out of her hands. He slammed the door shut with his foot and strode down the hall. Christmas music was playing, and the scent of freshly baked bread was so heavy in the air Essence licked her lips in hungry anticipation.

Essence paused in the living room and took a whiff of the poinsettias in the oversized glass vase on the end table. She'd been to Lincoln's home several times over the past three weeks, but every time she saw the grand staircase, arched floor-to-ceiling windows and imported Italian furniture, Essence felt as if she'd just stepped into the pages of *House Beautiful* magazine. The rooms were grand, the earthy decor was rich with warmth and color and the oil paintings on the main floor were striking, but Essence's favorite room in the house was the kitchen. It was twice the size of her apartment, filled with top-of-the-line stainless-steel appliances, and so clean that guests could eat off the gleaming hardwood floor.

"I wasn't expecting you to be home," Essence said, resting her purse on one of the chairs around the raised breakfast table. "What are you doing here?"

"I live here. Name's on the deed and everything."

"Quit being a smart-ass. You have a meeting with Microsoft at four, and it's quarter to."

Surprise showed on his face. "I can't believe you remember something I mentioned in passing a couple days ago."

"Of course I remember. It's important."

"The VP is out sick, so we rescheduled for next Friday. We'll meet up at the Entrepreneurs Business Conference in Washington and hammer out a deal then." Lincoln fixed his gaze on her. "I hate that I'm going to miss your birthday, but we'll celebrate when I get back home. I promise."

"Lincoln, my birthday's on December 23, not January 2."

"Then come with me to Chocolate City," he joked, winking at her. "You're a sexy, savvy entrepreneur who loves to network, so the conference will be right up your alley."

"I can't. I'm catering a brunch on Saturday, and in the evening I'm attending the Christmas Gala at the Cook Convention Center."

"You're going to be so busy next week you'll hardly notice I'm gone."

"Oh, I'll notice," she said in a singsong, her expression

coy. "I love when you tuck me in at night, and you give the best foot rubs ever."

"Is that why you keep me around? To pamper you?"

Essence licked her lips. "You know it!"

They shared a laugh.

"Just because I won't be here doesn't mean I won't be thinking about you." Lincoln pulled her into his arms. "When I return from my trip we can celebrate your birthday anywhere you want. How's that?"

Sobering, she blinked back the tears that had snuck up on her—the hot, blistering kind that stung the back of her eyes. Essence averted her gaze, looked everywhere but at his face. She knew she was acting like a big fat crybaby, but she didn't want Lincoln to go to Washington. She wanted to celebrate her birthday with him, alone at home. Essence didn't tell him that though, she couldn't. They weren't serious, weren't a couple, and she had no claims on him or his time. That's why Essence pushed all thoughts of their relationship out of her mind and posed a question at Lincoln that she'd asked him a dozen times before. "What do you want for Christmas?" she asked, tilting her head back so she could stare up at him. "I need you to point me in the right direction, because I'm having a hard time finding something for a man like you."

"A man like me?" he repeated, frowning. "What does that mean?"

"You have everything a guy could want. You said so yourself."

"But I don't have you."

Essence hid a smile. "Lincoln, quit fooling around and tell me what you want."

"I want to unwrap *you* on Christmas morning."

"That's going to be mighty difficult with you all the

way in Climax, Georgia," she said, deciding to play along with his sexy little game.

"I'll fly you in on Christmas Eve."

He's joking, right? Has to be, because meeting his family is a huge deal and we're only lovers. Essence stood there, completely bewildered by his words, and several seconds passed before she surfaced from her mental haze. As she glanced aimlessly around the main floor, she spotted the large evergreen tree standing beside the front window and gestured to it with an index finger. "When did you get a Christmas tree?" she asked. "And why is it completely bare?"

"I got it last night, and I was hoping we could decorate it together."

"Aww, sweet." Essence touched a hand to his cheek and gave him a peck on the lips. "Why don't you get started, and I'll join you after I pop the appetizers into the oven."

"You have lots of time to cook. The party doesn't start for several more hours."

"I know, but if I don't prep the food it won't be ready on time, and I'd be mortified if guests arrived early and nothing was ready," she said. "Besides, my staff will be here any minute now, and I don't want them to catch me slacking on the job."

Lincoln poked out his bottom lip. "Come on, Essence, live a little!"

"Hey!" she hollered, poking him in the chest with her index finger. "That's my line and I never gave you permission to use it!"

His hearty chuckle was infectious and caused her to giggle, too.

"I know you like to oversee what's happening in the kitchen, but I don't want you stuck in here all night. I want you by my side, meeting my friends and associates."

"You do?"

"Of course. Why does that surprise you?"

"Because you prefer me being behind the scenes," Essence said, blown away by his confession. "At least that's the impression you gave me at the office mixer a few weeks back."

"That wasn't it. I just hated seeing you with Jared. He's not good enough for you."

I know, but you are. You're all the man I need. Why can't you see that?

"I have to get down to work," Essence said, sneaking a look at the oven clock. "I'm running behind schedule and need to start baking pronto."

"So that's it. You're just going to leave me to decorate alone?" Lincoln stared down at his hideous multicolored sweater and sadly shook his head. "I've never decorated a Christmas tree before, and without your help it's likely to look as ugly as this sweater!"

Essence cracked up. "Help me prep the food, and I'll help decorate your tree."

"You're putting me to work at my own dinner party? Wow, that's cold."

"If you do a good job, I'll give you a treat." Taking his hands, she guided them to her butt and pressed her body flat against his chest. "Want to take a wild guess what it is?"

Lincoln raced over to the counter, ripped open the grocery bag and dumped the vegetables on the cutting board. "All right, let's get down to business!"

For the next hour, Essence and Lincoln worked side by side, preparing appetizers and drinks. They fed each other, danced to the Christmas songs playing on the kitchen radio and laughed about all the fun, exciting things they'd done over the past three weeks. "I can't believe you put me to work in the kitchen," Lincoln said, glancing up from the cutting board. "And that I actually went along with it."

"Why? Because successful businessmen don't cook?"

"No, because I haven't cooked since my mother died." Lincoln cleared his throat and then continued, "She had a heart attack on Christmas Eve, and passed away three days later."

"Lincoln, I'm so sorry. I had no idea. Is that why you hate Christmas so much? Because it brings up painful memories?"

"I didn't just lose my mom, Essence. I basically lost my dad, too."

Essence lowered the temperature on the stove, cleaned her hands on her apron and wrapped her arms around Lincoln's waist. Listening to him speak about the loss of his beloved mother broke her heart. His voice was filled with raw, untamed emotion, and the heart-wrenching expression on his face brought tears to her eyes.

"Just days after my mother's funeral, my father dumped me on his parents and took off to Florida. I haven't seen or heard from him in years, and I don't know if he's dead or alive."

Essence tightened her hold around him, ever so slowly caressed the length of his face.

"During the holidays, the pain of losing her, even after all these years, is overwhelming. We used to prep and cook together all the time, especially during the Christmas holidays, but after she passed I lost interest, and stopped doing the things I loved."

"Have you ever tried talking to someone about how you feel?"

"You mean like a shrink?" The muscles in his jaw tightened. "I can't do it. People will think I'm weak."

Essence paused, searched for the right words to make

Lincoln understand the value in seeking professional help. "When my best friend died a few years back, I had a really hard time coping with her death. I couldn't eat or sleep and there were mornings I just couldn't get out of bed. Attending grief therapy sessions made a world of difference."

"How?" he asked, his tone curious. "In what way?"

"Hearing other people's stories of loss made me feel less alone, less hopeless."

"Essence, it's been almost seventeen years since my mom passed and my dad left. I'd feel stupid going to therapy about it now after all this time has passed."

"There's no time line on grief, Lincoln, and it's never, ever too late to seek professional help," she said, lovingly touching a hand to his cheek.

Lincoln nodded, but didn't speak. He blew out a deep breath and rested his hands on the kitchen counter. He looked drained, unsteady on his feet, and for a second Essence feared she'd pushed too hard, said too much.

"I could come with you to a grief therapy session if you'd like."

Shock covered his face. "You'd do that?"

"Of course I would, Lincoln. I love—" Essence caught herself before she revealed the truth in her heart. Touching a hand to his cheek, she gently caressed the length of his smooth, brown face. "I love spending time with you and I'd do anything to make you happy."

Lincoln folded his arms around her and dropped a kiss on her forehead.

"I never had the pleasure of meeting your mom, but I think she'd want you to create new memories and celebrate the Christmas holidays in a way that's special and meaningful to you."

"You're the only person I've ever talked to about the pain of losing my mom," he confessed. "I've always been a loner, and never felt like I fit in anywhere, but then I met you, and something deep inside me changed."

He cupped her chin, stared so deep into her eyes that Essence lost all sense of time. The warmth of his smile and the tenderness of his embrace sent shivers down her spine. In his arms she felt safe, cherished, like his one and only. A crazy thought, considering they were nothing more than lovers.

"I want to be out with you, doing things and going places. Whenever you're around I feel like a kid in a candy store."

"That sucks," Essence said, faking a scowl. "Because you hate sweets!"

Chuckling, he pulled her closer to him with one hand and pointed at her with the other. "See, that's what I'm talking about. You're funny, you never take yourself or life too seriously and your positive, upbeat attitude is infectious."

"It is?"

"Damn right, it is! Thanks to you, I discovered Irish coffee, a whole slew of outrageous reality shows that are quite entertaining and the joys of eating dessert *before* dinner."

Essence opened her mouth with a saucy retort on her lips, but when Lincoln kissed her she forgot what she wanted to say. His tongue was sweet, flavored with peppermint, and searching. It moved slowly around her mouth, inciting her hunger and stirring her passion. Locking her hands around his neck, she pulled him closer, holding him tighter than ever before. His closeness was so overwhelming, so intoxicating, she could get drunk just from being in his arms.

"Sorry I'm late, suga', but all these fancy schmancy houses look the same, and without my glasses on, it was hard to make out the numbers."

Essence felt Lincoln release her, and surfaced from her mind-numbing haze. She glanced over her shoulder and saw her aunt Zizi standing in the doorway with a scowl on her face and a hand hitched to her hip. "Hi, Aunt Zizi."

"Who are you?" she demanded, her eyes glued to Lincoln. "The butler?"

"I'm Lincoln Davenport, and this is my home. It's a pleasure to meet you, Ms. Sinclair."

Aunt Zizi waved a hand absently in the air. The widower was only five feet tall, but she had a larger-than-life personality and a youthful air that beguiled her age. "Be a dear and fetch my bags from the car. It's cold as hell outside, and I don't want the vegetables to freeze."

Amusement colored Lincoln's face, but he didn't laugh. "No problem, ma'am. I'll go get your things right now."

Essence shot Lincoln a grateful smile. He winked at her and then strode out of the kitchen. "I'm so glad you're here," Essence said, sliding the tray of sugar cookies into the oven. "I'm running behind and I could really use your help finishing up the shrimp cakes."

"He seems sweet on you."

Essence played dumb. "Who, Lincoln?"

"No, Saint Nick!" Aunt Zizi shook her head so hard her dark brown curls flopped around her heart-shaped face. "I don't like him."

"You don't even know him."

"Yeah, but I know his type. He's one of those arrogant rich men who think women were put on this earth to cater to their every whim," Aunt Zizi said, scowling. "Take it from an old lady who's been around the block a few times. That man is no good."

"You're wrong," Essence argued. "Lincoln's smart, chivalrous and incredibly romantic. I've never met a man quite like him, and—"

"Good Lord, I hope you haven't taken up with that horribly dressed man," she said, her long, thick eyebrows crawling halfway up her forehead. "You need to get back with Rashad. That boy would do anything to make you happy, and he loves you dearly."

"No, he doesn't. He loves fast cars, wild parties and loose girls."

"Hush yourself, chil', he's just going through a phase. He'll grow out of it."

"When?" Essence questioned, growing exasperated. "When he's fifty?"

"You guys grew up together, and Rashad knows you inside and out...."

Essence stared out the window and spotted Lincoln striding up the walkway holding two large brown paper bags, and licked her lips. Seeing him made her mouth dry and her body weak in three places. *God help me,* she thought, grabbing a recipe card off the kitchen counter and fanning her face. Essence was in so deep, so hot for Lincoln, she could hardly stand to be away from him. Not seeing him for a week was surely going to kill her.

"Rashad's music career has taken off," Aunt Zizi pointed out. "And the entire family loves him. We'll be crushed if the two of you didn't end up getting married one day."

"You'll get over it."

"You'll never find someone better than Rashad."

Essence couldn't hold back her smile, and when Lincoln caught her staring at him out the window, she winked at him. "You know what, Aunt Zizi? I already have."

Chapter 9

"Mr. Davenport, your speech was outstanding!"

Lincoln glanced up from the lavish buffet table inside the Hotel Palomar's banquet hall and admired the dark-skinned sister in the chic red business suit. She was striking—a tall, leggy beauty with Afrocentric jewelry, thick braids and a smile that could outshine the morning sun. "Thank you," he said, reading her nametag. "I'm glad you enjoyed it, Mrs. Ohaji-Bishop."

"Call me Yasmin." She joined him at the buffet table and filled her plate with fresh fruit and vegetables. "I found your talk fascinating, and admired how you spoke candidly about your humble beginnings. No one in here would have ever publicly admitted to being dirt-poor."

At her words, thoughts of Essence flooded his mind. She was the one who'd encouraged him to kick his speech off with a poignant childhood memory. He'd balked at first, told her no one would care about his formative years in Climax, Georgia, but she'd insisted. Good thing he'd taken her advice. The audience seemed to relate to his rags-to-riches story, and all morning people had been praising his speech and patting him on the back. Talking about his childhood was surprisingly therapeutic, and Lincoln knew if it wasn't for Essence, he'd still be walking around in a miserable funk, cursing carolers, store Santas and eggnog.

"Let's share a table," Yasmin proposed, falling in step beside him.

They walked over to one of the many tall mahogany-brown tables and chatted amicably over lunch. They discussed their hometowns, their favorite haunts in and around Washington and the sessions they enjoyed the most over the course of the conference.

"I come from a family of overachievers," Yasmin confessed, popping a piece of pineapple into her mouth and chewing slowly. "I've always been a bit of a workaholic, and strive to be the best in my field, but your speech reminded me of what's important in life."

Lincoln raised an eyebrow. "It did?"

"Absolutely. Since being named Tampa's Business-woman of the Year, life's been an endless stream of interviews and public appearances, and although my husband's proud of me, he's not happy about me being away from home so much." A pensive expression covered her face. "Rashawn says the kids cry every time I leave the house, and that tears me up inside."

"How many children do you have?"

"Three little ones under the age of five, and we've only been married for four years!"

Lincoln released a slow whistle. "You and your husband have been a *very* busy couple."

"You can say that again!" Yasmin laughed, and when she threw her hands up in the air her silver arm bangles jingled loudly. "Some days I don't know if I'm coming or going, but I wouldn't change anything about my life. My children are my greatest accomplishment, and I wouldn't be the woman I am today without them. Your speech inspired me to be a better wife and mother, and to relish the beauty of every single day."

It did? Her words shocked him, threw him for a loop. He didn't set out to inspire anyone, and never imagined his speech would touch this woman in such a real, profound way.

"I loved when you said, 'We weren't put on this earth to acquire wealth. Success is a byproduct of being your true, authentic self and if you're living your truth, you will always be successful.'" Yasmin shook her head, her expression one of awe and disbelief. "That's deep."

Lincoln wore a proud smile. He'd said the words, wholeheartedly meant them, too, but he hadn't created them, Essence had. Last Saturday, after the rousing success of his dinner party, they'd stretched out on the living room couch with a bottle of Sambuca between them, and talked until the sun broke through the horizon. The things Essence told him about her past had stayed with him for days—played over and again in his mind. And when he'd sat down at the desk in his executive suite last night to pen his speech, her words had poured onto his paper.

It was there, sitting in his suite, writing his speech, that the truth had hit him. He loved Essence and didn't want to live without her. Meeting her had lifted that dark, cold cloud hanging over his head for the past ten years, and for the first time in his life Lincoln was thinking about marriage and children. He didn't want to work sixteen-hour days anymore, or spend his free time alone at home, either. He wanted to overcome the pain of his past, wanted to give himself wholeheartedly to the woman he loved. A woman who filled his days with so much fun and excitement he felt like pulling a Tom Cruise and hopping onto the nearest couch to proclaim his love.

Only Essence wasn't there. She was back in Memphis, getting glammed up for the Christmas Gala. He'd called her the second he'd stepped off the stage, and hearing her voice had made his heart swell. Love had made him soft, literally turned him into a poetry-reading, chick-flick-watching, squeezing-and-cuddling-and-kissing-by-the-fireplace fool, but he'd never been happier. And as long as he had Essence he'd never want for anything, or spend another Christmas Day feeling melancholy and blue or agonizing over his mother's untimely death.

"Is your wife here?" Yasmin asked, glancing around the room. "I'd love to meet her."

"I'm not married."

"You're not? That's great! I get a kick out of playing matchmaker, and I have friends who'd give up their entire shoe collection to meet a guy like you!" Laughing, she opened her purse, took out a business card and handed it to him. "Next time you're in the Tampa Bay area let me know. I'd love to have you over for dinner."

Lincoln examined the glossy white card. "You're a therapist?"

"Yes, why, is that a problem?"

"No, sorry, it just took me by surprise. I thought you were a model or a designer—"

"Oh, my. Now I *really* love you. Just don't tell my husband!"

They shared a loud, hearty laugh.

"Maybe I can call you one day to talk," Lincoln said with a shrug of his shoulder. "Essence thinks it would be a good idea for me to talk to a professional about some of the things that happened in my past."

"Essence sounds very wise. You should listen to her." Wearing an amused expression on her face, she studied him for a long, quiet moment. "Think she might be the one?"

I don't think, I know.

"You *definitely* don't need me to play matchmaker for you," she said, patting him on the shoulder. "You're so in love, Mr. Davenport, you're beaming!"

Lincoln chuckled. "Men don't beam."

"The ones in love do." Yasmin shot him a wink and swiped her conference information packet off the table. "I better run. I promised my husband I'd be back at noon so we could take the kids to the Christmas parade, and if I'm late we won't get good seats."

"You're probably the only person in here who traveled with their family."

"I know. Sad, eh?" Shaking her head, she glanced slowly around the crowded banquet hall. "These people think they have it all, because they have mansions and yachts and private jets, but if you don't have family and friends who love you unconditionally you have nothing."

"I couldn't have said it better myself."

"You have my business card. Use it." Yasmin flashed a friendly smile and a wave. "It was wonderful meeting you, Mr. Davenport. Take care of yourself and your lady friend!"

Lincoln stood alone at his table, reflecting on all the things Dr. Yasmin Ohaji-Bishop had said. His thoughts slipped back to last weekend, to the night he took Essence dancing at the Rumba Room. As they reached the front doors, she'd stopped to put on her leather jacket and he'd used the moment to put the moves on her.

"How fortuitous," he'd said, pulling her into his arms and glancing up at the ceiling. "We're standing under the mistletoe."

"If you didn't hate all things Christmas, I'd lay one hell of a kiss on you."

Lincoln had felt his mouth dry, and his pulse race a hundred miles an hour. "You would?"

"Damn right, I would." Essence licked her lips. "You're one incredibly gorgeous man, and although I've always thought kissing under the mistletoe was a bit cheesy, I'd make an exception for you."

"Then what are you waiting for?" Lincoln hadn't waited for an answer. He'd pressed his mouth against hers, lightly nibbled on her bottom lip, and when she'd passionately returned his kiss, he'd felt a rush of desire shoot straight to his groin. And the longer they'd caressed each other the harder it was for Lincoln to control his feelings.

It was those moments, those lighthearted memories that made Lincoln want to be with Essence every second of the day. And as he stood there, drinking his orange juice, he realized he had no business being in Washington, D.C. The truth was, he didn't want to be at the Entrepreneurs Business Conference and wasn't interested in going to Climax for the holidays. He wanted to be with his girl, his love, the saucy, sassy woman who'd changed his life for the better.

Deciding to take a page out of Yasmin's book, he grabbed his briefcase off the floor and strode out of the banquet hall and through the hotel's gleaming sliding glass doors. A sleek black limousine was idling at the curb and, when Lincoln peered into the passenger-side window, the thin gray-haired driver waved him inside.

"Where to, sir?"

"The airport, and step on it." Lincoln took his cell phone out of his jacket pocket and dialed Essence's number. Before the call could connect, he hung up. Why spoil the surprise? He couldn't wait to see the look on her face when he strode into the Cook Convention Center and whisked her into his arms. The image made him grin, and when Lincoln boarded a private charter plane for Memphis two hours later, he was *still* smiling.

Chapter 10

Essence turned her face toward the raised stage inside the Cook Convention Center's grand ballroom and patted back another yawn. Her third one in seconds. Essence was so bored, so sick and tired of hearing Rashad drone on and on about his West Coast tour, she considered faking cramps. It was a sneaky thing to do, something Essence couldn't believe she was actually considering, but anything was better than sitting between Rashad and the smooth-talking VP from Urban Beats Records. The flashy, bushy-browed music mogul was working her last nerve, and if he "accidently" brushed his hand against her thigh one more time she was going to "accidently" slap him.

The holiday spirit was alive and well in the ballroom, and everywhere Essence turned well-dressed people holding champagne flutes and blowing noisemakers were living it up. Guests snapped pictures in front of the ten-foot Christmas tree, kissed passionately under the mistletoe dangling from the ceiling and danced cheek to cheek out on the dance floor.

As Essence looked on, thoughts of Lincoln overwhelmed her.

What else is new? Her desire for him knew no bounds, and she couldn't go five minutes without thinking about him. She wondered if he was thinking about her, or so busy networking at the conference in Washington he'd forgotten all about her. He'd called her that morning after his keynote address and thanked her for helping him nail his speech, but the connection had been so poor they'd been forced to cut their conversation short. Lincoln wouldn't be back home until New Year's Day, and although they talked and texted each other countless times throughout the day, Essence didn't think she could survive a week without seeing him, without touching him, without sleeping in his arms.

I should have gone with Lincoln to Washington, Essence thought, her gaze drifting absently around the extravagantly decorated ballroom. *My parents are on a Caribbean cruise, my friends are busy with their boyfriends and families and Christmas dinner at Aunt Zizi's house is going to be the same ole, same ole.*

Blowing out a deep breath, Essence touched the nape of her neck and fingered the ends of her thick auburn-brown mane. It was the first time in years she'd gone to the hair salon and left without a silky, bone-straight weave, but she was ready for a change and loved how chic and mature her hairstyle looked. Rashad hated it, but Essence didn't give a damn what he thought. From the moment she'd opened her apartment door, he'd complained about her look and even begged her to change into a tighter, shorter dress. She didn't, of course, and told him if he dissed her one more time she was staying home, *and* keeping his money. That put an end to his rant, but his funky attitude remained.

"Sweet cheeks, go to the bar and grab me another Heineken."

Essence shot to her feet and snatched her clutch purse off the table. Normally, she'd put Rashad in his place for bossing her around, but since she had no intention of returning to the table, she decided to let his rudeness slide just this once. She'd done her part, earned her money and then some, and was glad to finally be rid of Rashad once and for all. He'd signed a lucrative recording contract with Urban Beats Records, and the VP was so impressed with how Essence carried herself, he'd hired her to cater the company's twenty-fifth anniversary party in February. The VP was a flirt, a man too touchy-feely for her liking, but he thought her ideas for the party were great and promised to contact her in the New Year to finalize the details. "See you later!" *Or in the next life,* Essence thought, shooting a wave over her shoulder.

Worried she'd wipe out on the slick, gleaming floor, Essence slowed her pace. Her gown, a strapless lace dress sprinkled with sequins, was so comfortable she'd schmoozed and danced with guests all night. By the end of cocktail hour, she'd handed out all of her business cards and booked three birthday parties on the spot. Things were looking up, and if everything went according to plan, she'd be out of her apartment and into her dream home by the end of next month. And if she didn't get accepted to the University of Memphis, she was going to apply to other universities, because she had every intention of finally finishing up her business degree.

Thanks to Lincoln she had a new lease on life, a new and improved attitude. The thought of him, the man she loved more than anything, warmed her all over. Essence couldn't wait to get home and call him, couldn't wait to hear his voice. She only hoped when she told Lincoln about attending the Christmas Gala with Rashad he wouldn't be mad. Or accuse her of being in love with her ex. That couldn't be further from the truth. Lincoln was the only man she wanted, the only man she loved with her heart and soul. He'd caused her to grow, strengthened her self-belief, but more than anything Essence loved how Lincoln made her *feel*. He made her feel as if she were smart enough to take on the world, and that was a heady feeling, one Essence could never, ever get enough of.

Essence was about to breeze past the bar and out the ballroom doors when guilt pricked her conscience. Leaving like this seemed wrong, juvenile even. The least she could do was order the Heineken and have it delivered to Rashad's table.

Making a quick U-turn, she joined the slow-moving line at the bar. To kill time, Essence opened her purse and took out her cell phone. There were dozens of new text messages from Lincoln, and as she read them the smile in her heart exploded onto her lips.

"You look so different, I almost didn't recognize you."

Essence felt an arm slip around her waist, and froze. A light, citrus scent fell over her. It was familiar, and soothing and so damn sensuous her eyes fluttered closed.

"I have never seen you look more beautiful, baby. For the first time in my life, I'm stunned speechless."

Essence glanced over her shoulder, saw Lincoln standing behind her wearing a sexy grin and threw herself into his arms. For a moment, Essence forgot everything else. She draped her hands around his neck, and showered his face with kisses. "Lincoln, baby, oh, my goodness, what are you doing here? You're supposed to be at the conference."

"I'm playing hooky," he said with a wink. "I couldn't

let you spend your birthday alone, so I decided to fly in to celebrate with you. Is that cool with you?"

"Hell yeah, it's cool with me! This is the best surprise ever."

"I have a feeling you'll like your birthday present even more." Lincoln brushed his nose playfully against hers. "When we get back to the house, I'll give you your present *and* show you in every imaginable way how much I missed you…."

Essence shivered. His words set her heart on fire. Lincoln wasn't a bad boy, and had never so much as received a parking ticket, but tonight his confidence was sky-high. He had killer swag, and looked so damn sexy in his leather coat and dark slacks Essence couldn't stop touching him. She loved seeing this side of Lincoln, loved how playful and fun he was, and moaned when he crushed his lips to her mouth. His kiss fanned the flames. It was so passionate and intense, Essence rocked back on her stiletto heels.

"God, I missed you so much," he growled, burying his hands in her hair. It was so soft and silky he couldn't stop touching it, playing in it, twirling the curls around his fingers. "It feels like I haven't seen you in months, but it's only been a few days."

Essence draped her arms around his neck. "Baby, I missed you, too."

"You look amazing, and I love your new haircut." Lincoln gave her the once-over and released a slow whistle. "It's a good thing I showed up when I did, or one of these wealthy, slick-talking politicians would have swept you off your feet."

"Why would I want a politician when I share my bed with the sexiest man in Memphis?"

"How do you feel about sharing more than just your bed?" Lincoln asked. He felt energized, charged up. But he always felt that way when Essence was around. His feelings for her were growing, deepening by the second, and holding her in his arms was the greatest feeling in the world.

"Lincoln, what are you saying?"

"I thought I had everything," he began, caressing her cheeks with his thumb. "I thought I was living the American dream, and had everything a man could want, but then you walked into my office and flipped my world upside down. I didn't realize what I was missing until I met you. Life means nothing if I don't have you to share it with, Essence—"

"Get your hands off my girl before I stomp your ugly grill into the ground."

Essence felt her heart plunge to her feet and shatter into a million pieces. She heard Rashad's voice, heard the profanity-laced insults he shot at Lincoln, and cringed inwardly. For a second, she thought of grabbing the water pitcher on top of the bar and throwing it in her ex-boyfriend's face. But she didn't want to do anything to embarrass Lincoln. Guests were shooting curious glances their way, and Essence feared if she didn't do something quick, things were going to get out of hand. Rashad loved attention, good or bad, and would do anything for free press. "Lincoln, let's get out of here."

"No, I want to hear what this guy has to say." Folding his arms across his chest, Lincoln quickly sized up his clean-cut adversary. The stranger was wearing a gray tuxedo jacket with blue jeans and sneakers, and enough bling to open his own jewelry store. His eyes were narrowed, his body looked stiff and he was so angry he was practically frothing at the mouth. A group of burly, gold-toothed men stood behind him, no more than a couple feet, poised to attack. The stranger grabbed Essence's wrist, but she easily broke free of his grasp.

"Rashad, knock it off," she snapped, her tone sharp

and her gaze lethal. "I'm leaving, and if you try to stop me I'll tell everyone in here how you persuaded me to be your date."

"His *date?*" His words came out in a shout, in a tone Lincoln had never used before. This couldn't be happening. Not again. The knot in the back of his throat threatened to choke him, to kill him dead. His breathing was heavy, labored, but he managed to ask the question circling his muddled mind. "You guys are…here…together?"

"Yeah, that's right, homey. I'm her date. Not you, sucker."

"It's not what you think. I promise. I'll explain everything later."

"No, explain everything now." Lincoln stared into Essence's eyes. He saw the pleading expression on her face, and knew she was begging him to be understanding, but he wanted answers and he wanted them now, not later. "Start by telling me who this guy is and why you're running around with him behind my back."

The stranger reached into his tuxedo jacket, took out a pair of sunglasses and slid them on. "I'm Rashad J," he said, smoothing is fingertips over his thick, dark eyebrows. "But my fans call me 'The Bedroom Maestro.'"

Lincoln gave him a blank stare. "I've never heard of you."

"I'm not surprised. You're not cool like that. Bet you don't even know who Jay-Z is!"

His entourage laughed.

"Baby, let's get out of here." Essence linked arms with Lincoln. "We'll talk in the car."

"Sweet cheeks, you're really going to leave with this clown?" His chuckle was loud, but sounded fake. "After all I've done for you? You wouldn't be nothing without me.…"

Ice spread through Lincoln's veins. His hands curled into fists and adrenaline propelled him forward, just inches away from the R & B singer's face. He wanted to deck Rashad for disrespecting the woman he loved, and didn't care if he had to take on the singer's entourage, too, but before he could throw a punch, Essence slid in front of him. She took his hands, wrapped them around her waist and pressed her back flat against his chest. Essence glanced over her shoulder and shot him a smile. One that instantly calmed him. Lincoln held Essence tight, realized he wouldn't let her go for anything in the world.

"Good luck with everything," Essence said to her ex. "I wish you and your family well."

"Sweet cheeks, we belong together."

"No, I belong with Lincoln. He's the only man I want, the only man I need."

"You're going to pick this suit over me?" Scowling, Rashad threw his hands in the air and gestured with his head to Lincoln. "I have the number one track on iTunes and just signed with one of the biggest record labels in the country. What does he have?"

"Compassion, sensitivity and a heart of gold." A smile touched her lips. "Lincoln's my soul mate, and I won't let anything come between us."

"Whatever, fine, then leave with him." Rashad shrugged a shoulder. "You'll come running back to me like you always do. Bet you're beating down my door by the end of the week."

"It's not going to happen," she shot back. "I plan to spend the rest of the Christmas holidays at home with my man and nowhere else."

Rashad cringed. He scanned the room, caught sight of the buxom waitress at the bar and pulled her to his side. "Want to party with me tonight?" His tone was smug, and his chest was puffed up with pride. "I have a stretch Hummer waiting outside stocked with Cristal and caviar. You down?"

The waitress shrieked. "Of course I'll kick it with you! You're Rashad J!"

Rashad swaggered off with his curvy, wide-eyed date and burly entourage in tow.

"Essence, you have some explaining to do."

Taking a deep breath, she turned around and faced Lincoln. She told him everything, didn't hold anything back. She told him about her tumultuous relationship with Rashad, and how she'd finally grown a backbone and dumped him last year. Lincoln listened quietly without interrupting, but the more she spoke the thinner his eyes got.

The expression on his face became grim, his tone guarded. "Why keep me in the dark about who he was?"

"Because it wasn't important. I don't love Rashad—"

"Then why did you get his initials tattooed on the back of your neck?"

Essence frowned. "I didn't. R.J. stands for Ramiyah Jones," she explained. "Rashad's sister Ramiyah was my best friend. When she passed away in a tragic Jet Ski accident, I got the tattoo in honor of her memory."

"Baby, I'm sorry. I feel like such an ass. I thought that tattoo was for Rashad."

"I'd never get a guy's name tattooed on my body."

Lincoln raised an eyebrow. "What about your husband's name?"

"Don't have one yet," she quipped, a grin tickling her lips. "Why, Mr. Davenport, are you applying for the permanent, full-time position?"

"Most definitely."

"Lincoln, quit playing."

"I'm not playing, baby. I'm serious." Fixing his gaze on her face, he blocked out all the noises and conversations swirling around the grand ballroom and focused his attention on her. "Did you mean those things you said to Rashad, or was that just talk?"

"I meant every word."

"I feel the same way. Have since our very first date."

Her eyes widened; not with excitement, but with disbelief. "Are you sure you're not confusing lust with the real thing?" she asked softly. "We have an amazing connection, and our lovemaking is incredible, but—"

"I don't care if we ever make love again. I just want you in my life forever."

"Liar!" she shrieked, sliding her hands up and down her curvy hips. "You know you can't live without this good loving!"

Lincoln chuckled. "All that matters to me is that we're together. That we *stay* together," he stressed, pressing his lips to her forehead, the tip of her nose and across her cheeks. "I never imagined I could fall this hard or this fast for someone, but from the moment you walked into my office, I knew you were the only woman for me. I fought my attraction to you like hell, but the more I tried to fight my feelings, the deeper they grew."

"Is that why you had your way with me after the holiday mixer?"

"Is that what happened?" Lincoln cocked his head to the right, then slowly shook his head. "I remember things a little differently. *You* cornered *me*."

"You're right, I did, but you loved every wicked minute of it."

They laughed, kissed and held each other fiercely.

Lincoln couldn't hold back his smile, couldn't stop touching and kissing her. Essence had captured his heart from the moment they'd met, and now he couldn't imagine his life without her. "I love you with all my heart and I want to have a future with you," he confessed.

His voice was low and the expression on his face was so earnest and sincere, tears filled her eyes and spilled down her cheeks.

"If my mom were alive, she definitely would have wanted me to marry you."

"Really? You think so?"

"For sure. My mother was sharp and saucy and had a big, bright personality, just like you." Lincoln touched a hand to her face. "Baby, I want to travel the world with you, and take care of and pamper you like crazy when you're pregnant with our first child."

"You want kids?"

"Two of each sounds good, don't you think?"

Essence squealed. "That sounds like heaven, especially the part about you spoiling me."

"Then let's get out of here. I have a special birthday surprise waiting for you back at the house and I can't wait to see the look on your face when you open it."

"I love you more than words can describe," Essence gushed, tenderly caressing his cheek. "Now that I have you in my life, Lincoln, I don't need anything else."

"Not even that diamond Cartier necklace unveiled in Paris last month?" he teased.

"Not even the diamond Cartier necklace unveiled in Paris last month."

A grin exploded onto his face. Chuckling, he scooped Essence up in his arms and spun her around the room. The couples standing around the bar pointed and laughed.

Essence shrieked, overcome with joy and happiness. "What am I going to do with you? You're crazy!"

"Only about you." Lincoln strode out the doors of the grand ballroom, holding Essence tightly in his arms, feeling on top of the world. "How do you feel about going to Climax for the Christmas holidays?" he asked. "I figured I'd take you out for an expensive dinner, ply you with tons of champagne and then take you to my grandparents' house to meet my wild kinfolk!"

"I'm game," she said, giving him a peck on the lips. "Let's leave tonight!"

A hearty chuckle burst out of Lincoln's mouth. He'd laughed more in the past six weeks than he'd laughed all year, and whenever Essence was around he felt energized, alive, like a brand-new man.

Holding Essence in his arms, he stalked through the crowded lobby, wishing everyone he passed a Merry Christmas and a Happy New Year. Lincoln knew he was acting out of character, but for the first time in his life he didn't care what anyone thought of him. He had finally found the woman of his dreams, a woman who completed him in every way. Essence made him feel whole, loved, and he was so excited about their relationship and their future together he wanted to shout it to the world.

Lincoln strode through the sliding glass doors of the Memphis Cook Convention Center and stepped out into the winter night. He looked up at the sky and admired the lone, twinkling star. "Thanks, Mom," he whispered, holding Essence close to his chest. "This is the greatest Christmas gift I could have ever asked for."

Then, for the second time in minutes, Lincoln lowered his head and kissed Essence with all the love and affection flowing through his heart.

* * * * *

SECOND-CHANCE CHRISTMAS
Farrah Rochon

For my sister, Tamara. Thanks for giving me the
idea for this story.

Chapter 1

Ayana Taylor placed her hand in the driver's outstretched palm as he assisted her from the hired car that had brought them to the Golden Ridge Resort and Spa. The sprawling lodge was nestled at the base of the Colorado Rockies' postcard-worthy Vail Mountain. Snow-covered pine trees and veins of ski trails along the face of the mountain completed the picturesque view.

The nerves that had been tying her stomach in knots eased as she took in the fragrant green garland that trimmed the resort's vaulted entryway. It was hard to remain anxious when faced with the sights and smells of the holidays.

"Hey, wait…wait up a minute," came a craggy voice from inside the car.

Ayana rolled her eyes as she waited for her on-again, off-again, don't-like-him-enough-to-ever-get-serious-about-him traveling companion, Keith Mitchell, to climb out of the backseat. She'd needed to bring a date with her to see her brother, Austin, get married; she'd decided that she didn't want to face this weekend alone, and Keith had seemed the most logical choice. He was well-educated, gainfully employed and if he walked into a room full of women he automatically became the main attraction.

They'd once been intimate, but not for a long time. It had been her decision.

Ayana figured Keith had jumped at the chance to join her because he was expecting something more serious to go on. Poor baby. She wasn't looking forward to his whining when he discovered that she'd reserved a room with double beds and he would be sleeping alone in his. She was grateful she'd had the forethought to do so, too. They had only been in Colorado for a couple of hours, and Ayana was already regretting her choice of travel companion.

"Hold on a minute," Keith said. "You know I'm not feeling well." He clutched his stomach with both hands and groaned. She had to admit he did look rather pale.

As the driver gathered their bags from the Lincoln's trunk, Ayana assessed Keith. Crossing her arms over her chest, she asked, "So if you knew you suffered from altitude sickness, why did you agree to come with me to Colorado?"

He shrugged. "It's been a while since I've been here. I'd forgotten how bad it can get. Besides, I figured being here with you would be worth a little upset stomach."

He tried to pull off a sexy smile. It didn't work, especially when, seconds later, he dashed to a garbage can and emptied the lunch they'd been served on their first-class flight from Dallas. He walked back toward her, wiping the back of his hand across his mouth and looking as if he'd just gone through a wash cycle.

Ayana retreated a step and held up both hands. "I don't mean to sound insensitive, but this outfit cost me a lot of money." She nodded to the bellman who had just finished loading their bags onto a luggage cart, and followed as he led the way into the resort.

The moment Ayana walked through the doors, her mood immediately lifted. The soaring atrium was bedecked with yards of the same pine garland that adorned the outside of the lodge. It was threaded with glittering ribbon and festooned with ornaments of deep brown, gold and bronze.

A massive tree that towered no less than twenty feet occupied the center of the lobby. At its base was a cozy village scene made up of miniature ceramic buildings, a train and even an ice-skating rink with mechanical people sliding across it. The entire scene was utterly charming.

Now she understood why Austin and Rachelle had chosen this as the place to hold their wedding. If you wanted to get married the weekend before Christmas, what better place to do it than one that captured the spirit of the holidays with such elegance?

"I need to find a restroom," Keith said, leaving her to check in to their room.

Trying not to roll her eyes at him again, Ayana started for the reception desk. Halfway there, her feet came to a sudden stop as she encountered the one sight she had been dreading since the moment Austin had told her about the wedding.

Jackson Richards.

The tangle of nerves that had twisted inside of her for months immediately made its presence known again, causing her stomach to pitch and roll and her skin to break out in an icy sweat. She'd known this moment would eventually arrive. Jackson was her brother's best friend and business partner, and there was no way he would miss Austin's wedding. In fact, Jax was the best man. Running into him this weekend had been inevitable.

But that didn't mean she had to like it, nor did it mean she had to talk to him.

Ayana jutted her chin in the air and continued her march to the reception desk. Three people stood in a line that was cordoned off by velvet-covered cables. Jax was at the far end of the counter, casually leaning against the polished wood under a sign that read Platinum Members.

Just then he turned, and their eyes connected. Ayana's breath caught as chills traveled along her nerve endings. She looked past him, pretending she hadn't seen him, then returned her attention to the line before her.

Clasping her hands in front of her, Ayana focused all her energy on appearing calm and serene. She stared straight ahead, engrossing herself in the argyle pattern woven into the sweater of the man who stood ahead of her.

As each person in line was tended to by front desk personnel, the angst building in her belly multiplied. It would be just her luck that she and Jax would finish up in line at the same time. Blessedly, just as she was being called to the desk, the person catering to platinum members returned, handing Jackson a dark-green portfolio emblazoned with the lodge's name in gold lettering. Ayana's bones nearly melted in relief. At least he would be gone by the time she was done checking in.

She should have known better.

Instead of sparing them both the awkward, unwelcome reunion, Jax seemed determined to make it happen. He stopped a few feet away from her and waited. Ayana didn't dare look back. She didn't have to; she could feel his nearness against her skin, as if he were physically touching her.

The front desk clerk slid her credit card and two plastic keycards across the polished wood, accompanied by a parting smile.

The thought of turning around and facing Jax after all these years caused a knot of unease to form in her throat. It took great effort to swallow it down, but she did. Stiffening her spine, Ayana wiped her face clean of all expression and turned. She was immediately bowled over by the sheer magnificence that was Jackson Richards.

God, but why did he have to look so much better than he had ten years ago?

He still wore his hair cut close, the small, natural waves rippling across his head. His brilliant, light brown eyes glittered with inviting warmth as a hint of a smile curled up the edge of his perfectly shaped lips.

"Hello, Ayana," he said in the rich, resonating voice that had turned her knees to jelly the first time she'd heard it. "How have you been?"

Just as she started to respond, Keith sidled up next to her and looped her arm through the crook of his elbow. "Are we all checked in?" he asked.

The light in Jax's eyes dimmed, and that trace of a smile thinned.

Ayana looked up at Keith. "Yes, we are," she said. Then she turned and allowed him to escort her to the bank of elevators, grateful to have made it through her encounter with Jax emotionally unscathed.

At least that's what she was telling herself.

As Jackson watched Ayana walk away, a sharp pain he hadn't felt in nearly a decade returned with an acuity that had him grimacing. He thought he had been prepared for this, but he had been wrong. Horribly, astoundingly wrong.

He'd underestimated the potency of the connection between them, which hadn't diminished one bit in all the time he and Ayana had been apart. She would deny it, of course. It was more than obvious that she had every intention of continuing the systematic avoidance she'd employed where he was concerned, but it was hard to dispute the undisputable.

Jax hadn't seen her enter the resort's lobby, he'd *felt* it. It had started with a buzz that traveled along his skin, sending pinpricks of something hot and sensual cascading down his spine. The moment he looked up and spotted her examining the Christmas tree in the middle of the lobby, everything around him ceased to exist. Every atom, every molecule, every part of his essence had focused solely on Ayana.

Then he'd noticed the man walking beside her.

Jax's nostrils flared with the fury that had taken hold of him and refused to let go.

Why hadn't he thought to ask Austin whether she would be bringing a date to the wedding? At least then he would have been prepared to see her with another man, instead of suffering what had felt like a two-by-four to the gut.

He wasn't unrealistic enough to assume that Ayana had spent the past decade pining away for him. She'd even been engaged once, although Jax had eradicated that news from his brain the moment Austin had mentioned it.

Still, having vague knowledge of her being with another man and actually seeing it with his own eyes were two entirely different things.

"Not your concern," he reminded himself.

He was the last person who had a right to begrudge Ayana happiness, not when he had been the one who had caused her so much hurt.

"Damn," Jax cursed under his breath. This weekend would be even more frustrating than he'd first thought.

The bubbly strains of "Let It Snow" floating from the harpist's talented fingers along with the cheerful holiday decor adorning just about every surface in the banquet room should have put Ayana in a festive mood. Instead, she'd spent the past hour vacillating between anxiety and annoyance as she studied the guests at her brother's wedding rehearsal party.

She had left Keith in their room, crouched over the toilet. She'd ordered room service to deliver a couple of bottles of ginger ale and saltine crackers, but that was where her caretaking duties ended. Keith had brought this upon himself. He had known his body didn't handle Colorado's high altitude well, and failed to mention it until too late.

Now she was stuck spending the weekend with a man who couldn't go ten minutes without throwing up, *and* she was dateless for the rehearsal party and more than likely the wedding. What little sympathy she had for Keith was quickly drying up.

Ayana forced a smile as she tipped her wineglass toward her cousin Lucien, whom she only saw at weddings and funerals. She drained the goblet, then motioned to the bartender for another white wine. Even though the alcohol had done a credible job of calming her nerves, she decided this glass would be her last. Getting tipsy would *not* be a smart move.

Ayana worked the kinks out of her shoulders, rolling them slowly. She'd maintained her rigid posture for far too long as she sat on the high-backed leather barstool. She should probably get up and mingle, but if she did, she would lose her excellent view of the banquet room. From where she was seated—the last stool in the far right corner of the U-shaped bar—she could keep her eyes on all guests, including the one she was determined to avoid. She was ashamed to admit it, but for several days she had actually considered missing her own brother's wedding if it meant not seeing Jackson.

"Hey, girl." Her cousin Shawntell walked up to her and enveloped Ayana in a hug. "It's been ages since I've seen you. You look fab."

"So do you," Ayana said. "Congratulations on your baby girl. I saw the pictures on Facebook. She's adorable."

Shawntell beamed with the glow of a new mother. "Her daddy is up in the room with her, but the minute she starts crying he'll be calling me to rescue him. Do you want to hit the buffet?"

Ayana waved a hand. "I'm good."

"We'll have to get together and chat. It's been too long."

"Definitely," Ayana said. She watched her cousin, who was a year younger than her own twenty-eight years, head for the generous spread of food, and Ayana had to fight off the instant stab of envy. She still had ample time to get married and have children of her own. She would never begrudge someone else's happiness just because it was taking her a little longer than she'd thought it would to find her own happily-ever-after.

There was one person in particular whom she held responsible for that. Ayana looked around the room for him again, but Jax was nowhere to be found.

It's been ten years, Ayana. Get over it.

But there were certain things time couldn't erase or heal, and the complete and utter thrashing Jax had rendered on her heart was one of them.

Ayana took another sip of wine as her eyes roamed the banquet room, looking for his well-over-six-foot frame. But she didn't see him meandering through the crowd, nor had she for at least the past half hour. For that matter, she hadn't seen her brother either.

Had those two skipped out on the rehearsal party?

It wouldn't surprise her if they had. But unlike most men, they wouldn't have skipped out for a wild bachelor party with sleazy strippers. They were probably somewhere talking about the latest news on technology stocks.

Ayana spotted her mother striding toward her, a frown furrowing her normally smooth skin, courtesy of the Botox she received from the Fort Worth location of Tranquil Pleasures, the string of day spas Ayana owned with her partner and best friend, Dana Parker.

"Ayana, have you seen your brother?" her mother asked.

"He left to check on something over an hour ago, and hasn't been back since."

"Check on what?"

"He wouldn't say. He just said he had to check on something."

"I haven't seen him since just after the toast." Ayana slipped her phone from her metallic gold Coach wristlet. "Let me call him."

"I've already tried. His phone is going straight to voice mail."

It was Ayana's turn to frown. Austin rarely let his phone go directly to voicemail. As the sales rep for the software company he and Jackson co-owned, her brother was always within reach. Ayana wouldn't be surprised if he'd figured out a way to shower with his Bluetooth in his ear.

"Have you asked Rachelle?" she asked.

"She hasn't heard from him either. I've been looking for Jackson to see if he knows where Austin went."

As if summoned by their simply speaking his name, Jax walked through the set of double doors closest to the bar. Unfortunately, Austin didn't enter behind him.

"Let me see if Jax has heard from him," her mother said.

"Denise!" They both turned to find her father waving his hand in a "come here" motion, a huge smile on his face. Ayana suspected he'd indulged in a bit more of the spiked eggnog than usual. "The photographer wants to take pictures of us. Come on."

Her mother rolled her eyes, then laid a hand on Ayana's arm. "Find out from Jax if he's heard from Austin, will you?"

"No...I..." She shook her head, a wave of anxiety washing over her.

But her mother was already heading for the area that was made to look like a winter wonderland. The display, which had been set up for picture taking, was second to the buffet as the most popular spot for guests.

Ayana retrieved her wineglass and downed the rest of the liquid in one gulp. Pulling in a fortifying breath, she climbed down from the stool and straightened her shoulders.

As she headed toward Jax, she ran both hands down the front of her winter-white cowl-neck cashmere sweater and smoothed the hem over her matching white corduroy leggings. She'd chosen the ensemble because she looked absolutely fierce in it, especially when paired with her knee-high stiletto-heel fawn-colored boots and matching belt. She looked good and she knew it.

And Jackson knew it, too.

The approval she'd witnessed in his eyes as their gazes had locked in the lobby earlier today had been unmistakable. The fact that she'd experienced even the slightest thrill from that approval had pissed her off. She didn't give a flying hell about Jax's approval—about *anything* concerning him.

To prove it, Ayana shook off her nervousness and walked right up to him.

"Have you seen Austin?" she asked.

Jackson slowly moved his arresting, light brown eyes from the spot in the corner he'd been gazing at and centered them on her. The rate with which her pulse escalated was both alarming and embarrassing. The left side of his mouth curved in that sexy half smile—something else that hadn't changed in the past ten years. The effect it had on her was the same, too. Her nipples instantly formed into tight, achy peaks.

Dammit! What happened to not giving a flying hell about him?

"Hello to you, too, Ayana. It's nice to see you after all these years."

She crossed her arms over her chest, affecting a bored look, and trying to hide her body's reaction to him. "Austin. Have you seen Austin?"

Jax's eyes darted over her shoulder, then came back to her face. "He's…um, not feeling well. He has a headache. I think he had a bit too much to drink last night."

"Wrong answer," she said. "Austin doesn't drink."

"Well, he did last night."

"And he's just now getting a headache from it?"

His eyes narrowed and an unmistakable note of irritation colored his voice as he said, "It was a late-onset hangover."

Ayana continued to stare, one brow cocked. Jax tilted his head back and let out a frustrated sigh. "What do you want from me, Ayana?"

"The truth would be nice."

He looked past her again, and the tense lines that bracketed his mouth put Ayana on edge. She peered over her shoulder in the direction that he was staring, finding Rachelle and her bridesmaids laughing and carrying on at the head table.

"What's going on, Jax? This isn't like Austin."

Ayana caught the trace of worry that flitted over his features, and her anxiety tripled. He hesitated a moment before gesturing to a quiet corner of the banquet room, away from the guests. He pulled out his cell phone, swiped his thumb across the touch screen and handed it to her.

"I got this text message from Austin a half hour ago."

I can't go through with this.

"What?" Ayana yelped.

"Shhh." Jax peered around the room.

Ayana did the same, hoping no one had heard her. She turned her attention back to the phone and pointed at the screen. In a lowered but just as fierce voice, she asked, "What in the hell does he mean by 'this'?"

"What do you think he means?"

Ayana's eyelids slid closed. "God, please." She prayed that her sensible, levelheaded brother had not developed the most untimely case of cold feet. "Where could he have gone?"

"Hell if I know." Jax ran a hand down his face. "I've been searching all around this hotel for him."

"Did you check his room?"

Jax slanted her a look, one she deserved. Of course Mr. Genius, Phi Beta Kappa, had thought to check Austin's room.

"Well, where else have you looked?" Ayana asked.

"I checked the bar—"

"He doesn't drink," she pointed out again.

He let out another frustrated breath. "Your brother and I have been best friends for fifteen years, Ayana. I know he doesn't drink. That doesn't mean he wouldn't go into the bar to hide out. I also checked the lobby and the ski lift area."

"What about the restaurants and roof deck? That's where the pool and hot tubs are."

"Those were next on my list. I only stopped in here to see if he'd come to his senses and returned to the party."

She gestured to the banquet room, which was still swelling with guests. "Well, as you can see, he hasn't, so let's go."

Jax put his hands up. "I've got this."

"The hell you do," she said. "I'm coming with you."

Those lines of irritation bracketed his mouth again. "I don't need your help, Ayana."

She fixed him with a sharp glare. "That's too bad, because you're getting it. Let's go."

Chapter 2

She was stubborn as hell.

Some things never changed, and that stubborn streak the size of the Mississippi River that coursed through Ayana Taylor's veins was one of them. The amazing way her butt looked in a pair of snug-fitting pants was another.

Jax sucked in another shallow breath, trying to get as much oxygen to his brain as he could. He'd been way too close to fitting his palm against the curve of her firm backside, a move he would surely regret. Instead, he settled for both torturing and pleasuring himself with the view as she strode ahead of him, that proud head rigid with determination.

They boarded the elevator, which was decorated with a lighted garland and filled with the scent of pine, as was just about everything else at this resort. The elevator quickly took them to the sixth-floor rooftop. The heated swimming pool was peppered with a smattering of guests brave enough to withstand the shock of cold they would surely feel when their wet bodies emerged from the water. However—and not surprisingly—Austin wasn't one of them.

Ayana pointed toward the rear of the roof deck. "The hot tubs."

"Do you really think your brother is relaxing in a hot tub while his family and friends are downstairs at his wedding rehearsal party?"

"No, what I think is that he's cracked up and lost his mind," Ayana said. "What other reason would he have for leaving in the first place?"

"Cold feet." Jax shrugged. "Happens to the best of 'em."

She peered over at him with a raised brow. Despite her silence, the unspoken "Did it happen to you?" came through loud and clear.

They were *not* going there.

Jax hitched his head toward the hot tubs. "Let's check to make sure he isn't there. No stone left unturned, right?"

Just as Jax had expected, the mission proved futile. He could tell Ayana's worry was escalating with every minute that passed. She spun in a slow circle, looking around the roof deck. The sun had just started to set, sinking behind the mountain range to their west.

"Where could he be?" she asked in a voice that trembled slightly.

"This is a huge resort," Jax reminded her. "I haven't checked the pub yet. Maybe he's hiding out there."

At least he hoped that's where Austin was hiding out, because the pub was the only other place Jax had yet to look.

Austin had hinted at some misgivings about his impending wedding, but it had never entered Jax's mind that he would pull a stunt like this. The two of them had arrived in Vail a week ago. With Jax running his end of the company from his hometown of Philadelphia, while Austin worked from his native Dallas, they rarely found time to meet face-to-face. They'd decided this would be a good opportunity for an uninterrupted meeting of the minds. Jax had rented a chalet about halfway up the mountain and the two had spent the week immersed in work.

On more than one occasion, Austin had questioned him about his short-lived marriage. He'd asked Jax several times whether he would do it again before admitting that he was having reservations about marrying Rachelle. Jax had immediately struck his statement down as the most ridiculous thing he'd ever heard. Austin and Rachelle had only been dating for a little over two years, but they got along better than any couple he knew.

Jax had written his friend's reservations off as the typical cold feet any groom suffered before pledging to spend his life with one woman. Never had he imagined Austin would do something like this.

He and Ayana took the elevator back down to the first level. Just to the right of the lobby was an Old World–style English pub. It wasn't Austin's typical hangout, but that was all the more reason to look there.

Five minutes later, he and Ayana walked out of the pub without Austin in tow.

She turned to him and the vulnerability that was so evident in her eyes pinched his chest. Jackson reached out and clasped both of her hands within his own. He was jarred by the current of electricity that raced through him at the feel of her soft skin, but quickly shook it off. This wasn't the time.

"Your brother is fine," Jax assured her.

She looked up at him and those soulful brown eyes hit him with the same wallop with which they'd struck him when he'd first spotted her this afternoon. What was it about Ayana Taylor that so readily snatched the air from his lungs? How could she still have this effect on him after all this time?

"Why would he do something like this?" she asked. "You've been with him all week. Did he give any clue that he was about to just pick up and leave?"

Jax hesitated only a second, but apparently that was all Ayana needed.

Her eyes widened. "He did, didn't he?" She pulled her hands away and started pacing in front of the pub's entrance. "Jax, why didn't you try to talk some sense into him?" She stopped and drilled him with a look. "Oh, wait, I forgot who I was talking to. You're not necessarily the best source when it comes to dishing out marital advice."

"And the lady hits her mark," Jax said with a sigh. He shut his eyes and pinched the bridge of his nose.

Before he'd come to Colorado, for the briefest moment he'd thought seeing Ayana for the first time in ten years would be a pleasant experience. What in the hell had he been thinking?

Her phone rang, and they both stopped short.

She pulled it from that ridiculously tiny purse she wore on her wrist and stared at the screen. "It's my mother. How can I tell her that Austin's missing?"

"Don't," Jax said. "Give her the hangover story."

"She won't believe that any more than I did."

"Make something up, but don't tell her that he's missing. And don't mention the text message."

She cut her eyes at him as she answered the phone, as if it was *his* fault Austin had gone AWOL. She shifted a few feet away, holding the phone to one ear and covering the other with the hand that held the tiny purse. With the lively music streaming from the pub, Jax couldn't hear what she was saying, but she'd pasted on a fake smile, which told him that she wasn't delivering bad news. Ayana had always blatantly worn her emotions for the world to see.

Jax took a moment to study her. To say she'd grown into a gorgeous woman was such a gross understatement it was ridiculous to even voice it. She was so far beyond gorgeous it was almost a crime.

And that body.

Damn, but that body was a thousand times more lush and sensual than it had been the last time he'd seen her, when she had been a fresh-faced eighteen-year-old recent high school graduate on her way to college.

Back then, during those frequent trips to the Taylors' Dallas home that he and Austin would take while attending the University of Texas, Ayana had stolen his breath whenever she'd stepped into a room. Now, at twenty-eight, not only had she stolen his breath, but when he'd first spotted her in the resort's lobby, she'd rendered him speechless.

It was too bad she hated him on what felt like a molecular level. With good reason, of course.

She ended the call with her mother and walked toward him on those pointy high-heeled boots that made his mouth water just looking at the way the smooth leather hugged her delectable calves. Jax doubted she'd worn the boots for the sole purpose of torturing him, but it sure as hell felt that way.

"What do you know, she actually bought the hangover story," Ayana said, slipping the phone back into her purse.

"Thank God," Jax breathed.

"But *we* know that he isn't in bed with a hangover," she pointed out. "What's the plan? How do we go about finding him?"

"*We* don't go about finding him," Jax said. "Go find your date and get back to the rehearsal party."

Jax grimaced at the bite in his tone, but he couldn't help

it. Since the moment he'd spotted the two of them earlier today, thoughts of her and the guy she'd brought to Colorado had filled his head. Imagining the two of them together was driving him crazy.

"I'm not thinking about Keith right now. I'm focused on finding Austin."

Keith. Stupid name.

Ayana held her hands out. "Come on, Jackson, what's the plan?"

"I'm going to look around Vail Square," Jax answered. "Hopefully he's in one of the shops or restaurants around here."

"I'm coming with you," she said. "I already told my mom I'm not coming back to the party. I told her I was tired after the long day of travel."

"Which you probably are."

"I'll survive," Ayana said.

Jax was about to make another pitch for her to leave the searching duties to him, but did he really want to send her back to the room where Keith was waiting?

"Jackson, come on," Ayana persisted. "We need to find Austin before others start to notice that he's gone."

Ten years later and he still knew better than to argue with her when she got that stubborn look in her eye.

Ten years later and that stubborn look still turned him on.

Jax ran a hand down his face. It was bad enough he had to spend his time searching for a runaway groom when he should be using this very rare downtime to relax and clear his mind. Now he would have to spend it fighting the strongest case of lust he'd had in God knew how long.

Actually, Jax *did* know how long it had been since his blood had burned this hot for a woman. It had been ten long years.

And it had been *this* woman.

* * *

Ayana buried her chin into the collar of her sweater. After her upbringing deep in the heart of Texas, the blast of cold that hit her the minute she cleared the resort's double doors was a shock to her system, despite having just experienced it when they'd searched the rooftop.

She struggled to keep pace with Jax's long strides as he headed for Vail Square. The all-inclusive community, with numerous restaurants, shops, entertainment venues and residences, resembled similar complexes that were popping up over the Dallas/Fort Worth area. This particular neighborhood boasted several quaint boutiques that sold products from high-end cookware to fashion to ski equipment.

Even though it was not even 6:00 p.m. yet, several of the shops had already closed for the evening. But the cafés, coffee shop and a number of retail stores were still open.

"Do you want to split up?" Jax asked. "I'll take the left side of the square and you take the right? We can meet at the ice-skating rink."

Ayana nodded. She was more than on board with that suggestion. She was having a hard enough time just breathing around him. Maybe if they separated she could manage a coherent thought.

"I'll also check that outdoor concert area," he said. "Why don't you look around the fire pits, and maybe the area around the Christmas tree?"

Jax took off toward the cluster of food establishments—quaint sandwich shops, a bakery and a café. Ayana went in the opposite direction. She dipped into the retail stores that were still open, searching for her brother's head of naturally wavy, dark brown hair. Austin wasn't as tall as Jackson, but she would be able to pick him out in a crowd with no problem.

Except there *was* a problem: he wasn't there. In fact, he wasn't anywhere.

With every shop she exited, Ayana's nerves ratcheted up another notch. What if Austin had done something really extreme, like left town altogether?

She shook her head. Her brother was way too sensible for that.

Although Ayana also thought he was too sensible to ever question marrying a woman who was obviously his perfect match in every way. If Austin was capable of developing such a drastic case of cold feet, who's to say what else he might be capable of?

"Austin Dennis Taylor, you are in *so* much trouble," Ayana murmured as she made her way toward the square's outdoor fire pits.

It was a good thing Rachelle was a traditionalist. She'd insisted on adhering to the custom of the groom not seeing the bride before the wedding, so Austin's absence shouldn't raise his future bride's eyebrows. For now.

If Austin didn't show up for his own wedding tomorrow evening, more than eyebrows would be raised. Ayana was pretty certain her mother's blood pressure would go through the roof as well.

Not spotting him around the stone fire pits, she plunked her hands on her hips and trailed her eyes over the square. A children's choir, which had gathered in the concert area, began the first haunting strains of "O Holy Night."

"Goodness, Austin," Ayana said. "Where are you?"

"Not here."

She yelped, spinning around and colliding with Jackson, who'd appeared out of nowhere. At the same time, her left heel slipped on a patch of slick ice covering the brick walkway. Ayana felt herself falling backward, but

Jax was there. He grabbed her arms and pulled her against his solid chest.

"Whoa there." His deep voice resonated along her skin.

Ayana was drawn in by the deceptively powerful arms surrounding her. Jax had always had more brains than brawn, but there was a strength there that she hadn't expected. He was leanly muscled, with corded, well-defined biceps that fit perfectly underneath her palms.

"I didn't mean to startle you," he whispered in her ear.

"It's…it's okay," Ayana mumbled. She found purchase against his chest and levered herself up. Then she took two steps back. Then another.

Distance. She needed much, much distance when it came to Jackson Richards. Because apparently ten years and more than a thousand miles wasn't enough to teach her body the lesson her brain and heart had learned when Jax had left her.

He blew into his hands and rubbed them together, his eyes casually roaming around the square. "No luck?" he asked her.

It was obvious that being wrapped up in each other's arms again, even by accident, hadn't lit every inch of *his* body on fire. No, she was the only one foolish enough to allow feelings that had been buried a decade ago to resurface within hours of being near him.

"No," Ayana answered, more brusquely than she'd intended. She didn't want to give Jax the satisfaction of knowing that he had any effect on her whatsoever. "Have you tried calling him again?"

He held up his cell phone. "At least a dozen times. It's going straight to voice mail, and he's not answering text messages."

Ayana brought both hands up and massaged her temples. "Do you think he maybe went to one of the other resorts?"

"That was going to be my next suggestion," Jax said. "Do you have a recent picture of him stored in your phone? We can go around asking people if they've seen him."

God, this was truly starting to sound like one of those missing-persons shows on television. The thought sent a tremor of panic cascading down Ayana's spine.

"He's okay, Ayana," came Jax's warm, calming voice. She stared up at him. "I can still read everything you're thinking just by looking at you. You're brother hasn't come to any kind of harm, so don't even think that way."

For a brief moment, Austin's well-being took a backseat to the knowledge that her feelings were still so transparent to Jackson. When Ayana thought about just a few of the things that had crossed her mind since she'd first encountered him earlier today, it made her skin pebble with unease and embarrassment.

"I…uh, I don't have a recent picture of Austin. I cleared everything off my phone to make room for pictures this weekend."

"What's your number?" Jax asked, pulling his phone from his pocket. "I'll forward the one I took a couple of days ago. His face is partially covered, but it'll have to do. And before you ask, he made me take the picture so he could send it to Rachelle."

Ayana gave him her cell number and, seconds later, heard the ding of an incoming text message. She opened the message and laughed. Austin, whose adventurous side peaked at going to the grocery store without a prewritten shopping list, was straddling a snowmobile. He wore a puffy jacket and a helmet, and looked as if he was ready for the ride of his life.

"Let me guess, he got off the snowmobile a minute after you snapped the picture."

"You know your brother well." Jax laughed.

Ayana joined him, but then sobered. "I thought I knew him. I don't know what he's trying to pull with this stunt, though."

The pensive lines bracketing Jackson's mouth became more pronounced. "When was the last time you talked to Austin about anything relating to TR Software?"

"Not for a while," Ayana said. "Why? Is something happening with the business? Are you two in trouble?"

"No, no." Jax shook his head. "It's the opposite. We're on the verge of landing our biggest contract yet, a deal with the U.S. Department of Education. But Austin has been feeling the pressure. I think with that and the wedding all coming together at the same time, he may have... I don't know..."

"Snapped?" Ayana provided. Her throat swelled with alarm over the implications that insinuated.

"I don't think he's gone off the deep end," Jax said. "Hopefully, he just needed some time to clear his head."

Ayana glanced at the clock on her cell phone. "He has a little under twenty-four hours. If he hasn't cleared his mind by then, he's going to have a lot to answer for."

"Let's hope we can find him before then," Jax said.

As the first pillow-soft snow flurries began falling from the sky, she and Jax made their way back to the resort. They entered the lobby and Jax had the valet bring forward the SUV he'd rented. He waited for Ayana to get in before climbing behind the wheel and pulling out. They then spent the next hour showing Austin's picture around three neighboring ski resorts on the stretch of Highway 6 in Vail.

The storm that had been threatening all day had finally

made its way to this part of Colorado, and those previous snow flurries had grown into full-fledged flakes. The wind had picked up considerably, blowing so hard that the snow looked as if it was falling horizontally.

Despite the heat rushing out of the air vents, Ayana was still chilled. She wrapped her arms around her upper body, cursing her stupidity at leaving her coat.

Jackson looked over at her and immediately pulled the car onto the shoulder of the highway. Without a word, he tugged off his well-worn leather jacket and handed it to her. Ayana wanted to turn down his offer, but she was too sensible, and too darn cold, to do that.

She accepted his jacket with a muted "Thank you" and quickly threaded her arms through the sleeves. It was still warm from his body and covered in his scent. Suddenly, being cold didn't seem like such a bad thing. It was better than being completely surrounded by Jackson.

"The only other place I can think of is the chalet," Jax said.

"Are you talking about the place you two stayed in this past week?"

He nodded. "It's about fifteen minutes or so up the mountain. I'll bring you back to the resort and head up there."

"It doesn't make sense for you to bring me all the way back to the resort. Let's just go to the chalet."

He gestured to the windshield. "Look at this weather, Ayana. You don't need to tag along in this."

"A little snow isn't going to kill me," she said.

It infuriated her that he thought a little inclement weather was enough to deter her. His coddling had always been the biggest bone of contention between them. Because he was four years older, Jax had spent most of the years they'd known each other treating her like a little sister. Except for the year she'd turned eighteen, when their relationship had taken a decidedly non-siblinglike turn.

Well, she was twenty-eight now, and she refused to allow him to treat her as anything other than a grown woman.

"I'm coming to the chalet," Ayana said. "Drive."

He slid her a glance. "Have you always been this bossy?"

She cocked an eyebrow. "Don't you remember?"

Jax blew out a deep breath and shook his head. "How could I ever forget?"

Chapter 3

He should have demanded she go back to the resort.

Jax bit back a derisive snort. As if he could ever demand Ayana Taylor do anything she didn't want to do. He could no more control Ayana than he could control this storm that had begun to rage even more as they gingerly made their way up the mountain.

Jax had opted to stay in the cabin for a few more days so that he could get some uninterrupted work done when he wasn't joining in on the wedding festivities, but Austin still had a key. He could only hope that Austin had decided to come up here when he decided to pull his disappearing act.

Jax chanced a glance at the woman seated beside him. Should he try to engage her in a bit of civil conversation? Just because things had ended badly between them, it didn't mean that things had to remain that way for the rest of their lives, did it? He would give just about anything if he and Ayana could go back to being at least friendly toward one another. He missed having her as a friend.

Okay, so he missed having her as a whole lot more than just a friend, but if that's all she was willing to offer, he was more than willing to accept it. So far, even that wasn't looking like a viable option.

Jax knew he would have to take baby steps, and the first step on the road to him and Ayana developing a friendship again was actually getting her to do something other than bark at him.

"That's a nice color on you," Jax tried.

Ayana looked over at him, then without acknowledging him, brought her attention back to the towering pine trees outside the window.

Well, so much for civil conversation.

Jax stared at the road ahead, but his mind remained on Ayana. As much as he tried, he couldn't blame her for feeling the way she did. If they were to present the case of what happened between them ten years ago to an impartial jury, Jax figured twelve out of twelve would vote in favor of him being named the biggest asshole of the decade.

He'd been an experienced, somewhat worldly twenty-two-year-old, and she an innocent eighteen-year-old fresh out of high school. He'd known Ayana had had a crush on him since the first time he'd accompanied Austin home over Thanksgiving break during their freshmen year at UT. Her doe-eyed, worshipful looks had been cute, and a bit of an ego boost.

Until the year she'd turned sixteen. That was the year everything turned upside down.

Jax could still remember the precise moment his view of Ayana changed. He and Austin had traveled up to Dallas for spring break because Jax couldn't afford the trip to Cabo San Lucas where most of the guys in their fraternity had headed. He and Austin had been lounging on the teak deck that surrounded the large in-ground pool at the Taylors' palatial home when Ayana and three of her friends had entered through the French doors. They had all been wearing cover-ups over their swimsuits.

Jax had been rising from the lounger to get himself another beer when Ayana had peeled the cover-up off her shoulders to reveal a shiny metallic gold bikini that had made her skin look as if it had been kissed by the sun.

He'd tripped over his chair. Jax remembered hastily coming up with the excuse of having one too many beers when Austin had asked what was wrong. If he'd answered his friend honestly and told him that the sight of his baby sister had given him an instant hard-on, Jax wasn't sure if their friendship would have made it past that day.

Ever since that afternoon at that pool, Jax had looked at Ayana in a considerably more carnal light. She had gone from being his best friend's kid sister to being a woman, with luscious curves and the kind of hips that were made for gripping.

Their relationship had taken a flirtatious turn. During that week, when Ayana would plop down on the couch between him and Austin while they were watching movies in the Taylors' basement rec room, Jax would have the hardest time concentrating on the screen. In the mornings, when she entered the breakfast room wearing nothing but a T-shirt that hit her midthigh—a sight he'd seen numerous times over the years—Jax would have to excuse himself from the table. He lost count of the number of times he'd locked himself in the bathroom so he could relieve the pent-up lust that rushed through his veins.

For an entire year he resisted her siren's call, maintaining his distance when he visited the Taylors, making sure there were always other people around.

But a man could only resist to a certain point.

He'd fallen victim to his baser instincts one weekend

when Ayana and her friends had made the trip to UT for the Longhorns' game versus Texas A&M. Coming upon Ayana as she sat behind her brother's computer, Jackson had given in to months of curiosity and kissed her for the first time.

A year later, the night of her senior prom, they had taken things even further—much further—than either of them had expected it to go.

Jax's grip involuntarily tightened on the steering wheel.

Ten years later and he could still feel the sensation of Ayana's smooth skin as he'd caressed every part of her. He could taste her flavor on his tongue, feel the snug fit of her untouched body closing around him as he introduced her to the pleasures that could be found between a man and a woman.

Then he recalled the devastation on her face when he'd broken her heart by marrying another woman just a few weeks later. It was an image he had never been able to shake.

They rounded a narrow bend in the road and the chalet appeared, nestled among a copse of snow-covered pines. The first thing Jax noticed was the absence of any lights shining through the windowpanes, which didn't bode well for finding Austin there. Not to mention the lack of a car parked outside. The only remote garage opener was clipped to the visor of his rented SUV, so Austin couldn't have parked in the garage.

But maybe he'd taken a cab up to the chalet instead of driving his rental car. And maybe he was sitting in the dark. They were here, they might as well search the place.

Jax climbed out of the SUV and shivered at the temperature, which had dropped considerably from when they'd left the base of the mountain. He rounded the vehicle to open Ayana's door for her, but she was already out and on her way to the wooden steps that led to the chalet's porch.

"Careful," Jax called. How she managed to walk through the snow in those spike-heeled boots was beyond comprehension. Actually, why she even wore them defied logic. Although Jax wouldn't complain too much. She looked absolutely amazing in those boots. And sexy. God, did she look sexy.

She wobbled on the first step and Jax caught her arm. He cupped her elbow as they walked up the stairs, then he unlocked the door to the chalet and held it open so that she could enter ahead of him. Jax flipped the switch and the room was bathed in light.

"Austin," Ayana called.

Jax knew it was futile. Everything was just as he'd left it that morning, from the coffee cup he'd forgotten to put away to the papers and contracts strewn across the table in the dining area.

"Austin." Ayana went into the kitchen, then into the sunken living room. She turned back to him. "Look upstairs."

"He's not here, Ayana."

"Would you please just look? Maybe he's sleeping."

Jax blew out a tired breath and took the stairs to the loft area two at a time. Just as he'd expected, he found the bed still a disheveled mess, with the boxers and T-shirt he'd worn to bed strewn across it. Jax lifted them from the covers and balled them up, pitching them into the corner with the other dirty laundry.

He made his way back down the stairs and found the space empty.

"Ayana?"

There was no reply.

He turned and spotted the door to the back porch

cracked open. Before he could get there, the door opened wider and Ayana walked back inside. Her dark-brown hair was covered with delicate snowflakes that glittered like iridescent lights. Dressed all in white with the faux-fur collar of his leather jacket bunched up around her chin, she looked as if she belonged on the cover of a travel magazine for the Colorado Rockies. No, she looked as if she belonged on *every* cover of *every* magazine. Period.

"He's not here," she said with a dejected sigh.

Jackson's cell phone rang. He pulled it from his pocket. "It's Austin," he said, then answered. "Where the hell are you?"

Ayana rushed to his side.

"I…fine…" came the voice on the other end of the line.

"Shit, you're breaking up. I can barely hear you." Jax covered his exposed ear. "What did you say?"

"Said…fine. Still not…married. Tell Mom…don't call."

"Austin, where are you?" Jax asked again.

"Give me the phone." Ayana went to grab his cell, but Jax pivoted out of her reach.

"Austin!" he barked. He was met with the hollow silence of a dead phone line. Jax didn't know if he'd hung up on him or if the spotty service was the culprit, but he was angry all the same.

"What did he say?" Ayana asked.

"I could barely make it out, but it sounds as if he's still determined not to go through with the wedding."

Ayana's hands fisted at her sides. "I swear I'm going to kill him when I see him."

"You'll have to wait until I'm through with him," Jax said.

"Not a chance." She shook her head. "I get first dibs. I've known him longer. Besides, I still haven't paid him back for chopping all the hair off my Barbie dolls when I was six."

Chuckling, Jax put his hands on his hips and shook his head. "Can you at least save some hide for me to chew up?"

"Depends on how mad I am when I see him," Ayana said. "Let's get back down the mountain before this storm gets any worse."

Nodding his agreement, Jax led the way to the front door and held it open for her. "After you," he said.

Then he shut the lights off, locked up the chalet and followed Ayana to the SUV.

She was no expert, but Ayana didn't need a degree in meteorology to know that the snowstorm was about ten times worse than it had been when they'd first arrived at the chalet twenty minutes ago. She did her best to maintain her cool, composed facade, but her right hand gripped the underside of the passenger seat as Jax drove at a painstakingly slow pace through the blinding snow. She was from Dallas. The biggest danger she faced on the roadway was I-20 traffic after a football game.

Jax held the steering wheel with both hands and hunched forward, his forehead nearly touching the windshield. "I can't see a damn thing," he muttered. "Was this storm supposed to be this bad?"

"I don't know. I figured that once I arrived at the resort I wouldn't be leaving until my flight Sunday afternoon, so I didn't pay much attention to the weather forecast."

A branch smacked into the windshield, and Ayana jumped so high her head would have hit the car's roof if she wasn't held down by the seatbelt.

"Shit." Jax swerved the SUV to avoid another flying branch. "Sorry," he said.

"It's okay. Just concentrate on what you're doing."

They covered another few yards before Jax slowed the SUV to a crawl. "What's that?"

Ayana peered through the windshield, making out red-and-blue police lights flashing through the thick snowfall. As they pulled closer, she was able to discern what had brought the police to this spot. A huge tree had fallen, blocking the entire roadway and at least eight feet on either side of it.

Jax stopped several yards ahead of the downed tree. Ayana noticed that the flashing lights were mounted to the front rack of one of those all-terrain four-wheelers. The officer driving it wore a slicker and a brimmed police hat that was covered in plastic and secured with a leather strap under his chin. He drove up to the driver's side of the SUV and motioned for Jax to roll his window down.

"There's no getting past," the officer said. "Slope is too steep on either side of the tree."

"How long will this be blocking the roadway?" Jax asked.

"The storm is predicted to blow through by midnight, so we should have a crew here no later than six."

"Six in the morning?" Ayana screeched.

"Yes, ma'am."

"Is there another way down the mountain?" Jax asked.

"Just the hiking trails, and you don't want to do that," the officer said.

"What about that thing?" Ayana asked, gesturing to his vehicle. "Can't you give us a ride?"

He shook his head. "Against department policy unless it's a dire medical situation."

"But we—" Ayana started, but then a strong gust blew so hard it rocked the SUV. Despite the chin strap, the officer had to clamp his hand on his head to keep his hat from flying off.

"I suggest you two head back up the mountain before this thing gets any worse," he called. "With this wind, there's no saying if another tree will fall. You don't want to get stuck on this road with no way up or down."

She definitely didn't want that. Ayana could hardly fathom the thought of having to spend the night in the chalet with Jax. How much worse would it be to spend the night stuck in this SUV with him?

Jax thanked the officer and rolled up the window.

"Is that it?" Ayana asked. "You're not going to even try to talk him into giving us a ride down the mountain?"

"You heard the man, Ayana. And be honest, do you really want to ride that thing down this mountain? You would be an icicle by the time you reached the resort."

At the moment it was better than the alternative. She would surely go up in flames if she had to endure the next twelve hours in the same house with Jax.

He executed a tight three-point turn in the middle of the narrow road and started back up the mountain.

Good Lord, they really were stuck together. The reality of it hit her with the force of the branch that had smacked into the SUV's windshield not long ago.

She could *not* do this; she would go crazy. Or do something even worse, like jump him when he wasn't looking and attack that mouth that had been calling to her for the past two hours.

How in the name of all that was holy was she still so ridiculously attracted to this man? She hadn't set eyes on Jax other than in pictures since the day of his and Austin's graduation from UT, just two months after he'd taken her virginity on the lumpy mattress of the guest room in her parents' home.

Their graduation day was the same day that Ayana had

learned that he'd married another woman just a week be-fore—a girlfriend she had known nothing about.

He should be the last man she was attracted to, but she couldn't deny what she felt. And God help her, they had to share a cabin while this winter storm raged around them.

Something else occurred to her that instantly caused her limbs to tremble.

"What if the power goes out?" she asked. "I noticed the firewood crate when I was out on the porch. It had only a few pieces in it. That's not enough to last the night."

"There's at least another twenty logs stacked in the iron trunk on the side porch," Jax said. "And you don't have to worry about the power. I made sure to rent a chalet with a backup generator. If the power does go out, all I have to do is flip a switch and we're up and running."

Of course he'd thought to rent a place with a backup generator. Jackson had always been the type of person to have contingency plans for his contingency plans. He was as methodical as her brother. The trait drove her crazy whenever she had to deal with Austin. For some reason, however, with Jackson it was sexy.

She dropped her head into her hand and emitted a groan.

"Spending the night in the same house with me is not the end of the world, Ayana. I know the cabin isn't that big, but I'm sure you'll figure out a way to avoid me." She heard the hint of frustration in his voice. He looked over at her and said, "That's what you're planning to do, aren't you?"

"Do you blame me, Jackson?" She twisted in her seat and stared at him. "Honestly, why should I give you the time of day after what you did to me?"

Her question was met with silence.

"Thought so," Ayana said.

He shook his head and returned his attention to the road. Minutes later, they were turning back into the drive that led to the chalet. Under different circumstances, she would have been excited at the prospect of spending the night in the quaint cabin. The picture it created was worthy of a postcard, surrounded by the snowy pines with the dark-blue velvet sky as its backdrop. The cabin itself wasn't huge; rather, it was the perfect size for a cozy, romantic winter getaway.

And here she was, preparing to spend the night with the one man who had crushed every romantic dream she'd ever held. The universe had a perverse sense of humor.

Jackson used a remote to raise the door on the garage located directly underneath the chalet. Ayana was grateful they had made it back to the cabin without skidding off the mountain road, but the thought of the upcoming hours here with Jax left her on the verge of full-fledged panic.

Jackson turned off the ignition but didn't get out of the car. Instead, he took a deep breath and said, "Look, Ayana, I know there is some really bad stuff in our past, but we're stuck here together, and even once we get back to the resort we're going to be in each other's company throughout the entire weekend. Can we please just call a truce?"

Ayana remained silent, ruminating over his statement, realizing that this was a definitive juncture. At this very moment, she had the ability to define their relationship going forward. Could she find it within her being to forgive Jax for the way he'd broken her heart all those years ago, and give them the chance to rebuild the friendship they'd once shared? Or did they continue as they had for the past ten years, virtual strangers?

Pulling in a deep breath, Ayana finally said, "If we're going to spend the next twelve hours avoiding each other, then there's no need for a truce, is there?"

With that she climbed out of the SUV and waited for him at the door that led to the chalet.

Chapter 4

He had never been one to give in without a fight, but Jax wasn't sure he was up for this. Being stuck with Ayana all night was punishment of the torturous, kill-yourself-because-death-must-surely-be-better-than-this kind. Of course, he didn't have to worry about coming up with creative suicide tactics. He would surely die of lust well before the Vail Police Department ever removed that damn tree.

They had to come to some kind of understanding. Jax would settle for just having the opportunity to clear the air about what had happened between them a decade ago.

He'd tried several times over the years to explain his side of the story, but early on it became painfully apparent that Ayana had no desire to hear anything he had to say. She'd had no desire to even be around him long enough to hear his side of the story. After the first couple of years, Jax had stopped trying, accepting the likelihood that he would probably never earn her forgiveness.

Austin's wedding had changed everything. When he'd

learned that she would make the trip to Colorado, he knew it would probably be the only chance he'd have to make things right between them. He'd vowed to figure out a way to get Ayana alone so that he could apologize—*really* apologize—for his role in what had happened between them all those years ago.

Jax just hadn't realized he'd have this much time with her. He also hadn't anticipated that, when finally faced with the opportunity to express his regret over breaking her heart, it would be so difficult to actually do it.

In a life filled with varying degrees of regrets, hurting the woman standing just a few feet away from him was one of his biggest. The timing of it all couldn't have been any worse. After years of a gradually escalating flirtation, on the night of her prom, he and Ayana had finally given in to the strong feelings between them. They had engaged in a love affair that rivaled anything he'd ever seen in the movies.

If Jax had known that a girl he had only casually dated would show up weeks later, pregnant and fearful of being disowned by her entire family, he would have handled things a lot differently.

He'd been left with an impossible choice: allow a baby he'd fathered to enter this world a bastard, the way he had, or break the heart of the woman he loved. Jax had done what he believed was the honorable thing, and Ayana had suffered because of it.

Guilt over the callousness with which he'd hurt her had haunted him for years. Ten years later, he was still trying to figure out the best way to make up for the pain he'd caused. He would, though. Jax was determined to make things right.

He led the way into the cabin from the side door that led up from the garage. When they entered, Ayana walked straight to the other side of the kitchen island. She rested her hands on the back of a barstool and looked around, a pensive frown pulling down the corners of her mouth.

"Is the temperature okay?" Jax asked. He'd left it set at seventy-eight, but with the bitter wind blowing outside, the central unit was having a hard time keeping up.

"It's fine," she said in an emotionless tone.

She was only a few feet away, yet she seemed so unapproachable she might as well have been in another town. It would be easier to go to their separate corners and wait out the storm. All they had to do was get through this weekend and they could resume their normal lives.

But Jax didn't want to just get through the weekend. He didn't want to go another ten years without seeing her.

If only she had given him the chance to explain, instead of letting all those years go by with nothing but animosity between them.

It wasn't for lack of trying on his part. Immediately following the demise of his short seven-month marriage, Jax had driven out to Lubbock, where Ayana was in school at Texas Tech. He'd been determined to set things straight between them. But Ayana had refused to talk to him, going so far as threatening to call the campus police if he didn't get away from her dorm.

Over the years she'd made a concerted effort to avoid him. Jax remembered the precise moment when it became apparent to him that the fact that they always missed each other was not happenstance. He'd taken a surprise trip to the Taylors' for Easter. Ayana had called her mother on her way to their home, but once Denise told her that Jax was in town, Ayana had all of a sudden remembered a girls-only weekend trip that she claimed had been planned by one of her friends. Jax would bet his last dollar that the spur-of-the-moment trip had been prompted by his arrival.

It was time to end this estrangement between them. At the absolute least, he wanted to rediscover the friendship they'd once shared.

Even more than that, he wanted to reignite the passion that had sparked that first night they were together, when the girl he'd been attracted to had become the woman he couldn't get out of his mind. He didn't know how serious she was about the guy she'd come here with, but she'd hardly mentioned him since they'd left the resort. She couldn't be *that* into him.

That thought gave Jax the impetus he needed.

"Ayana, can I just say something?" he opened.

She looked over at him. The cynicism he'd sensed in her earlier had diminished. Whether it was because she was softening toward him, or because she was just tired after a long, exhausting day, Jax didn't know, but he planned to take full advantage.

"If you will allow me, I want to apologize," he said.

She folded her arms over her chest. "For?"

She was not going to make this easy.

"For the way things went down between us ten years ago."

She dropped her arms and blew out a weary breath. "Jackson, I just want to get through tonight."

"And I just want to apologize for hurting you."

"Fine, I accept your apology," she said. Then she turned on her heel and walked into the sunken living room.

Jax followed, but stopped at the threshold of the room. He stared mutely as Ayana sat down on the sofa, crossed her legs and picked up the remote. She clicked through the channels until she stumbled upon an episode of *Friends*. She tossed the remote on the coffee table and that was that.

Jax ran both hands down his face.

What had he expected? That she would run into his

arms and immediately forgive him for the heartache he'd caused her?

Rubbing at the ache that had settled in his chest, Jax made his way to the dining area. The alcove had served as his and Austin's war room over the past seven days. He still had enough work to keep him busy for the next two weeks straight, and then some. If he wasn't going to play host for his guest, there was no excuse not to work.

He fired up his laptop and logged in to the system of algorithms he'd been working on for the past five months. The software he and Austin had developed for streamlining the ordering system for school lunch programs wasn't sexy, but if they were able to sell it to the Department of Education, it would be, by far, their most profitable product.

Jax believed in the software he'd created, but it was the effectiveness of the sales pitch that would win them the contract. The fact that Mr. Missing in Action himself was their salesman had him a bit on edge. With the stunt Austin pulled today, Jax wasn't sure he trusted him with something so crucial to the future of their company.

He felt guilty even thinking that way. TR Software Design had been Austin's original concept, and Jax knew the company's well-being was just as important to Austin as it was to him. This year, only nine years after opening its doors, they had grossed eight figures. If they won the contract for the school lunch software, their profits would double.

But they had to win the contract first.

No, first Austin had to come to his senses and get married. If he foolishly allowed Rachelle to slip through his fingers, Jax knew his friend would regret it for the rest of his life.

Experience had taught him that piece of wisdom.

Shaking off the sobering thought, he pulled up the algorithms and attempted to work, but his mind kept wandering to the woman sitting not even ten yards from him. A few minutes ago he'd heard a clacking sound and realized that she had taken off those lovely boots that would fill his dreams for many nights to come. Apparently, she was making herself more comfortable.

Jax ran a hand down his face and bit back a groan.

How many nights had he dreamed of having Ayana in his home, getting more comfortable? He'd lost count of the number of times he'd walked into his empty condo and just stood in the doorway, imagining how different his life would have been if he had taken a different course of action when Kandace had come to him, pregnant and afraid. He understood now that the choice he'd made had been the wrong one for everyone involved, most of all Ayana.

But Jax was a firm believer in second chances. He'd given one to his dad, who had found him through an internet search about six years ago. If he could find it in his heart to give the man who'd abandoned his mother while she was pregnant a second chance, Jax knew that Ayana, whose heart was as pure as they came, could do the same. He just needed to give her a little push.

So why was he sitting in here?

Jax closed his laptop and pushed away from the table.

He only had a few hours to repair years of damage. If he had any chance of making things right with Ayana, he had to get to work.

Like a Christmas miracle, he had been given a second chance to win back the woman who owned his heart. He wasn't going to waste another minute.

Ayana had tried her best to keep up her stony facade, but it was getting harder as time ticked by. For one thing, it had never been in her nature to be this cold, unfeeling person. Even when she was not trying to, she always saw the best in people.

Secondly, Jax had been nothing but a gentleman since they had reached the chalet. It would be easier to maintain her frosty attitude if he was behaving like the bastard she'd made him out to be in her mind all these years.

Instead, he was acting like the Jackson she'd fallen in love with.

Ensconced in this cozy, romantic setting with him, it would be all too easy to shut out the memory of their estrangement and pretend they were those two young lovers who couldn't get enough of each other.

But where would that leave them tomorrow, when reality set in? More importantly, where would it leave her heart? Whenever the tiniest thought arose that even hinted at opening herself up to Jackson again, it was immediately followed by recollections of the pain he'd put her through. Why would she ever purposely set herself up for that kind of fall?

Her stomach interrupted her thoughts as it let out a loud, rolling rumble. Ayana covered it with both hands, instantly regretting not going through the buffet line with Shawntell when she'd asked earlier at the rehearsal party.

Pushing up the sleeves of her sweater, she levered herself up from the sofa and headed for the kitchen. She stopped short as she encountered a pitiful pine branch in a small trash can that she hadn't noticed tucked into the corner. A string of popcorn had been wrapped around it and a paper star was stuck on the top.

Ayana shook her head, unable to stop the smile that stretched across her face. This must have been Jax and Austin's attempt at a Christmas tree. She recalled the Christmases they'd all spent together and how Jackson would constantly compare it to the Christmases he'd had as a child: lonely holidays he'd spent with his grandmother because his mother was always working. Ayana's heart pinched at the memory.

Her stomach let out another angry grumble and she went into the kitchen to find something to fill it. The refrigerator was frighteningly bare, with only a couple of bottles of Pellegrino, a wedge of cheese and white grapes. She opened what she thought was the pantry, but found a broom, mop and bucket instead.

She then went from cabinet to cabinet, hoping to find something. She had been so concerned with finding ways to fill the hours she would be cooped up in here with Jackson that she hadn't given much thought to other important things, like not starving. She opened a top cabinet and spotted a box of crackers. She reached up, tapping her fingers on the shelf.

She whipped around at the sound of a low, deep chuckle behind her.

Jax was leaning against the thick wooden logs that separated the kitchen from the rest of the downstairs area. His arms were crossed over his chest, and the most devastating smile in the history of mankind graced his lips. Once again Ayana was hit with a wave of longing that arrested the breath in her lungs. When was the last time someone had made her feel this way, simply with a smile?

In that moment, she was forced to admit that her life had not been as bright without him in it.

"Vertically challenged, just like your brother," Jax said.

He walked over to her and reached into the cabinet. As his long body stretched up, it brushed against hers.

Ayana's legs turned to water at the feel of all the solid muscle pressing against her, despite the layers of clothing between them. She looked over her shoulder and found Jax staring down at her. His breathing had ramped up and his eyes had taken on a decidedly smoldering look. She didn't even have to ask, she knew just by staring at him that he'd felt the same current that had rocketed through her.

Over the years she'd tried to tell herself that it was just a schoolgirl crush, but Ayana could no longer deny the depths of her feelings for him. A crush didn't linger this long.

Jackson held up the box. "Is this what you were looking for?" His voice was huskier than it had been just moments ago.

Ayana swallowed and nodded. "I didn't have dinner." As if to put an exclamation point on the statement, her stomach let out another loud growl. She clutched her hands to it.

Jax grinned. "You didn't have to tell me twice."

If mortification was money, she could retire in style right now.

Her sleeves rolled down again, and she pushed them up to her elbows.

"Are you hot?" Jax asked.

Scorching. Especially in one place in particular.

"No, the temperature's fine. It's this sweater. It isn't made for lounging around." She looked down at her ensemble. "For that matter, neither are the pants."

"Both look amazing on you," Jax said. When she started to speak, he put both hands up in a gesture of surrender. "I'm just stating facts, Ayana."

She folded her arms over her chest, and with a defensive lift of her chin, said, "For your information, I was going to say thank you."

It was a lie. "Thank you" definitely was *not* what she was preparing to say, but Ayana was grateful that Jax had stopped her before she'd spoken. All evening her antagonism toward him had been met with affability. In fact, Jackson had gone out of his way to be agreeable when she had done the exact opposite. She was starting to question the justification of her staunch resentment. As much as he'd hurt her, what happened between the two of them had taken place so long ago. Surely the statute of limitations had expired.

Besides, did she really want to come across as this bitter, grudge-holding person who had not been able to get over something that happened when she was eighteen? Did she want Jackson to think that he had that much power over her?

He set the crackers on the kitchen counter and stuffed his hands into the front pockets of the dark-blue corduroy pants he wore.

"Uh, if you want to change into something more comfortable, I have a couple of pieces of clean laundry left. Go upstairs and grab a T-shirt and some sweatpants." Another of those half grins drew across his face. "You'll have to roll the cuffs up about a dozen times, but at least you'll be comfortable."

"Ha, ha," Ayana deadpanned. "Everyone knows the Taylors are short. Stop rubbing it in."

"I prefer *petite*," he said. "Your brother just *loves* it when I call him that."

Ayana let out a crack of laughter, then quickly covered her mouth with both hands.

Jackson sobered. His expression turned bittersweet as he titled his head to the side and quietly said, "You know, Ayana, it's okay to laugh. You're not committing some grave sin just because you let down your guard for a moment and felt something other than disgust toward me." He looked down at his feet before bringing his eyes up to hers again. "I'm not the enemy you're making me out to be," he finished in a strained voice.

Emotion tightened her throat as she considered his words.

Letting go of past hurts and the bitter feelings she'd held toward Jackson was simple in theory, but there was a tiny place inside of her where the pain was still raw, as if it was just yesterday that he'd introduced his new wife to the Taylor family. Just the chance of unleashing that kind of hurt on her heart again was enough to make Ayana think twice before letting Jax into her life again.

But she was older now, wiser. She was so far removed from that love-struck eighteen-year-old she had been the last time she'd seen him. She knew to protect her heart this time around.

"I truly am sorry," he said, his eyes and voice filled with remorse. He reached out and captured her upper arm, as if he was afraid she would escape. "I know you don't want to hear it, but if you never grant me anything else ever again, please just give me a chance to apologize. To *really* apologize."

Ayana pried his fingers from around her arm, but she didn't leave. She took a couple of steps back, let out a deep breath and said, "Okay. I'm listening."

Jax's head reared back slightly, as if he had been expecting another fight. Finally, with a hapless hunch of his shoulders, he held his hands out and said, "I'm sorry. I know the words don't even begin to make up for my actions, but at this point they're all I can offer. You have to know that I never meant to hurt you, and knowing that I did has haunted me all these years."

It took several attempts before she was able to push words past the knot of emotion that had wedged itself in her throat. "You did hurt me," she said. After a moment she added, "But I also know you didn't mean to."

Jax's eyes widened with cautious hope, exposing just how much her acceptance of his apology meant to him. Ayana's chest pinched at the naked vulnerability he wasn't even trying to hide.

"I came to that conclusion a long time ago," she continued. Shaking her head, she stared at him, a rueful smile tilting her lips. "It's just not in you to do something so heartless just for the hell of it, Jax. I knew there had to be a reason for you to walk away from me the way you did. I don't know the circumstances surrounding what happened between you and your wife—"

"Ex-wife," he interjected. "She was my wife for such a short period of time she doesn't deserve the title. And what happened—"

Ayana held up her hands. "It doesn't matter."

"Yes, it does."

"No, really. It doesn't." She sucked in a deep breath. "It was ten years ago, Jax. It shouldn't even matter anymore. I've allowed your marriage to affect my life for much longer than I should have."

He pinched his eyes shut and tilted his head back, expelling a harsh breath toward the ceiling. He returned his gaze to her and, holding both hands out in a pleading gesture, said, "That's just it, Ayana. My marriage—if you can even call it that—has been the wedge between us all this time. If we're really going to put this behind us, then I need you to hear this. Please."

It was the plea in his voice that was her undoing, along with the utter misery in his eyes. She wasn't prepared to hear this, had told herself that it didn't matter why he'd made her fall in love with him, then crushed her. But when faced with the raw emotion emanating from Jackson, she didn't have the strength to deny his request.

Backing up until the small of her back met the kitchen counter, Ayana braced herself for whatever he was about to share.

Jackson rubbed his hands down the sides of his pants. Ayana recognized the nervous gesture and said, "Just spit it out, Jax."

He began to pace in the small area in front of the kitchen island. Clearing his throat, he started. "One of my biggest fears all these years is that you might have thought the time we were together was just some…some…"

"Random hookup of convenience?" she offered.

Jax stopped and turned to her, his eyes teeming with regret.

"No," he said on a ragged sigh. "God, Ayana. Is that what you've been thinking all these years?" He dragged his palms down his face, his expression the epitome of pure misery. "Do you know how long I fought the feelings I had for you? If it had only been about convenience, do you think I would have waited so long to be with you?"

Her lungs expanded with the deep breath she pulled in. Her throat tight with emotion, Ayana pointed out, "There was also the matter of me being underage."

"I'd like to think that would have stopped me, but it wouldn't have." Jax shook his head, and with a humorless laugh, admitted, "For two years before I ever laid a hand on you I went to bed dreaming about you every single night." His gaze captured hers and held it. In a devastatingly soft voice, he said, "I was so in love with you, Ayana. My heart belonged to you way before you ever knew it."

Ayana wrapped her arms around her stomach, desperately needing to ward off his words, unable to handle his honesty. When she thought about all the time she'd spent loving him, the nights she'd fallen asleep dreaming of him, hoping and wishing and praying that he could somehow be hers. To learn that he'd had those same feelings for her… only to throw it all away.

"Why, Jackson?" The words came out on a hoarse whisper. Ayana pulled her bottom lip between her teeth in an effort to stop its trembling. "How…how can you tell me you loved me, yet you married someone else? How could you get some other girl pregnant if that's how you really felt about me?"

"Because you were off-limits! Dammit, Ayana!" He

rubbed the back of his neck as he resumed his pacing. "You were Austin's baby sister. Put yourself in my shoes for a minute. Here I was, sharing an apartment with my best friend and sneaking into his room when he wasn't there so I could stare at the picture of you he kept on his desk. I felt like a damn pervert. I was so messed up inside, I didn't know what to think."

"So when did your ex-wife enter the picture? I didn't even know you were dating anyone at the time, Jackson."

"Because it was never anything serious," he said. Ayana gave him an unconvinced look. "Okay, it was serious enough for her to get pregnant."

He blew out a frustrated breath. "Kandace was my failed attempt to prove to myself that I wasn't destined to be in love with somebody that I knew I could never have. I thought I could bury the feelings I had for you if I tried hard enough. We dated for a few months, but mutually decided to break things off. She could tell that my heart wasn't in it." He looked up at her. "Because my heart belonged to someone else."

Ayana tilted her head back and stared at the beams that stretched across the vaulted ceiling, trying to digest all that she'd just heard. She returned her attention to Jackson, willing herself to not be affected by the naked pain so evident in his eyes.

"So…so you weren't still sleeping with her during the time we were together?" she asked.

He shook his head. Taking a step toward her, he said in an achingly gentle voice, "The night we first made love was the first time in months that I'd slept with anyone. And I never slept with Kandace again, even after we were married. The baby was the only reason I married her."

"What happened to the baby?" Ayana asked. She had never gathered the courage to ask Austin about Jax's child.

"He was stillborn. Kandace went into labor at twenty-six weeks. I stayed with her for a few weeks after she got out of the hospital, but there was no reason to pretend that our marriage was going to last. We got a divorce and went our separate ways."

Jax held his hands out to her. "You were it for me, Ayana. From the minute my lips first touched yours, I knew I was done." He took her hands in his and brought them to his lips. Grazing her skin with the gentlest kiss imaginable, he whispered, "I am so sorry I ever hurt you. You have to know it's the last thing I ever wanted to do."

It was hard to hold back the emotion threatening to overcome her.

All these years she'd spent despising him, blaming him. And why? What had her hatred of Jackson really gained her?

She had allowed herself to grow so bitter that she had obliterated all of the good memories the two of them had shared. And there had been many.

Things didn't have to be this way between them. Ayana didn't know if they would ever find the friendship they'd once shared, but what good would it do for the two of them to continue living with such animosity between them?

"I'm sorry, too," she said.

Jax's eyes met hers. "For what?"

"For never giving you the chance to apologize, or to explain your side of the story. Thank you for making me listen," she said. "And I really do accept your apology. I've spent so much mental energy hating you all these years, and nothing good has come of it. I'm done living with this negativity, Jax.

"Earlier you asked for a truce, but I want to go a step further." His eyes widened with unmistakable interest and Ayana let out a crack of teary laughter. "Not that," she said. Some things never changed.

"Look, Jax, before we crossed that line ten years ago,

we were good friends. Years ago, I resigned myself to the fact that I would have to live my life without you, but I've evolved enough to admit that my life was happier when you were a part of it."

His palm came up to cradle her face. "Ayana." Her name came out on a plea as he leaned toward her.

She took a step back and held her hands up. "Friendship," she said. "I'm offering friendship, Jackson."

A flash of disappointment crossed his face. He retreated a step and sucked in a deep breath. "Okay," he said. "I'll gladly take anything you're willing to give. Thank you," he said.

"Thank *you*," she replied. "I meant what I said, Jax. I'm glad to have you back in my life."

Jackson nodded toward the stairs. "Why don't you go up and change. My clothes are in the top drawer of the chest. I'll make us something to eat."

Ayana stared at him for a moment, almost unable to believe how just deciding that she was done hating him had changed her entire outlook. It felt as if a weight that had been pressing down on her shoulders for years had suddenly lifted.

"Thank you," she said. "I'll only be a minute." Then she bounded up the stairs, her heart feeling lighter than it had in more than a decade.

Chapter 5

Jackson focused all of his concentration on carving the wedge of Parmigiano-Reggiano into paper-thin slices. He tried to ignore the sound of the water rushing through the pipes in the wall, and how that same water would eventually cascade down Ayana's naked body. Just a second ago, she'd called down to him from the loft that overlooked the bottom floor, asking if he was okay with her taking a shower. Now he couldn't focus on anything but the thought of her bare, dripping-wet skin.

At the moment, Jax couldn't think of a single possession he owned that he wouldn't gladly trade for the opportunity to join her in that shower. He gripped the edge of the countertop, trying to stave off the tidal wave of wanting that crashed into him.

He thought after the conversation they'd had just a few minutes ago that things would be easier, especially after he'd accomplished part of his goal without even trying. He'd apologized for the way he'd hurt her ten years ago, and she had accepted. It was more than he had been able to achieve in over a decade. It should have been enough.

But it wasn't. He wanted so much more from her.

He wanted Ayana to want him again, the way he wanted her. He wanted her to be okay with him stepping into that shower with her. No, he wanted her to be the one to invite him inside.

It was asking for far too much, far too soon. He knew this, but it didn't stop him from craving it all the same. He just hoped there was a chance in hell that she could one day feel the same way about him.

Just a few hours ago Jax wouldn't have believed it possible, but just a few hours ago he also didn't believe he could ever convince Ayana to look at him with anything other than disgust.

'Twas the season for miracles. Maybe there was one in store for the two of them.

As the water beat down on her head, Ayana's bones practically melted. She felt more relaxed than she usually did after a ninety-minute hot-stone massage at one of her day spas. Now that she and Jax had come to an understanding, the stress that had been building over the past several hours had plummeted. She was ready to move forward.

With caution, of course.

Ayana was wise enough not to let down her guard completely. Although she would never admit it to him, she knew exactly the kind of power Jackson wielded over her heart. She wasn't foolish enough to make herself that vulnerable again.

But now that she had yielded just this small bit to him, it was all too easy to recall the effect Jax had on her, mind, body and soul. Especially after discovering that he had been struggling with the same feelings she had struggled with all these years.

As she rubbed soap over her body, her mind focused exactly where she knew it would...on the man downstairs. Ayana smoothed both of her hands over her flat stomach, imagining they were Jax's. She brought her right hand up and across, to her left breast, cupping it, squeezing it, applying pressure to her aching nipple. Her left hand traveled down her belly to the spot between her legs that was bare after the Brazilian wax treatment she'd received just a few days ago at Tranquil Pleasures's Plano location.

Ayana bit her lip as she slipped one finger between the folds that had already become slick with want. She rubbed up and down, swirling her finger around the protruding bead of nerves that pulsed and ached at her cleft. Leaning back against the shower's stone-tiled walls, she opened her legs wider and brought her right hand down to join the left. As one continued to massage her aching clitoris, the other rubbed up and down her soaking sex before slipping inside.

Her shoulder blades burned as she pressed them against the wall. Her legs quivered, her knees growing weaker as her entire body began to tremble with her impending orgasm. She stroked herself faster, harder, moving her fingers in and out until she was nearly blinded by a burst of white-hot pleasure.

"Oh, my God," Ayana breathed as she slumped against the shower wall. She pulled in several deep breaths, trying like crazy to draw air into her lungs.

On legs that were still shaky from the cataclysmic release, Ayana stepped out of the shower. She took one look at herself in the mirror and cringed in mortified horror. How was she going to face Jackson after what she'd just done?

She kept her eyes averted from the bed as best she

could as she entered the bedroom in search of clothes. She opened the top drawer and found a faded Philadelphia Eagles T-shirt along with black-and-green plaid pants. As far as fashion statements went, it was a disaster, but at least she would be comfortable.

She padded down the stairs, finding Jackson standing at the sink, his back to her. He'd taken off his sweater, leaving him in a T-shirt and his dark-blue corduroy pants. Her stomach flipped at the sight of the thin fabric stretching taut across the muscles of his upper back and shoulders. Computer engineers were not known for their fine physiques, but Jax dispelled the common computer-geek stereotype. He had the perfect body. Always had.

He turned. "Hi," he said, his eyes bright with energy that had not been there before. "You feel better?"

Oh, if he only knew.

Ayana nodded. "Much. Thanks. Although you were right about the pants." She stretched out one leg. "They're about twelve inches too long."

Jax laughed, but then his forehead wrinkled with his frown.

"What?" Ayana asked.

"I was planning on wearing those tonight."

"Oh. Sorry. I can put on something else."

"No." His eyes traveled the length of her body. "They look a whole lot better on you." The huskiness in his voice traveled down her spine like a gentle caress, but there was nothing gentle about the heat in his eyes. It was hot enough to scorch.

Suddenly the chalet seemed a thousand times smaller.

Ayana tried to tear her eyes away, but Jax's intense stare drew her in, causing all the feelings she'd thought long buried to resurface. The naked desire on his face, the fierce passion resonating from his entire being grabbed hold of her and refused to let go.

Despite her vow to hold her cards close to her chest, to not reveal just how much his earlier words had affected her, Ayana couldn't keep the vulnerability from showing through her eyes. She loved him. She'd loved him since she was fourteen. And just like that, he'd barreled his way right back into her heart.

"Ayana—" Jax started.

"That bedroom and bath are amazing," she said, cutting him off, grateful that her voice didn't shake with the yearning that was coursing through her. "How did you and Austin decide who would sleep in the master bedroom?"

Jax just continued to stare at her with those intense brown eyes that saw too much.

"Did you two flip a coin?" she asked.

"Ayana, don't," Jackson said. "We need to talk about this."

"Talk about…" Ayana took a moment to swallow past the lust collecting in her throat. "Talk about what?"

"About what's happening here. About you and me."

Ayana brought both hands up to her head and massaged her temples. "Jax, I told you I was open to friendship. That's all. You can't expect us to just go back to the way things were after ten years."

"Even if we feel the same way about each other?"

"Who said I feel the same way about you?" she argued. "For God's sake, Jackson. I came to Colorado with another man! Do you really expect me to just fall back into your arms?"

"What about the guy you're with? You've hardly mentioned Kenneth."

"Keith."

"Whatever." He folded his arms across his chest.

"Things can't be that serious between you two. You've been away from the resort for hours, and he hasn't even called."

"He's sick."

Jax just continued to stare at her.

God, how could he still see right through her?

"Fine," she blew out on an exasperated breath. "Keith and I aren't serious. But that's beside the point. This is about the two of us. And the only thing we'll ever have between us is friendship. If that's not good enough for you, we can go back to being strangers."

Ayana could practically see the war taking place in his head. She wasn't sure which side she wanted to win. Her brain knew it was imperative that she keep Jax a safe distance from her heart. Unfortunately, her heart was having none of that. If only he knew how close her heart was to opening to him again.

"What will it be, Jackson?"

Without another word, he lifted a wooden tray filled with various plates and led the way into the sunken living room. Ayana sat, folding her legs underneath her on the sofa as Jax settled the tray on the coffee table.

Before he took his seat, she captured his forearm. When he looked down at her, she said, "Are we good, Jax? I don't want the rest of this night to be awkward."

After a moment's hesitation, he gave her a slight nod, and said, "We're good."

Relief fluttered through her chest. She wasn't sure she could face another tension-filled minute, let alone an entire night of it.

"Wow, look at you," Ayana said as she took in the spread before her. He'd sliced the wedge of cheese she'd spotted in the refrigerator, along with a roll of hard salami she'd apparently missed. There were also the grapes, crackers and a bowl full of almonds.

"I had to work with what I had," Jackson said with a shrug. "I only bought enough food to get through the few days I have left at the cabin, and I figured I'd have a few meals at the wedding."

"And you weren't expecting company."

He looked over at her. "I don't mind the company."

Ayana was doing her damnedest to prevent her heart from melting, but her damnedest wasn't good enough. She should have been mortified at how quickly she'd fallen under Jackson's spell again, but wasn't this the reason she'd avoided him all these years? She had always known that with very little effort Jax could worm his way back into her heart.

He held up a bottle of wine—something else she hadn't seen when she'd rummaged through the cabinets.

"Please," she said when he gestured to her glass.

He filled both, then lifted his glass. "To your brother's wedding."

"May it still go on as planned," Ayana said, clinking her glass with Jax's.

"It will," Jax said after taking a sip. "Austin is too smart to call off the wedding. It's just cold feet."

"I hope you're right."

"I am. I've known him a long time."

"You have," she said. She tipped her head to the side and a wistful grin drifted over her lips. "Do you remember that first Christmas you spent with us?"

"The one when your mom had to order pizza because the stove went out just as she was preparing to bake the ham?"

"Yes." Ayana laughed. "We thought that would be the

first and last time you'd ever come to the Taylors' for a holiday."

"Are you kidding me? I used to live for holidays with your family. They were a helluva lot better than anything else I had going for me."

Ayana instantly sobered. Jax had not kept his upbringing a secret from them. His father had left before he was born, and his mother had spent much of his childhood working two—sometimes three—jobs. He'd been raised by his maternal grandmother, who, after several years enjoying the freedom of being done with childrearing, had not been very enthusiastic about having to raise her grandson.

Jax had told them during that very first Christmas that he would have probably spent it by himself in their empty dorm room if Austin had not extended the invitation for him to join their family. He'd spent every major holiday with them throughout his college years.

Ayana had fallen harder and deeper in love with him with every visit he'd made to their home. He had been so easy to love back then. As she sat next to him right now, she feared that not much had changed on that score.

Rubbing the stem of the wineglass between his palms, Jax quietly admitted, "I envied your family so much. I thought families like yours only existed in the movies. I had no idea real people lived that way."

"It wasn't always sunshine and roses," Ayana said. "There were a few epic fights between me and Austin."

"Yeah, but even when you fought, you knew your brother always had your back, and vice versa. And you both had parents who would do anything for the two of you." Jax sipped his wine, then placed it on the tray. "I was so jealous of you and Austin. I wanted what you all had—the laughs, the joking around, even the arguments.

But then after a while, I realized I had it. You all made me feel as if I was a part of the family."

"You were," Ayana said. "When Mom would put together those care packages to send to Austin, she made sure to include your favorites, too."

"Yeah." He huffed out a humorless laugh. "That just added to the guilt I felt for feeling the way I did about you."

Ayana's shoulders stiffened. "Guilt?"

"Hell yes, I felt guilty," he said. He ran a hand down his face and let out a weary breath. "From the first time I visited your family, Denise and Carl made me feel as if they would do anything for me. Especially your dad. He accepted me into his family, treated me like I was his son, and how do I pay him back? I took his baby girl's virginity in his own house. I felt guilty as hell."

"Yet it didn't stop you from sleeping with me again," she pointed out.

His gaze locked with hers, those light brown eyes darkening with desire. "No, it didn't," he murmured, his voice gruff with need. "And if circumstances hadn't changed, I would have continued doing it, again and again and again."

He leaned toward her and brushed her lips with his. At the first feel of that sensuous mouth, Ayana's entire being melted. It was like finding a treasured gift that had been missing for much too long. She angled her head to the side, remembering that they fit better that way.

"Oh, God, Ayana," Jackson breathed against her lips. He ran his hand up the side of her face and into her hair, holding her head in place as his tongue licked along the seam of her lips. He urged them to part, applying more and more pressure until she relented, opening her mouth and letting his tongue slip inside.

The moment it did the kiss exploded. Jackson slanted his body over hers and captured her face in both his hands.

He held her close as his tongue jousted with hers, plunging and retreating, licking around and around, sucking her tongue into his mouth.

A distant warning bell sounded in her head, telling her to put an end to this before things went further than what was safe. Not for her body, but for her heart. Ayana knew she was barreling down a road that could lead to disappointment and heartache.

But it had been so long since she'd felt his lips against hers, and as much as it pained her to admit it, even to herself, she'd dreamed of doing this for years after they'd parted. She didn't know when, or if, she would ever get the chance to indulge in Jax's unique flavor again. So instead of pushing him away, as she should have, Ayana allowed herself to fully enjoy this momentous reunion.

She linked her hands behind his head as she opened her mouth wider and swirled her tongue inside his mouth. It was warm, and soft, and spicy, just as she remembered.

His kiss had set the bar for every other man, and no one had ever measured up. For years Ayana thought that she'd exaggerated her memories of Jax's skill based on her long-time infatuation with him, but as she kissed him again, she realized that she hadn't inflated anything. Jackson was masterful when it came to pleasing a woman.

He wrapped his arms around her and angled his body over hers. Without much prodding, he coaxed her into lying back and quickly covered her body with his own. Ayana relished the feel of his strong, impossibly hard body flush against her. She felt him on every inch of her skin, and when his hands tunneled underneath the T-shirt's hem to travel up her belly and to her breasts, which she hadn't bothered to cover with a bra after her shower, a desperate moan climbed from her throat.

She was catapulted back in time, to a place where her entire world had revolved around this man.

And just as quickly, Ayana remembered how her world had imploded when he'd crumpled her heart.

"Jax, wait. Stop!"

His head popped up. "What?"

Ayana flattened her palms against his chest and pushed. "I can't do this," she said. "I won't do this with you."

She levered herself up from the sofa and stood. Folding her arms over her chest, she walked over to the fireplace, putting distance between them.

"Ayana, what's wrong?" he asked.

She shook her head and pulled her lip between her teeth to halt the cry that nearly spilled forth. "I've been down this road with you before. I would be a fool to go there again. I'm no fool, Jackson. We're not doing this."

Chapter 6

Jackson rested his head against the back of the sofa, his eyes pinched shut. He tried like hell to ignore the ache in his groin. He'd have a better chance of ignoring someone blowing a horn directly into his ear.

It was as if he'd plummeted back to his teen years, getting turned on by a simple kiss. But there had been nothing simple about that kiss, nor about the woman he'd shared it with.

The first time he'd kissed Ayana like that, she had lit his body on fire. Jax was pretty sure if he looked hard enough he'd find wisps of smoke floating up from his skin right now. There wasn't another woman on the face of the planet who could ever affect him the way she did.

"God, Ayana, you're going to kill me." With a groan he collapsed back onto the sofa, his wrist falling to his groin to rest limply next to a body part that was the complete opposite of limp.

"I can't, Jax," she said, her voice even more resolute now

that she wasn't underneath him. "Twenty-four hours ago I was determined to never speak to you again. I can't go from that to letting you grope me on the sofa like we're still kids. I hope you can understand where I'm coming from."

Jackson ran both hands up and down his face, then over his head. "I guess I do," he said. It didn't bode well for the situation below his waist.

Resigning himself to the state of unfulfilled lust he was destined to remain in for the rest of the night, Jax pushed up from the sofa and started picking up the remnants of their dinner.

He tortured himself by looking over at Ayana again. His stomach tightened at the thought of what they could be doing right now if she hadn't called an end to their kiss. Actually, if he had his way, the two of them wouldn't be on the sofa, exploring each other's mouths. They would be upstairs, making use of that king-size bed.

Jax pitched what was left of the cheese in the fridge and closed the door with more force than he'd intended. Then he unleashed his frustration on the dishes, stuffing them in the dishwasher with such violence it was a wonder he didn't break anything. He shut the door to the dishwasher, then gripped the edge of the counter, pulling in several deep breaths in a failing attempt to get his body under control.

The fact that he'd even let his mind wander in the vicinity of sleeping with Ayana showed that he was a glutton for punishment. It had only been a few hours since she'd managed to speak to him after a ten-year silence. Why would he even allow himself to imagine making love to her again?

But, dammit, how could he not?

Especially after holding her and tasting her again. Especially after that sweet reminder of just how perfectly her body fit against his. She was so soft, so incredibly sexy.

She'd driven him crazy as a teenager, but now, in all her firm, lush, womanly glory? Goodness, the woman had him on the verge of losing his mind.

Just the feel of her soft curves against him had set his body on fire. Combined with those little mewls of pleasure that escaped her throat as his tongue had gained intimate knowledge of her hot mouth again, it was enough to leave him in a perpetual state of arousal.

Too bad Ayana had better control over herself.

He returned to the living room, stopping at the edge of the shallow steps. Ayana was over by the pitiful excuse for a Christmas tree Austin had insisted they bring into the chalet.

"That was your brother's idea," Jax said.

She turned and a gentle smile lit up her eyes. "I'm not surprised. This has always been Austin's favorite time of the year."

Jax continued down the steps. He wasn't sure where they should go from here; he just knew that he didn't want them both reverting to their separate corners of the cabin for the rest of the night.

"Look, Ayana, I don't want what happened a few minutes ago to spoil our night. If all you want to do is talk, then please, let's just talk." He gestured to the wine they'd enjoyed with their sparse meal. "And drink."

"Actually," Ayana said, one brow lifting. She nodded toward the sitting area in the corner where a chess game was set up on a small table fashioned out of a thick tree trunk. "You game?"

"You still ruthless?" Jax asked.

"Absolutely." She laughed. "But only because I learned from the best."

He'd taught her how to play chess during her sophomore year of high school, and she had quickly surpassed him in skill. She spent the rest of that summer kicking both his and Austin's butts.

They finished off the bottle of wine over a game of chess and lighthearted conversation.

"It's a good thing I ate something before you cracked open this bottle." Ayana topped her glass off with the last of the wine. "I'll have to remember this brand."

"It's from Napa," Jax said. "It goes well with the Pecorino Toscano I had, but Austin and I finished that wheel earlier this week."

"Your tastes have certainly graduated from cheese puffs and microwave pizza rolls," she remarked, her eyes bright with amusement.

"I'm sorry I didn't have much food to work with. I would have loved to cook you one of my specialties," Jax said as his rook captured one of her knights.

"Dammit." She studied the board for a moment, then looked up at him, her brow creased in a frown. "You have specialties?"

"Yeah. I've become something of a foodie. Well, more than something. I spent several months in Paris a few years ago, taking a Cordon Bleu course."

Her eyes widened. "You? Really? The guy who couldn't cook a can of soup?"

"Yeah, that guy." Jax laughed. "After we stopped getting those care packages from your mom, it was pretty much learn to cook or starve. And once I started to learn, I realized I liked it."

Awe widened her eyes. "How did I not know this about you?"

"I'm guessing there's a lot you don't know about me."

She nodded, bringing her glass to her lips. "I made it a point never to ask Austin about you." She hunched her shoulders. "What was the point? I was determined to never see you again."

A sharp ache pierced his chest. Whether it was caused by the devastating words she spoke, or the matter-of-fact way in which she said them, Jax wasn't sure. He just knew the pain was real.

"We were such good friends, Ayana. That's what's so messed up about this." Jax sat back in his chair, his eyes focused on a heart-shaped knot in the pine wall paneling. He looked back at her and admitted, "I still don't regret it."

Jax leaned forward and rested his elbows on his thighs. Clasping his hands together, he said, "Over the years, I've debated whether or not, if given the chance, I would give up those weeks we had together if it meant having you back in my life. I wouldn't. As much as I've missed you all these years, there is nothing that would ever make me regret the time we shared, Ayana."

She caressed the goblet's stem, leisurely running her finger up and down the thin stalk. Finally, in a voice that was a shade huskier than it had been a few minutes earlier, she said, "I wouldn't give them up either." A sad smile pulled at the edge of his lips. "You owned my heart for so long, Jackson. I guess that's why it hurt so much when you broke it."

"I will never be able to apologize enough," he said.

Her finger moved to the rim of her wineglass, gently circling it. For a brief moment, Jax found himself jealous of a piece of stemware.

"All these years I told myself that I didn't want to hear any apologies from you, that it wouldn't change anything. But it does," she said. "You never meant to break my heart."

He shook his head. "Never. I swear to you, Ayana. Hurting you was the last thing I wanted to do."

"Thank you, Jax. It really does help to know that."

The sincerity in her eyes gave him a renewed sense of ambition. Ayana had insisted that all she wanted was friendship, but mere friendship would never be enough. They had always meant more to each other.

Ayana returned her attention to the chessboard, but Jax's interest had shifted from the game. He wanted to learn more about *her.* They would never make up for the ten years they'd lost, but he had a driving need to learn all he could about her.

"I told you about the time I spent in Paris," he said. "What about you? How is the spa business treating you? Austin told me about the newest location in North Dallas."

He moved his bishop and, too late, realized he'd put it right in line with her queen.

"Weak move, Richards. Weak, weak move." She laughed as she knocked his bishop out of play. "The North Dallas location is our biggest site yet, over seven thousand square feet."

"Seven thousand square feet? You really need that much space to wash hair?"

She gave him a censorious look, but it was ruined by her grin. "We don't do just hair. Tranquil Pleasures is a full-service salon and spa. We offer both beauty and re-laxation services."

"How did you even get into the spa business? The entire time you were in high school, all you could talk about was becoming a lawyer."

"I know," she said. "I was going to take the law profession by storm, but my heart was never in it. After I finished my undergrad, I took a summer job as a receptionist in a high-end salon and spa in Dallas. I impressed the boss lady with the way I handled the clients, so instead of going on to law school as I'd planned, I took on the role of customer service liaison for her five locations."

"I know that didn't go over well with your dad. I can remember Austin talking about some big blowup you two had."

She chuckled. "No, it did not. He'd already had an engraved nameplate made for my desk." She shrugged. "It didn't go to waste. I have it on my desk at our flagship salon."

"So how did you end up moving from customer service liaison to co-owner?"

"The original owner developed an aggressive form of breast cancer. She put me in charge of managing the entire company while she went through treatment. She eventually decided that she didn't want to run them anymore, and my friend Dana and I bought her out. We just started making plans to branch out to the Houston area."

"Wow." Jax's head reared back. "I didn't know about the expansion plans. That's great, Ayana." He looked across the chessboard, a smile drawing across his face. "It's amazing what you've been able to accomplish in such a short amount of time. Most twenty-eight-year-olds are still trying to figure out what they want to do with their lives, but look at you. I'm proud of you."

Her shoulders stiffened, and her eyes narrowed as she frowned. "What exactly is that supposed to mean?"

The sudden sharpness in her tone threw him. "It means exactly what I said. I'm proud of your accomplishments."

"So should I feel validated now? Want to give me a high five the way you used to do when I passed a calculus exam you helped me to study for?"

Was she serious?

"Are you actually biting my head off for paying you a compliment?"

"When you do it in that condescending way? Yes."

"Wait, wait, wait." He put his hands up. "How was that condescending? I said I was proud of you."

"Like a big brother is proud of his little sister. It's exactly the way you used to treat me back when I was in high school, Jax."

"That's not how I mean it."

"Well, that's how it sounded," she said. "Next you'll be telling me that you're sorry you kissed me. Like it was incestuous or something."

That wasn't going to happen.

"Look, Ayana—"

But she didn't give him a chance to finish. She set her wineglass down next to the chessboard and hopped up from her chair, striding toward the kitchen.

"Dammit." Jax followed her into the kitchen. He walked over to the refrigerator she'd just opened and slammed the door shut, then wedged himself between her and the fridge. "I can't believe you're still doing this."

"Still doing what?" she asked, affronted.

"Blowing the smallest thing out of proportion."

"*Excuse* me? When did I ever blow anything out of proportion?"

Jax's eyes widened. "Are you kidding me? You were the queen of blowing things out of proportion. Remember that trip to New Orleans?"

She choked out a horrified laugh. "Are you really bringing that up?"

"Hell yes. With all the drama you caused after we told you that you couldn't come with us? You would have thought Austin and I had asked you to watch us drown puppies."

"I was fifteen years old."

"Exactly. Too young for a trip to Mardi Gras with two

college-age men, but that didn't matter to you. You went off like some crazy person, the same way you did earlier today when you found out Austin was gone. I told you I could handle it, but you—being you—had to make a big deal out of it."

"My brother had gone missing! Of course I made a big deal out of it."

"But I told you that I could handle this."

"Oh, and you're doing *such* a fine job. I'm sure Austin is about to walk through the door any minute. Oh, wait! No, he isn't, because he is *still missing.*"

She stood there with her hands on her hips, her chest heaving.

Jackson blew out a frustrated breath. He'd forgotten how hot she was when she got all worked up.

She put both palms up. "You know what? I don't have to put up with this. Thanks for dinner. I'm going to bed."

She pivoted and stalked up the stairs.

Jax was about to call her back, but then thought better of it. Anything he said would probably just set her off again, and the angrier she became the more he wanted to attack her mouth. He had a feeling that at the moment, that wouldn't go over so well.

Of all the things he loved about her, Ayana's passion had always held the most appeal. Whether she was excited or angry, she wasn't afraid to let you see it.

Instead of following her upstairs, the way certain parts of his body wanted to do, Jax returned to the dinner table. He might as well get a little work done, since he apparently wouldn't be getting much of anything else tonight.

Ayana stood at the edge of the loft's banister, looking down at the floor below. She wanted to feel justified in her rage, but just moments after she'd stormed up here, she admitted to herself that there had been merit to Jackson's accusations. She *did* have a reputation for blowing things out of proportion. Her dad used to tease her, telling her that he was sure there was a volcano named after her somewhere in the South Pacific.

She considered going downstairs to apologize, but something stopped her. A little something called self-preservation.

After that kiss she and Jax had shared, Ayana realized it was safer to maintain her distance, both physically and emotionally. Being around Jackson made her do things that she normally wouldn't do, made her make mistakes she thought she was too smart to ever make again.

Was it any surprise that she'd completely melted the moment his lips had touched hers? She'd reacted just as she always feared she would; she'd completely given in to his kiss. It was the reason she'd so doggedly avoided him all these years.

Still, that didn't give her the right to bite his head off. The man had paid her a compliment, for goodness' sake!

With a frustrated sigh, Ayana plodded down the stairs.

Her feet halted on the second-to-last step, her insides warming at the sight of Jackson hunched over his computer, completely immersed in his work. How many times had she found him like this during his and Austin's visits from school, when he was supposedly on a break? She would come downstairs for a late-night snack and see the telltale glow from the computer screen. She could walk right up to him and he wouldn't even realize she was there until she spoke.

Ayana knew that his strong work ethic was deeply rooted in his quest to build a better life for himself. Despite the hardships he'd faced, or, more than likely, because of them, he'd done all he could to succeed.

Ayana noticed him grimace as he worked his neck from side to side and rolled his shoulders. She continued down the stairs and came around to the opposite side of the table.

She put her hands up. "You were right."

He looked up from his computer, his right eyebrow quirked in inquiry.

"I may have blown things out of proportion."

Jackson lifted his forearm and gave himself a pinch. "I must be dreaming."

"Ha, ha," Ayana deadpanned. "This isn't easy for me."

"No shit. You never admit that you're wrong. Ever."

"So not true," she said. "And how would you know? We haven't seen each other in a decade."

"I talk to your brother almost daily. I've heard enough stories over the years to know that you're as stubborn as you used to be as a teenager."

Ayana narrowed her eyes. Why did he insist on making this hard for her?

His lips hitched in a grin. "Don't change," he said. "Stubborn looks good on you. It always has."

The ice around her heart instantly melted. Only Jackson could do that to her.

Her own lips twitching with a wry smile, she walked around to the other side of the table. "Come here," she said. She put her hands on his shoulders.

Jax jerked out of her reach. "What are you doing?"

"What's the matter?" Ayana laughed. "Do you think I'm going to kill you?"

"I don't know. Maybe. You were pretty pissed when you went stomping upstairs."

"You outweigh me by at least seventy pounds. I'd never be able to dispose of the body," she said. Jackson's eyes cut to hers. "I was going to give you a massage," Ayana said. "You probably spend more than half your day hunched over a computer. I can only imagine the awful shape those shoulder muscles are in."

"A massage?" he asked.

"Yes, a massage. I'll treat you to the Tranquil Pleasures experience."

"I didn't think owners took such a hands-on approach."

"I like to know all aspects of my business. How else can I evaluate if my employees are doing the job correctly?"

"Sounds like the key to a successful operation." Jackson pushed away from the table and stood. "Let me see what those magic fingers can do. Where do you want me?"

"You can sit right back in that chair. You're not getting a full-body massage, just neck and shoulders."

"How much for the full body?"

The wickedly sexy drop in his voice did very naughty things to her lower region, but Ayana managed to regain control over her libido without falling prey to his charms.

"It's not on the menu," she said. "Now sit."

With an exaggerated sigh, Jackson obeyed, sitting back in the chair. Ayana got behind him and rubbed her hands together to warm them up. "Now, this won't be the true experience, because we don't have any of the oils that we use at the spa, but you'll get the idea."

The minute her hands touched him, he let out a groan.

"I haven't even started yet," Ayana said.

"I know. But it still feels good."

Using the techniques she'd picked up over the years from the numerous clinical massage therapists who'd worked for her, she worked the knots out of Jackson's shoulders with deep, sure kneads. His head lolled back and he let out a moan of pleasure.

"Jax, it feels as if you've got speed bumps underneath your skin. Seriously, how much stress are you and Austin under?"

"Too much," he said. "But it will all be over soon enough."

"When?"

"After he makes his pitch to the Department of Ed in a few weeks. The stress isn't going anywhere until that's done. I'm not even trying to fight it. This is making me feel a helluva lot better, though." He moaned again. "God, your hands really are like magic."

The simple compliment sent a bevy of tingles cascading up and down her spine.

"If you know you're going to be stressed, you need to figure out ways to combat it beforehand. This isn't healthy, Jax."

He peered up at her over his shoulder. "What other stress-relieving activities do you suggest?"

Ayana's heart rate escalated at the deep, seductive lilt to his voice. She knew how his mind worked, knew exactly what stress-relieving activity he would propose.

As his light-brown eyes connected with hers, Ayana sent up a silent plea for the strength to resist him. Accepting his apology for what he'd done to her all those years ago was one thing, but exposing her heart to that kind of pain again by sleeping with him? That would be the actions of a pure fool.

She was *such* a fool.

Still kneading his shoulders, she summoned courage she had to dig much too deep to find and asked, "What type of things did you have in mind?"

Jackson's body stiffened. He turned and caught her by the wrist. "What are you offering?"

Ayana didn't say anything, just stared at him, letting her eyes speak for her.

Jax blew out a shuttered breath. "Ayana, don't give me permission to do something that you're going to regret in the morning."

"Will I regret it?" she asked.

"You did the last time."

"No, I didn't," she said. "I told you before, Jackson. I never regretted the time we spent together. Never."

Jackson stood, taking both her hands between his palms. "Does that mean you're willing to do it again?"

She shouldn't. Lord knew she should pull out of his reach and escape to the safety of the second bedroom upstairs. Instead, Ayana flattened her palms against his chest and said, "Even if it's just for tonight."

"What if I don't want it to be just for tonight, Ayana?" His velvety-soft voice caused her skin to pebble with want. "What if I want more?"

She put her finger against his lips. "All of that can wait, Jax. This can't."

Capturing his face between her hands, she pulled him in for a slow, deep kiss that resonated throughout her entire body. Ayana melted against him, loving the feel of his strong chest against her aching breasts. His hands slid down her sides to her waist, then around to her backside. He gripped it, his fingers digging into her fleshy rear end. He pulled her against him and Ayana's breath caught at the bulge pulsing behind his zipper. He was so hard; heat and wetness pooled between her legs at the thought of all that power being unleashed on her.

"Are you sure you want to go through with this?" Jackson whispered as he traced his lips along her jaw.

"Yes," she breathed, letting her head fall back so that his mouth could travel down her neck.

He nipped at her skin, peppering it with unhurried kisses. Then he took her by the hand and guided her up the stairs. Ayana's heart beat so hard within her chest she was sure Jackson could hear it.

Did she really want to do this? Could she handle it?

The last time she'd given her body to this man, her heart and soul had been included, and he'd managed to rip them both out and leave her emotionally bruised and battered for years. Did she want to give him that kind of power over her again? Had she already done so?

As if he'd read her thoughts, Jackson took her hand and brought it to his lips. With a gentle kiss, he said, "I promise not to hurt you this time."

He guided her to the huge bed in the chalet's master suite, which was much too high for Ayana. A sexy chuckle rumbled from Jax's throat and he scooped her up by the waist, setting her onto the chocolate-brown comforter that complemented the room's masculine theme. He caught the hem of her T-shirt—his T-shirt—and pulled it up and over her head.

Jax let out a low, animalistic growl as his eyes fell to her breasts. Ayana felt a measure of feminine pleasure at the thought of eliciting such a sound from him.

"God, Ayana. You're as beautiful as ever."

He zeroed in on her neck, pulling in a deep breath before running his tongue along her skin. He trailed the moist tip from just behind her ear to her collarbone, peppering her skin with light licks and gentle bites.

Ayana's head fell back. As she stared up at the ceiling, those questions started to swarm around her head again. She mentally swatted them away, closing her eyes and focusing on the pleasure that radiated from every point on her skin. Jax's hands found her waist again. His palms spanned across her stomach before he brought them behind her and plunged south to grip her butt. He hooked his thumbs into the sides of her waistband and pulled both the pajama pants and her panties off her hips. Ayana levered herself up so that he could pull the pants down her legs, baring her body to him.

Jax dove for her breasts, capturing her right nipple between his lips and sucking it into his mouth. The moan that climbed up her throat echoed against the high ceiling.

She flattened her palms against his chest and pushed. Unlike the first time they did this, she refused to sit around while he ran the show. She was no longer the timid, awestruck teenager who was too afraid to express what she wanted. The memory of the pleasure Jax was capable of unleashing on her body was never far from her mind, and finally, after far too many years of dreaming about it, she was about to experience it again.

"Take this off," Ayana said, pushing his shirt up his torso.

Jax's brown eyes darkened with heat at her command.

"One minute." Holding up one finger, he turned and headed for the bathroom. Ayana heard rustling, then Jax returned, tossing several condom packets on the bedside table before picking up where he'd left off. He pulled the shirt over his head and let it fall to the floor to mingle with her discarded clothing.

Lying naked atop the downy bedding, Ayana spared a moment to take in the sight before her: the chiseled contours of his chest and stomach, the thin, sexy trail of hair that disappeared into his waistband, the undeniable bulge hidden behind his zipper. The picture he created caused her stomach to tremble with delicious need.

His eyes still locked with hers, Jackson unbuckled his pants and tugged at the zipper. Then he shoved both his pants and underwear down his legs and climbed into the bed, stretching his body over hers.

"Ayana, you have no idea how many times I've imagined this."

"We don't need to imagine anymore," she whispered against his neck. "We're here now." She hooked her hands around his neck and brought him down on top of her, savoring the feel of his hard, fit body pressed up against her bare skin. When his lips met hers, Ayana closed her eyes and plummeted to another place and time, to that period long ago when she'd had fantasies of spending her life with the man in her arms.

But there was no reason to fantasize anymore. Jackson was here, and for the moment, he was hers.

Ayana opened her legs for him, a mewl of pleasure escaping her lips as he settled between her thighs. Reaching between them, she wrapped her hands around his erection, running her palms up and down his silken skin. Jax reached over and grabbed one of the condoms, and together they guided the latex over his hard flesh.

Levering himself above her, he stared into her eyes as he slid his entire length inside of her with one deep thrust. They let out twin cries of mutual pleasure as their bodies reconnected in that most elemental way for the first time in ten years.

Ayana fitted her hands to his back, pulling him closer as he began to move slowly inside her. She closed her eyes, focusing on the feel of his powerful erection sliding in and out of her, sinking deeper with every thrust, pushing her higher, to a place coated with unrivaled pleasure.

Only Jackson. He was the only person who could ever take her here.

Ayana shifted her hips, taking him deeper into her body. Jax's lips found her breast again, going from one to the other. He tongued her nipple, sucking the tip into the moist warmth of his mouth. Every tug set off a tiny burst of sensation that ricocheted within her belly.

Their lovemaking turned from languid to fiery. Jackson buried his head against her neck and began to pump with a fervor that pushed her back until her head met the headboard. Over and over again he plunged, the breadth of his solid erection stretching her body in ways that surpassed the physical level. Jackson had a way of reaching her soul.

The feeling started low in her belly, the heavy, tingling sensation of something on the brink of happening. Ayana tried to stave it off, wanting to bask in the anticipation of it for a little while longer. But then Jackson's teeth sank into her shoulder and her entire body went up in flames.

Ayana flew apart, her world exploding in a burst of white-hot light as waves of pleasure crashed into her. Jackson's hips continued to move, pumping harder and faster, until his entire body went stiff. He threw his head back and growled toward the ceiling, his limbs shaking with the force of his climax. She joined him, her body going up in flames with a second orgasm that she felt throughout her entire being.

Slowly she floated back down to earth, her body replete with a sensual satisfaction she had not felt with anyone else.

"Only you," Ayana breathed. "Only you."

Chapter 7

Ayana's eyes popped open. She looked up at the unfamiliar ceiling and frowned, then she looked over at the man occupying the bed next to her and shuddered.

"Oh, God," she groaned into the pillow.

How stupid could she be? How incredibly, unbelievably, outright foolish could a woman be to deliberately put herself squarely on the road to heartache again? She knew what sleeping with Jax would lead to, yet she'd gone ahead and slept with him anyway.

Stupid. Stupid. *Stupid.*

Jackson Richards was not good for her peace of mind. He created dreams that would never come to fruition. He reduced her to being that lovesick teenager who was willing to do whatever she could to win his love and affection.

Well, she wasn't that girl anymore. She would not fall victim to the kind of thinking that had made her such a mess for years after Jax had left.

Ayana peeled his fingers from around her waist and

scooted off the bed. She went into the bathroom and showered, washing her body and her mind of the memories of
last night.

It was easier this way.

Ayana stepped out of the shower and used a hand towel
to wipe the steamy moisture that had collected on the mirror. She stared at the reflection looking back at her, telling herself she would not cry. She'd shed enough tears
over Jackson to last her a lifetime. She would not give in
to those threatening her right now.

She also would not make a big deal out of what had happened between her and Jax last night. They'd spent a few
hours together, and that's all it would ever be. Despite the
revelations of last night, in the light of day it was obvious
to her that too much time had passed for there to ever be
anything between them. They were different people. Their
time had passed.

When she reentered the bedroom, Jackson was leaning
back against the headboard.

"Good morning," he said. His forehead furrowed as he
took in her appearance. She was fully dressed, down to
the suede belt around her waist. She held his T-shirt and
pajama pants folded neatly in her hands. Ayana placed
them on the dresser.

"We need to get back to the resort as soon as possible,"
she said. "I'll be downstairs."

She didn't give him a chance to speak, just walked out
of the bedroom with as much dignity as she could mus-
ter. Ten minutes later, Jackson came downstairs in dark
jeans and a hooded sweatshirt with the University of Texas
Longhorns logo embroidered across it in burnt orange.

"Ayana," he began.

"Are you ready?" she cut him off.

"We've got time," he said. He reached for her, but Ayana stepped out of his reach.

"Don't," she said, putting her hands up. "Please, Jackson, just don't." Ayana sucked in a deep breath and said, "Look, I let my guard down last night. It was foolish, yet understandable, I guess, given the circumstances. But it was a one-time thing. Nothing has changed."

Jackson pitched his head back and expelled a harsh curse. "Are we really back to this?"

"Jax—"

"Everything has changed, Ayana." He started to pace in the small area in front of the staircase. "How can you think we can just go back to being nothing to each other?"

"Jackson, please."

"Dammit, I'm not the enemy! When are you going to realize that?"

"Yes, you are, Jax."

He stopped pacing and stared at her, his expression stormy.

Ayana pulled her bottom lip between her teeth, her refusal to cry a matter of pride and self-preservation. "When it comes to my peace of mind—when it comes to my heart—you are the enemy, Jackson. I won't allow you to hurt me again."

"No." Jax shook his head. "I'm not letting you do this to us."

"You don't have a choice," she said.

Jackson stared at her for several moments, a number of emotions playing across his face: anger, annoyance and finally, resignation.

"We need to get going," Ayana said.

With a frustrated curse, he pivoted and started up the stairs.

While she waited for Jax to finish whatever he was

doing upstairs, Ayana looked around the chalet. Memories of the previous night assaulted her. The sparse dinner he'd made for her, the back rub she'd treated him to, the two of them making love over and over again.

She closed her eyes and soaked them in, filing the memories away for years to come. She knew from experience that she would be calling on them soon.

One disobedient tear managed to escape. She quickly dashed it away from her cheek and dared any others to fall.

Jackson came down the stairs with an overnight bag over his shoulder. "Give me a minute to warm the car up. I'll come up and get you."

Ayana nodded.

She went into the downstairs bathroom. When she came back out, she spotted Jackson through the window on the door. He was on the front porch, pacing back and forth, his cell phone to his ear. She heard him mention Austin's name and headed for the door so she could chew her brother out for all he'd put them through, but the next thing she heard stopped her dead in her tracks.

"You don't want to make the same mistakes I made," Jackson said.

Ayana's hand halted on the door handle.

"I loved a woman and foolishly let her go. It was the biggest mistake I've ever made. If you really love Rachelle, and I know you do, don't hurt her this way, Austin. Marry that woman today, and get started on your lives together."

Emotion clogged Ayana's throat as she slowly backed away from the door. She covered her lips with trembling fingers.

How easy would it be to indulge in the fantasy his words had sparked? To imagine how life would have been if he had not made the choices he'd made? Of the life the two of them could have had together all these years?

But he *had* made the choice.

Even though he'd married his wife out of obligation, it had still been Jax's choice to make. Ayana would not allow herself to get caught up in the could-have, would-have, should-have cycle. There was no point to it. Things were what they were.

Jackson came inside and stopped short. "Uh, are you ready?" he asked.

Ayana nodded.

"I just talked to your brother," he said.

"Oh?" she said, feigning surprise.

"Yeah. I think I finally convinced him to go through with the wedding."

"How did you manage to do that?"

He shrugged. "I told him to imagine life without Rachelle. That was enough."

Ayana swallowed audibly. "I guess he didn't like the prospect of that."

He stared at her for several moments before saying in a hoarse voice, "It's not easy having to live your life without the person you love, and knowing that you're the one who messed it up." He ran a hand down the back of his head and lingered on his neck, massaging it. "We should probably get going," Jackson said. "The garage door was barricaded by snow. I shoveled it away and brought the car around front."

He held the door open and locked the chalet behind her after she walked out. He helped her navigate through the considerable snow that had fallen overnight, and then helped her into the car. Ayana took several deep breaths as he jogged around the front of the SUV.

Once behind the wheel, he turned over the ignition, but left the car idling. He gripped the steering wheel, pulled in a deep breath and said, "Ayana, we need to talk about this."

"Jax, just drive. Please."

Ayana could feel the frustration flowing off him in waves, but he did as she'd asked. Without another word, he put the car in gear and started down the driveway.

It took everything Jax had in him not to stop on the side of this narrow mountain road and demand Ayana talk to him. After everything that had passed between them last night, after everything they'd shared, the fact that she could hardly look at him this morning ripped a hole through his very soul.

This woman owned his heart. She had for years. But she didn't want it, and the knowledge of that hurt so much more than Jax ever thought possible.

The raging snowstorm of last night had dissipated, leaving only a few flakes falling from the sky. They passed the area where the tree had blocked the roadway. It was now located on the side of the road in huge chunks, cordoned off with yellow police tape. A few yards later they heard a huge thump as the front driver's-side tire rolled over something. The front end of the SUV immediately slanted toward the side.

"Shit," Jax cursed.

"What was that?" Ayana asked.

"I have no idea." He guided the vehicle to the narrow shoulder and got out. Ayana did the same, rounding the side of the car. Jax dropped to his haunches and inspected the tire. Just under the rim, he spotted the culprit. A decent-size piece of tree bark was wedged in the tread, causing the instant blowout.

"Damn," he said, pushing himself up. "I guess it's a good thing I made sure the rental company checked the spare before I rented the car." He rounded the SUV and opened up the back. Removing the panel, he cranked the pulley, lowering the spare tire from underneath the back of the vehicle.

"I would offer to help if I could," Ayana said, "but these pants cost me two hundred dollars, and the boots four times that much."

Jax looked up at her over his shoulder. "I think I can manage. These jeans were only about forty bucks. I can sacrifice them if necessary."

Ayana gave him a soft smile before stepping away from the SUV. He captured that smile in his mind and locked it away so that he could call on it in the months ahead.

God, would he really have to go back to living without her?

He couldn't fathom going another decade without seeing Ayana's smile, smelling her hair, tasting her body. He needed her the way he needed air, and water, and food. How could she not see that?

He rubbed the spot in the middle of his chest that had been aching since the minute she'd walked out of that bathroom this morning, fully clothed, her barrier firmly up between them once again.

By the time Jax got the tire changed, it was already after eleven. The wedding wasn't set to start for another six hours, but he wanted to keep his eye on Austin just in case those frigid feet made a return appearance. Jax was ready to tie him to a chair until five o'clock if he had to.

They arrived back at the resort twenty minutes later. Before he pulled up to the valet, Jax turned to Ayana.

"Look, I know you don't want to talk about last night, and I respect your choice, but I need you to know that I'm going to cherish every memory of it, Ayana."

The brief look she shot his way was full of longing.

Why was she fighting this?

For a moment, Jax was tempted to drive straight through the resort's circular driveway, head back up to the chalet and lock himself there with Ayana until she admitted that her feelings for him were true. How could she not see that?

"We should go and check on Austin," she said, her face turned to the passenger-side window.

Letting out a frustrated breath, Jax drove up to the valet and handed the keys over. In silence he and Ayana made it to the elevators. As she watched the numbers go up above the door, Jax watched her, even though it hurt to look at her, knowing that in just a few short hours she would be gone from his life again.

They got off on the fifth floor and headed down the hallway to room 512. Jax found out during their conversation this morning that Austin had booked this room under his middle name after he'd left the rehearsal party. That was why he hadn't been in the room he'd originally booked two floors below when Jax had gone in search of him yesterday evening.

Ayana arrived first, pounding her fist on the door. "Austin, open up. Right now." The door opened and Ayana barreled in. "What in the hell is wrong with you?" She accosted her brother, punching him on the shoulder.

"Ouch." Austin rubbed his arm.

"Do you know what you put us through? And all this time you were right here, two doors down from my room."

"I'm sorry," he said. Austin looked from Ayana to Jax. "Really, I'm sorry for putting you both through hell. Jax told me you got stuck on the mountain last night."

Ayana glanced over at him, then returned her attention to her brother. "Don't worry about that. I just want to know whether or not you've come to your senses."

He nodded. "I have. It was just… I was… I don't know.

Blame it on too much stress. I guess it got to me. But I'm ready to get married." He turned pleading eyes to his sister. "Please don't tell Rachelle about this. I want to be the one to do it, but not right now. I don't want to spoil her big day with the news that it almost didn't happen."

"Ayana?"

They all turned toward the still-open door. Keith, the date Ayana had come with to Colorado, was standing in the hallway.

"Keith," she called, heading for him. Jax had to avert his eyes. He'd rather jump out the damn window than watch her greet this guy with a kiss or something.

Having no interest in seeing Ayana reunite with her date, he carried his duffel bag into the suite's bathroom. He dropped the bag and kicked it in the corner. Then he slouched down on the edge of the tub and cradled his head in his hands, trying to resign himself to life without the woman he loved.

The Golden Ridge Resort prided itself on hosting the perfect wedding, but during this time of the year it wasn't just perfect, it seemed magical. Yards of silky white-and-gold fabric draped from the thick beams that crisscrossed the chapel's peaked ceiling. Several dozen high-backed chairs were lined up in rows on either side of a center aisle covered in white rose petals. The altar was adorned with trees twinkling with hundreds of white lights, and to infuse even more of the festive holiday spirit, huge potted poinsettias were distributed throughout the room.

The harpist from last night was back, her fingers gently gliding over the delicate strings, the soft strains of "Silver Bells" wafting through the air. Ayana found herself getting misty-eyed. She rarely cried at weddings, but this was her only brother. She was allowed this one.

She stood in the back of the room. Since Keith had not been feeling well enough to come down from the room, Rachelle's younger brother, who was serving as usher, was to escort her to her seat right before the wedding party marched in. The minister entered the room from a side door, followed by Austin, her cousin Victor, who was serving as a groomsman, and Jackson.

Ayana let out an audible gasp at the sight of him.

Jax was devastating in jeans and a hooded sweatshirt. Dressed in the dashing formalwear, he was heart-stopping.

"You may want to drag your tongue into your mouth."

Ayana turned to find her mother standing behind her.

"What are you doing here? Shouldn't you be preparing to walk up the aisle with Dad?"

"They won't start without me," her mother said, her eyes roaming over Ayana's face. She tucked a strand of hair behind her ear. "I just wanted to make sure you were okay."

"Why wouldn't I be?"

"I know about last night," her mother said.

Ayana's mouth fell wide open. "How do you know about last night?"

"When I went to your room to look for you, I found Keith there, sick and alone. When I went looking for Jackson, he, too, was nowhere to be found." Her mother put up her hands. "Now, I don't know what happened between the two of you last night, so don't go spilling any secrets. But I do know that when it comes to Jackson Richards, this—" she lightly tapped the center of Ayana's chest "—has a history of getting involved, probably more than you'd like."

Ayana's eyes slid shut. "How long have you known?"

"Since you were about fourteen." Her eyes were full of concern. "*Are* you okay?"

Ayana pulled her lower lip between her teeth and shook her head. "I don't think so," she whispered. She released a pitifully defeated breath and held her hands out. "How can he still have this kind of effect on me? It's been ten years. I should be over him."

Her mother cupped her cheek in her palm and looked at her with those wise, knowing eyes. "Ayana, honey, it could be a hundred years. It wouldn't matter. The two of you were connected from the very first time Jackson came to the house." Her mother let out a small laugh. "You can ask your father. He had to stop me from sending Jax to spend that weekend in a hotel."

Ayana choked out a laugh. "Really? Why?"

"I saw the way that nineteen-year-old boy was staring at my fourteen-year-old baby, and all I could think about was getting him away from you. But I doubt Jackson even recognized how much he loved you back then."

Ayana's shoulders wilted with indecision. "What am I supposed to do now?"

"You need to figure that out," her mother said. "You've purposely cut him out of your life for the past ten years. Are you okay living the rest of your life without him?"

"I don't know."

"You're a smart girl." Her mother leaned forward and placed a kiss on her forehead. "You'll figure it out. Now, let's get your brother married before he loses his good sense and runs off again."

Ayana forced a smile, but her heart wasn't entirely in it. The decision looming ahead of her weighed on her soul, threatening to crush it. Would it be foolish to give Jackson a second chance to break her heart?

Ayana wasn't sure she even had the choice, and when her gaze returned to him, she knew for certain. She didn't have to give Jackson anything. Her heart already belonged to him. Always had.

* * *

Jackson tried to pay attention to the ceremony, but the entire time he stood at Austin's side, all he could think about was getting Ayana alone. They had to talk. He had to find a way to make her understand something that had become abundantly clear to him over the past few hours.

He couldn't live without her.

He would not go the rest of his life in the same unfulfilled fog he'd spent the past ten years wandering in. He and Ayana were meant to be together. The connection between them was too strong, the feelings he had for her too powerful. He didn't care how long it took to make her see that, but Jax wouldn't relent until he did. She owned his heart; he refused to give it to anyone else.

The ceremony ended and they were led to an adjacent room for the cocktail hour. Jax suffered through twenty minutes of formal pictures with the rest of the wedding party. The moment they were released, he headed straight for Ayana, who was standing at one of the chest-high cocktail tables with her cousin Shawntell and her husband.

"Excuse me," Jax said. "Ayana, can I see you?"

She looked up at him, and for a moment Jax thought she would refuse. She didn't. Instead, she set her drink on the table and followed him out into the hallway. The hum of chattering voices dissipated as he led her toward the wall of French doors that opened onto a balcony that wrapped around the entire second floor of the resort.

"Jax, why are we going out here?"

"Because I can't have any distractions when I tell you this." He took her hands in his and brought them to his lips. "Ayana, for the past ten years something has been missing from my life. I knew what it was, but I didn't want to admit it, because I knew you were determined to never see me again. Now that I have, I can't go back to the way things were. You complete the missing parts of me, Ayana. Please don't make me live my life without you."

Tears streamed down her face, making her luminous eyes even more radiant. "I don't want to go back there either," she said, her voice heavy with tears. "God, Jackson." She sucked in a deep breath and let it out with a sigh. "I've loved you more than half my life. As much as I tried to deny it, it's always been you. You owned my heart from the very beginning."

"Can I still have it?"

After a moment that seemed to last an eternity, she nodded and said, "It's yours."

Jax's eyes fell closed as he pulled her into him, crashing his mouth to hers. He put everything he possessed into that kiss: the love, the passion, all of it.

"I love you so much," he breathed against her lips. "Thank you, Ayana."

"For what?"

"For giving me a second chance."

Epilogue

Ayana sat with her back against the headboard of the bed in the chalet's master bedroom, studying the chessboard that sat between her and Jackson. It was his move, and even though he apparently didn't see it yet, she'd just noticed that she was in danger of being checkmated.

"Aren't you hungry?" she asked, trying to divert his attention away from the board.

"We just ate two hours ago," Jax said, his brow furrowed in concentration.

"Yes, but we've done a few things since then that made me work up an appetite."

A wicked smile inched up his lips. "Give me a minute," he said. "I'll whip something up as soon as we're done with this game."

Ayana squelched a frustrated curse. She was in danger of seeing her perfect record against him broken if she didn't figure out a way to stop this game.

She straightened her back, pushing herself up more

firmly against the headboard. As she did so, the sheet slipped slightly. Ayana went to straighten it, and then thought better of it. She sat up straighter, allowing the sheet to fall away from her breasts as she did.

Jax stopped with his hand hovering over the chessboard.

"I know what you're trying to do," he said.

"Is it working?"

He shoved the chessboard off the bed and covered her body.

Ayana wrapped her arms around his neck and pulled his head down. "I'd take that as a yes," she said. Then she crushed his mouth to hers.

* * * * *